Praise for the

Also by D.D. Ayres

Explosive Forces
Irresistible Force
Force of Attraction
Primal Force
Rival Forces
Necessary Force (novella)

PHYSICAL FORCES

D.D. Ayres

St. Martin's Paperbacks

This is a work of fiction. All of the characters, organizations, and events portrayed in this novel are either products of the author's imagination or are used fictitiously.

PHYSICAL FORCES

Copyright © 2017 by D.D. Ayres.

All rights reserved.

For information address St. Martin's Press, 175 Fifth Avenue, New York, NY 10010.

ISBN: 978-1-250-08699-0

Our books may be purchased in bulk for promotional, educational, or business use. Please contact your local bookseller or the Macmillan Corporate and Premium Sales Department at 1-800-221-7945, ext. 5442, or by e-mail at MacmillanSpecialMarkets@macmillan.com.

Printed in the United States of America

St. Martin's Paperbacks edition / June 2017

St. Martin's Paperbacks are published by St. Martin's Press, 175 Fifth Avenue, New York, NY 10010.

10 9 8 7 6 5 4 3 2 1

Rose Hilliard: There'd be no K-9 Rescue Series without your inspiration and spot-on editing skills. Thank you!

CHAPTER ONE

Macayla Burkett was about as prepared as a private detective could be. At least, one who specialized in locating lost, runaway, and abducted domesticated animals. To be exact, she was a Pet Detective. Three dog leashes encircled her waist. A high-beam flashlight hung from her utility belt, along with two dog muzzles, small and large, clipped there for easy access. The pockets of her cargo pants bulged with dog treats, a Kong, and a small first-aid kit. A pair of twelve-inch-long side-cut wire clippers, Velcroed to her pant leg, bumped her thigh with every step. The canister of pepper spray fogger hung from the right side of her utility belt for protection against aggressors of both the four- and two-legged variety.

She worked as an animal recovery specialist for Jefferina Franklin, a former police officer who now owned Tampa/St. Pete Recon, a fully licensed private investigation agency. It was part-time work, depending on the number of missing animal cases that came in. So far, the job had consisted mostly of coaxing once-sheltered pets out of swampy areas or abandoned structures, or off medians in rush-hour traffic. It was hot, fatiguing, and sometimes dangerous work. Occasionally she wasn't fast enough on the draw with the pepper fogger. This month alone she'd been bitten by an accidentally cornered squirrel and sprayed by a startled skunk.

Not a glamorous life.

Still, rescuing missing pets gave her a real sense of satisfaction. The looks on their owners' faces would be almost thanks enough if she didn't have rent to make. But she did have to earn a living. So this job, supplemented by the dog training classes she taught, plus the occasional pet-sitting job, made her bill collectors happy.

Mac, as she was known to her friends, was barred from real PI work until she qualified for a Class "CC" license, which would allow her to be hired as a PI intern. That meant a semester of general investigative training at the nearby community college. But Mac wasn't at all certain the PI business was for her. Tracking men who owed child support and catching cheating spouses didn't appeal at all. She liked the anonymity of working with animals on an assignment-by-assignment basis. Nobody owned her time, or kept track. Her responsibilities were clear and short-lived. That way she didn't owe anything, or anybody, a full-time commitment. Life had taught her that being responsible could carry a terrible price.

Jefferina Franklin had been doubtful about her abilities until she'd offered to follow up on, for free, several requests to locate missing pets that Tampa/St. Pete Recon routinely turned down. After logging a nearly 100 percent recovery rate, she had the job. That was more than ten months ago.

Tonight, however, her assignment didn't require her to trap or retrieve a runaway dog or cat. This was actual investigative work. Emphasis on intelligence gathering.

One week ago, the night before a big race, three racing greyhounds had disappeared from the kennels of Derby Lane racetrack, the oldest continuously operating greyhound track in the country. Their owners told police they thought the dogs were taken to keep them from competing in a big-money race. They hoped that afterward, the dogs would be returned. Not a trace of them had been seen since. Officially, the trail had gone cold.

Worried about the damage that could occur to professional animals missing their diet and training regimen, the owners had turned to Tampa/St. Pete Recon to develop and follow up on any new leads. Jefferina called Mac.

"If anyone asks, you're just tracking missing pets. Not trying to locate dog thieves. This is still officially a police matter. I won't have my license revoked because an unlicensed amateur screwed up. So don't." Jefferina was hard but fair. "You're only to collect evidence. No contact. No actions."

"Right," Mac murmured to herself. She'd need hard evidence of the dogs' whereabouts, if she found them. In this case, that meant photos.

She patted her left pants pocket. It contained her boss's newest bit of geek gear, a thermal image attachment for a cell phone. She had never used it before, and was much more worried about losing or damaging it than any possible danger to her personal safety.

The thrill of her first real PI assignment spurred her on as she made her way under the canopy of moss-draped trees a few blocks northwest of downtown St. Petersburg, in a modest area known as West and East Lealman. She'd done her due diligence, even if the sergeant at the precinct treated her like a cub reporter as she grilled him on the details the police had gathered.

The greyhounds hadn't bolted on their own. The

padlocks had been cut through, and leashes and muzzles were missing. They had been taken. Dognapped. That was all he could, or would, tell her.

Next she'd contacted her usual missing-animal sources. Word on the street had been very slow in filtering back to her. That worried her. After months of tracking lost, abandoned, and occasionally taken pets—mostly by good people who thought the animal abandoned—she'd developed a network of people who regularly funneled information to her about stray-animal sightings. In a community that sometimes couldn't agree on much, nearly everyone thought that a person who'd mistreat an animal was a lower order of human being.

As she crossed the grass of an empty lot, the earth beneath her booted feet squished, softened by the curtain of rain that had swept in off Tampa Bay at sunset and dampened the area before moving on to anoint more lucrative real estate. The August shower had cooled the air just enough to discourage the gnats and mosquitoes that usually hovered in the warm night air. Illuminated by the city lights from Tampa, across the bay, the sky was never completely dark. Tonight the low clouds magnified that glow so that she didn't need her flashlight to guide her steps.

Mac paused in the shadow of a palmetto shrub to get her bearings. The sign across the road read KING OF THE ROAD MOBILE HOME PARK. Her first landmark.

Thankfully, the rain shower had driven the inhabitants inside, lessening the chance she'd be sighted. But the park wasn't her goal. It was the source of the only clue she'd developed so far about the missing greyhounds. It had come to her via Cedric, a man who lived on the street with his dog Dougie. While turning in his weekly aluminum can collection this morning at County Sanitation, located a few blocks from here, Cedric said he'd overheard residents of this trailer park complaining about hearing dogs howling pitifully several nights ago. One resident thought she spied a greyhound when she went to investigate. But when the police came they found nothing suspicious in the neighborhood. This morning, Cedric told her one of the mobile home residents was complaining about the smell that seemed to be emanating from a house on the block directly behind them. As thanks for the information, Cedric asked for and got three hot dogs from Doc's Haines Road Hot Dogs, one for him and two for Dougie.

Mac adjusted her belt. One complaint plus one complaint might add up to zero, but she was hoping for a solid sighting. She'd love to be the one to solve the mystery of the missing greyhounds. A high-profile case would give her legitimacy with law enforcement who, so far, seemed to see her as nothing more than an amateur dogcatcher. Emphasis on amateur.

Just get the pictures and get out, she reminded herself. Taking an animal off the premises was not authorized. This was still, technically, a police matter.

Keeping inside the line of shrubbery that ringed the area, she skirted the trailer park, and was slapped in the face with a wet palm frond twice for her efforts. Finally, she came face-to-face with the barrier between the park and the nearby neighborhood. She was prepared for wire fencing. She was unhappy to discover that it was a wood fence. Everybody was into upscaling their bit of turf.

It was times like this that she allowed herself to admit that being five foot nothin' was a bit of a handicap. But she didn't dwell on it. Two years of being the flyer on a middle school cheer team had left her still limber enough to scale a wall, even if her physical therapist recommended that she not do such demanding activities anymore. And mostly she didn't.

Well, not if she discounted her so-called date last week, which involved rock climbing at Vertical Ventures.

Mac groaned under her breath. Chasing dogs was more interesting than that date had been.

Luckily, the fence wasn't more than six feet. She was over it without much effort, despite the fact that her wire cutter handles had forked over the fence top, leaving her struggling for several seconds.

Note to self: Remove big hardware before climbing.

But once she was on the ground, her swallowed curses evaporated. The smell emanating from somewhere ahead was impossible to ignore.

Peering out through the limbs of an unpruned jacaranda tree, she could make out a block of small houses, many no larger than the double-wide trailers on the other side of the fence she'd shimmied over. She heard a dog bark, sharp and sudden, a warning that it, at least, was aware of a stranger on the street.

Hunkering down out of sheer instinct, she made her way in the deepest shadows toward the source of the stench. Why hadn't neighbors called this in? Why hadn't the city responded?

She reached for her cell phone, popped the infrared device into place, and held it up. The dark house was instantly rendered in vivid colors of blue and green with hints of yellow. Nothing red, which would indicate warmth and life. Not even the possibility of an electrical device like a TV or computer left on. Just to make certain it was working correctly, she swung it away from the house.

As she panned into the yard next door, two images that had been in deep shadow jumped vividly to life on her cell phone screen. Hot oranges and reds outlined two people facing off behind the yellow-green contours of a pickup truck parked in the driveway. They were arguing, the hot

red ovals of their mouths issuing sounds that barely registered with her as she watched. They must have just exited
the house, Mac thought.

The device's dual imaging allowed her to see a natural
image of the men overlaid on the thermal imaging, giving
her enough detail to tell one wore a hoodie while the other
wore a suit or sport coat.

Watching in fascination to see the gadget at work, she
knew the exact second it all went wrong. She saw the man
in the suit reach into the bed of the pickup. And then she
was looking at the pale-blue flare of the barrel of a pistol
aimed at the second man.

Unable to believe what she was seeing, she pushed the
RECORD button to capture the images she couldn't look
away from.

She flinched at the brilliant flashes that exploded from
a pinpoint in the middle of her screen. Yet the sound of
the shots barely registered. Was that why the other man's
silhouette barely moved? His only response was a hard
grunt, as if he'd been punched in the gut. Hers was to stop
breathing.

The first man moved quickly, lowering the tailgate of
his truck even as the neighborhood came to life with barking dogs and doors banging shut. One brave soul turned
on a porch light. But no one came running over in answer
to a shot fired.

The shot man tried to stagger away. His assailant
wheeled and struck the man with the pistol butt, its barrel
still glowing eerily bright orange on Mac's screen from the
heat generated by the bullet's passage. As the wounded
man collapsed, the gunman caught and struggled to get
him up into the bed of the truck and shut the tailgate.

Mac bit down hard on her lip to stop the instinct to cry
out as he jerked open the truck's driver's-side door. But

then he paused, as if listening. With her heart banging in her chest, the need for air was pushing her hard but she resisted breathing, because the man was moving again. He closed the driver's door, moving in quick strides past the hood to come straight in her direction. He must be wearing boots because he made little clicking sounds as he moved.

As he neared, Mac lowered her phone, effectively blinding herself. It was a childish move, as if she thought that by no longer being able to see him, he wouldn't be able to see her, either.

Go away! she thought wildly, repeating the phrase under her breath. This couldn't be happening. He couldn't have seen her crouched down in the shrubbery. She wouldn't have known he was there if not for the infrared device. All she had to do was hold still and be silent.

He came quickly toward her, moving into the shadow of shrubbery that flanked the near-side sidewalk. Though she quaked with fear, she couldn't resist raising the camera once more to figure out what he was doing. Everything after that disappeared behind the metallic glare of that still-glowing hollow-eye pistol aimed in her direction.

No time to scream. He must have seen her, as unbelievable as that seemed.

Not again. Please, not again.

She didn't cry out. There was only the impulse to throw herself further into the bushes. To shield, protect, and block herself from what she knew, all too well, came next.

The sound of a siren wailing in the night sounded like her own smothered scream.

CHAPTER TWO

Three weeks later

"Engaged? Crikey!" Oliver Kelly stroked his short, thick beard. "That's—"

He glanced at his partner Jackeroo, an Australian shepherd lying on the hotel carpet a few feet away, as if his partner would know what to say.

The dog lifted his head, ears cocked expectantly.

"*Congratulations* is the word you're looking for." Kye McGarren sounded amused as his voice came through the cell phone.

"Yeah. That's it." Oliver motioned Jackeroo to him and began stroking the dog as he talked. "Good on ya, mate. But it's a bit sudden, isn't it?"

"It's been a year. Yardley's been tough to nail down."

Okay, so Kye and Yardley being in love wasn't news. They lived together when not on assignment for BARKS. Still. "Marriage. It'll change you."

"God, I hope so. It's time I settled down."

Oliver grunted. "You might have given a mate a heads-up, is all."

"You would have told Yardley."

"Never."

"Admit it. You gossip like a girl."

"Say that to my face."

Kye sighed. "That's the other reason I'm calling. I can't leave Yard right now. You're on your own this weekend."

"Fair dinkum. I'll give 'em right bloody hell." Oliver bit off the next sentence. He only went "all Aussie"—as Kye called it—when he was annoyed. "You know I hate these dos with everyone crawling up everyone's butt trying to drum up business. That's your department. You schmooze, I demonstrate. Public speaking gives me hives."

"Imagine your audience in their underwear."

"Fuck you very much. Now all I'll be able to visualize is a bunch of hairy-assed law enforcement alphas in Speedos."

"You that worried about going solo this weekend?"

Oliver was tempted to tell him the truth. Public speaking terrified him. He could regale a pub full of patrons with wild tales. But put him behind a podium and his throat closed up tighter than a sphincter. Of course that would be admitting vulnerability.

"Don't get your knickers in a twist. It's this sudden talk of settling down. You'd think—" He sucked in a breath. "Yard's in a family way."

Oliver could practically hear the grin that spread across his friend's face. "We're betting it's a boy. I'll send you the photos as soon as we get the sonogram done."

Oliver shook his head. "I'll pray for you, mate. You've fallen a long way from the path of the heathen brotherhood."

Kye laughed. "You'll tire of it one day. Bye, Uncle Ollie."

When the call had ended, Oliver looked over at his constant companion. "It's sad, really. A good man taken out in his prime. By love."

Jackeroo thumped his tail.

"Oh, you would side with Kye. That's because Yardley spoils you rotten when I'm not looking. Who gives a working animal T-bone steak?"

Jackeroo barked. One of his favorite words was *T-bone*.

He was a gorgeous example of the breed. His coat was longish and silky, with a white front that ran from his chin down both forepaws. His back and haunches were glossy black with touches of honey underneath, and he had white back feet. But it was his face that never failed to draw comment. A white blaze swept down from his forehead between high, flopped black ears, and around either side of his muzzle. Honey-brown fur covered his cheeks and circled his eyes, one brown and one blue. Dramatic kohl lines rimmed his eyes and mouth so that when he panted, everyone swore he was really smiling.

Oliver agreed. His K-9 partner was a handsome devil, and he knew it. Those floppy black ears peaked and swiveled like semaphore flags, signaling his moods. Right now Jack was very pleased with his world. He loved the beach.

Oliver shook his head as he pulled on board shorts. Being reminded of why he was in St. Petersburg Beach lowered his own enthusiasm for the beach resort several notches. He could really work up a resentment toward Yardley if she didn't make his partner so happy. It was fuckin' weird the way Kye's face lit up when she appeared. He became a big Day-Glo hunk of burnin' love. Pitiful.

"Uncle Ollie." He grinned suddenly as he hunkered down next to his K-9 and kissed him on the nose. "Think I'll make a good uncle?"

Jackeroo barked and licked his handler's face.

"Right. When the kid's old enough, I'll teach him every

bad habit I know. How to drink. Roll his own veggie cigs. How to surf and pull women. A real terror of an uncle, that'll be me."

Let Kye do the dutiful heir-apparent Prince William married-bliss thing. He was Prince Harry.

"Dirty Harry. Yeah." He liked the sound of that.

Oliver worked hard, putting in all the time and sweat his job required, and then some. If he wanted to mess about another ten or twenty years before settling down, then he right well would.

Except that the boast sounded lame. Like he was trying to cover up something. Or maybe he was just more tired than he realized. Burnout was an ever-present danger for people in his line of work.

Bolt Action Rescue K-9 Service was the full name of his and Kye's company, shortened to BARKS, which trained and supervised professional K-9 Search And Rescue teams worldwide. That often meant bugging out with an hour's notice to a place in the world where things had gone bad or deeply wrong. Be it a hurricane, an earthquake, a tsunami, mudslides, volcanoes, wildfires, floods, any and every kind of natural and some man-made disasters—BARKS was ready to go, bringing expertise and some of the best scent- and sight-trained K-9 teams on the planet to save lives.

He and Jackeroo, a K-9 team for three years, specialized in difficult search-and-rescue missions. The latest job had been enough to make a man shrivel inside. It was an off-the-books job involving the extraction of medical personnel from a war-torn area. They'd arrived too late. The hospital had been flattened by a bomb. All they extracted were corpses, many of them small children. What they'd left behind still haunted his sleep.

Oliver shook his head, willing the ugly images away.

He didn't always enjoy his job but he knew he or Kye would get it done the best way possible. Many didn't last long in a business that dealt with horror on a regular basis. Or else they became people you didn't want to know. Kye and he worked at keeping a sane balance.

That's why, when he could play, he played harder and faster and looser than most. Women were his recreational drug of choice. Strictly an off-duty short-term pleasure.

This weekend wasn't going to be any different. Here at St. Petersburg Beach, leggy women lounging on chairs in tiny bikinis would be as common as flowers in a florist's window, all stretched out before him like a personalized buffet for fun in the sun.

Oliver looked down at his K-9 partner. "Time to get out and search out some fun."

Jackeroo sprang up from his lying position and barked twice, his tail making wide sweeps of approval.

Oliver slipped his feet into beach runners and grabbed his sweatshirt from the back of a chair before heading for the door.

The other reason he was in town, the International Professional Search and Rescue conference, could wait until later. Much later.

Oliver shook himself like a wet dog to try to throw off the public-speaking willies.

An amazing swimmer, Jackeroo loved the beach. It didn't matter whether it was the pounding surf of the Hawaiian Islands, the clear waves of Bondi Beach, or this new experience of the American Gulf. He bounded along beside his owner as Oliver jogged along the water's edge, only to occasionally swerve suddenly and leap into the curl of an incoming wave. Oliver let him play, knowing his dog would eventually catch up as he ran his daily four miles.

Jackeroo had learned the hard way as a puppy not to drink salt water. After lapping up the sandy surf a few times and heaving it back up on his first seaside visit, he'd learned to just swim in the surf.

After a minute or two, Jackeroo came sprinting up beside his handler and fell into stride for a serious run on the beach.

"Good on ya," Oliver pronounced and received several bright barks of joy from his sodden dog. He'd have to bathe him to get the sand and salt out of Jackeroo's thick tricolored coat.

Oliver scanned the still-empty beach as they returned the way they'd come. Right now it was still too early for beach babes. He was just about to turn his attention back to the shoreline when he caught sight of a shabbily dressed woman on her knees in the sand beside one of the dumpsters in the shadow of a beachside hotel.

Even so, he jogged on a few yards until his mind replayed exactly what he'd witnessed.

A woman.

Scrounging for food in a dumpster.

Not in some hellhole on earth. In a first-world tourist Mecca.

It was that last thought that brought him up short. It made him backtrack and tie Jackeroo to a palm before he went to investigate.

CHAPTER THREE

"Come on, sweetie. Come to Mac. I've got something good just for you."

Macayla scuffled around on her knees and elbows in the sand as she maneuvered for a better view of the dog she'd been trying to coax out from under a row of hotel dumpsters for the past ten minutes.

Ordinarily, St. Petersburg Beach at sunrise was the last place Mac would be. She'd been roused out of bed an hour ago by a call from a security guard about a stray Pomeranian skulking around one of the beachside resort hotels. Luckily, the caller knew to contact the Pet Detective, as Mac had become known to the locals. One glimpse of the little dog and she knew she'd found Wookie, the Pom who'd disappeared during a vacationing family's excursion to the beach three days earlier.

If a lost pet was found quickly enough, a friendly face and kind tone was often enough to lure him into the arms of even a stranger. However, after only a few days and nights on the streets, many pets became too afraid to approach anyone, sometimes even their owners. When dealing with a pet out of his element, there was always the possibility of being bitten or scratched. That's why Mac wore long-sleeved shirts and her oldest pants on the job.

Ignoring the nearly overwhelming stench from the full garbage bins that had her breathing through her mouth, Mac bent down so that her cheek was almost touching the sand. All she could see of her canine suspect was a shiny black nose and two black marble eyes in a foxy face surrounded by a thick coat of reddish hair. His furry body, glimpsed when he dashed from under one dumpster to another, was matted with sand and seaweed, and something else suspiciously gooey. No doubt from the seepage collecting under the dumpsters.

Mac calculated her options. Wookie had ignored the dish of water she offered. The kind of squeaky toy that made most dogs delirious with joy lay untouched on the sand. Obviously, Mac had not offered the right bait. Or Wookie was too strung out by his ordeal to recognize a good deal when it was offered. Sometimes the more direct approach was needed.

Mac pulled kibble out of her pocket, then scooted her hand, holding three pieces of dog food, slowly toward the edge of the dumpster. Surreptitiously, she readied her animal control pole with the adjustable loop on one end. "Come on, Wookie. Your nice family is worried sick about you."

Wookie growled as Mac slid her hand inch by inch nearer. Then he darted out and grabbed a bite, only to drop it and scurry backward to safety before Mac could slip the noose over his head.

"You little brat." Mac collapsed belly-first in the sand, letting her frustration out in a huff.

Wookie, equally annoyed, banged around under the dumpster, barking frantically.

Great. Now she'd upset the poor little guy.

"Okay, okay. You calm down. I'll calm down. Then we'll think of something else." Mac sat back on her haunches with a chuckle.

Poms were notoriously stubborn. She didn't want her efforts to become a test of wills, or she might be here all day. Patience was the greatest virtue in her job.

Hoping for a breath of fresh salt air to cleanse her lungs, she glanced over her shoulder at the beach. Close in, cabana boys raked the sand and set up beach chairs for the hotel guests who would descend later in the day. Near the shoreline a few early risers were jogging or strolling along the wet packed sand. Above them a full moon in a fading night sky hovered just above the darker slate-blue water of the bay.

Swinging her head in the opposite direction, she saw that the rising sun had formed a golden aura behind the towers of the pink wedding cake structure better known as the Loews Don CeSar beach resort. It was going to be a nice day. But a low out in the Gulf promised rain later in the week.

Her attention came back to the dumpster just as the Pom darted out and grabbed the bite of food he'd dropped.

"So you are hungry." As she reached for more kibble, her own stomach cramped in sympathy. She'd left home so quickly she hadn't even stopped to grab coffee. Animals were notorious for disappearing before she reached a reported sighting location.

Remembering that she kept a protein bar in her pocket for just such emergencies, she pulled it out. Her mouth began to water even before she tore the corner of the wrapper.

A foxy face peeped out from under the dumpster. Shiny dark eyes watched attentively as she unwrapped the bar. Maybe Wookie had a thing for blueberry pomegranate acai bars.

Mac gazed at her snack. Should she sacrifice it? What if he licked it, got it full of sand, and then didn't eat it? What was it that flight attendants said? Make yourself secure before you try to help someone else. That was a good rule to apply to hunger, too.

She took a big bite of the bar.

"You really shouldn't do that."

Mac swiveled her head in the direction of the beach. The view was now blocked by a manly silhouette. Even as her eyes adjusted, the sun crept up over the top of the hotel to the east and spotlighted him in its golden light.

Startled, she let her gaze travel up yards of tanned skin and rippling male architecture, bisected by a pair of board shorts the color of a school bus. Those shorts just managed to hang on to the cliffs of his lean hips, where a tip of colorful ink peeked out above the waistline. The sleeves of a hoodie were tied loosely a little higher, at his waist. Emerging above, his broad-shouldered, ripped-muscle torso was balanced by two powerful arms, one decorated in a half sleeve of colorful tattoos.

Maybe it was the thick pile of sun-streaked hair, haphazardly twisted into a man bun on top of his head. Because, honestly, not every man could pull off that look. Or his red-gold beard, trimmed short but thick enough to be a statement. Or the warm intensity of his gaze, a rich blue somewhere between Caribbean Sea and desert turquoise. He looked like a superhero disguised as a surfer dude.

Stifling a laugh, she lifted her hand to shield her eyes. No, her eyes weren't deceiving her. He could be the model for that comic-book character Thor, so beloved by her nephew. If Thor was inked.

His expression was dead serious as he held out his hand. "Give that to me."

"No." Instinctively, she clutched the bar to her chest as she continued to kneel in the sand. Something about his voice intrigued her but she was too busy fencing with his gaze to give it much thought.

His expression altered, something like sadness or even pity entering those beautiful eyes. "I won't hurt you. Promise. I just want to help."

Help? Did she look like she needed help? Oh yeah. Suddenly she was seeing herself from his point of view.

She was wearing cargo pants with more holes than could qualify as fashionable. The rest of her attire included a man's button-down shirt several sizes too large, scuffed boots, fingerless gloves, and a tangle of thick dark waves under a cap. To top it off, she was kneeling before a smelly dumpster with food in her hand. She must look like a bag lady to him.

When his gaze came back to her face its intensity magnified. "If you need a meal, love, I'd be happy to stand you for breakfast."

Yep. The sun god thought she was dumpster-diving.

"I'm fine, really. Thanks for asking." Embarrassment washed through her middle and then rapidly receded, leaving her weak in the knees as she tried to stand.

He caught her by the elbow to steady her. Which was probably a good thing, because she'd been about to trip and fall right into the middle of his admirable pecs. Not that she was paying that much attention. They were just at eye level and, well—hell. They were firm and nicely sculpted under tanned skin that her palms itched to touch. Not that she went around touching strange men's pecs, or abs, or anything else. The beaches in St. Pete all had their share of gorgeous on any given day. But, honestly. He was more like an advertiser's idea of Surfer God. So not her type.

Mac mentally rolled her eyes. Who the heck was she kidding? He was every woman's type. The appeal was 3-D high-frame stereo-surround-sound male. The earth trembled a little. Or maybe it was just the sand shifting beneath her boots.

She was seldom caught off guard by her attraction to a man. That alone rattled her. Even on her feet, she was more than a foot shorter than he.

That's when it dawned on her that she was in an alley formed by walls lined with large metal containers on one side and a row of tall canebrake on the other, meant to shield the bins from the public. He was big, and as solid as carved stone. Not the sort of man she'd want to tangle with.

A nervous tic pulled at her mouth, which she instantly regretted because he noticed. His gaze narrowed in assessment. She took a deep breath, needing all the oxygen she could get to clear her senses as she tilted her head back, a long way, and met his gaze directly. "I'm not here looking for food."

Without comment, he glanced at the half-eaten bar still clutched in her hand.

She felt the burn deepen in her cheeks even as she offered an explanation. "This is for the dog I'm trying to lure out from under there." She made a vague wave toward the nearest dumpster.

The man followed her gesture in time to see Wookie make a Hungry Hippo lunge for another nugget of kibble she'd left in the sand.

A big grin revealed his nice set of teeth. "Your dog?"

"No. I do this for a living." She didn't need his raised

eyebrow to tell her that that sounded a bit off. "I locate missing pets. For their owners."

He frowned. Damn. Even his frown was cute. "You're a dogcatcher?"

"No. I'm a pet detective."

He didn't laugh. But his mouth crimped in an effort to hold it in.

This wasn't the first time she'd felt the need to defend her career choice. "To be more accurate, I'm an animal recovery specialist for Tampa/St. Pete Recon. That's a private investigation agency located in . . ."

"Tampa or St. Pete?" He was grinning now.

Damn. How lame could she sound? She shrugged. "Both."

"Animal recovery. How's that different from dog-catcher?" His voice had a pleasing growly aspect with some kind of accent she didn't intend to waste time trying to place. In her experience, golden boys like him used conversations with women as an excuse to show off. *Don't you think I'm sexy?* was implied in every word.

"It just is. Now if you'll excuse me, I need to get back to work." She glanced at the protein bar, thought about her surroundings, and tossed it into the dumpster.

The bar missed, bounced off the rim, and dropped into the sand. Now it was a total loss in more ways than one.

Mac bent to pick it up.

At that moment a puff of dirty red furry dog burst from under the dumpster barking furiously.

Mac quickly dropped to her knees and held out the bar. "Is this what you want?"

The Pomeranian sniffed it delicately then backed up and decided to make a run for it.

She leaped to grab the little dog as he sped past her but

missed, and ended up on her knees in the sand while Wookie headed straight toward the beach.

"Crap!" She scrambled to her feet, knocking sand off her clothing as she started after him. "Wookie! Wookie! Heel!"

Masculine laughter brought her head around sharply.

Something in her expression must have signaled the signs of a woman on the edge. More likely, barking-mad crazy female. He lifted both hands in defense, though his stage-perfect smile didn't dim a watt. "Looks like you got a real killer on the loose."

The way he said "a *reel keel-lar*" finally pegged his accent for her. He was Australian. Probably. And then who he was clicked into place for her. The looks. The body. The attitude. Of course.

She was tempted to ask, to make certain. But Wookie was making amazing progress across the sand. For a short-legged pup weighing less than six pounds, he was fast. In a minute, he would get away completely. She grabbed her pole off the ground and pelted after her quarry, not nearly matching the dog's speed in her boots on the dry, shifting sand.

She couldn't outrun the dog, but if she kept him in view he would sooner or later wear himself out and pause to rest. With a little luck—something she was having too little of this week—she would be able to snag him with her pole.

But the Pom was proving to be a canny little animal, zigzagging past the few strollers on the beach who tried to stop or slow him down. When he'd rounded a couple who'd paused to kiss at the shoreline, Wookie turned and cut back toward the row of hotels.

Panting heavily, Mac redoubled her determination not to lose sight of him. Maybe he was headed back to the safety of the dumpsters. That would be the best-case scenario, because she could wait him out once he was cornered again.

Almost before she could form that thought, Wookie veered off again, crossed the patio at the back of a hotel, and zipped into the adjacent parking lot.

Mac's heart lurched as she scrabbled up stone steps rising off the beach to cut him off. "No, Wookie. Heel."

She saw a waiter emerge from the row of private cottages opposite the parking lot and shouted, "Help me! The little dog. Stop him!" But the dog zipped past.

"No worries," Mac heard a man reply from behind her. "We got him."

She glanced back as the stranger from the dumpsters trotted up beside her with a medium-sized black, white, and tan dog on a leash. She hadn't noticed a dog before. Where had he come from?

He bent and unclipped the dog's leash, then gave a command. "*Go by*, Jackeroo."

Before she could protest, the dog whizzed past Mac, kicking sand on her legs as he ran. It took a few seconds longer for her to realize he was after Wookie.

She swung around. "Is that your dog? Call him back."

The man grinned and shook his head. "My shepherd will bring the little fella back to you. Watch."

Ignoring his calm assurance, Mac took off after the pair. Even as she neared them she saw that the other dog had come up fast behind Wookie and then cut quickly to the right, coming around in front of the Pom. He barked, several short sharp sounds that brought Wookie up short a few feet shy of the sidewalk and the street.

Far from being intimidated by an animal easily ten times his size, the little dog erupted in a fury of barks, unwilling to back down. The larger dog wheeled to the right again, coming up behind the smaller dog, forcing the Pom to turn away from the street in order to keep an eye on his attacker. Confronted by the other dog, all six and a half pounds of Pom barked furiously and tried to run past. But each time he tried, the shepherd blocked his path with a bark or a quick run at him, until Wookie became so agitated he was bouncing on the asphalt in alarm as he barked.

Mac watched, pole at the ready for her moment, as the dog kept Wookie from bolting to the street.

The shepherd's owner, who had come up to stand by Mac, suddenly whistled, a soft clear sound that must have been heard several blocks away.

The shepherd immediately stilled, no longer maneuvering as Wookie bounced around in front of him. Even so, the shepherd watched the smaller dog with a penetrating stare that seemed to say, *Don't even try it.*

Frustrated and panting heavily, Wookie turned one direction and then another, trying desperately to find a way past his nemesis. Finally, he swiveled toward Mac, and realized that the path to her was the only avenue open. He made a desperate dash toward her.

Dropping the pole, Mac grabbed and lifted Wookie into her arms, just to make certain she had firm and full control of the situation. "Okay, big boy. The fun's over."

The little dog didn't argue. Breathing heavily from his exertions, he eyed his tormentor from the shelter of Mac's arms.

Mac stroked him until he stopped shivering. As she did so, she heard the shepherd's owner say, "That'll do, Jack."

The dog immediately ran to his master's side, short tail wagging and tongue lolling from a wide-open mouth. He was a gorgeous black-and-white animal with a short bushy tail and tan markings around his two-color eyes, along his cheeks, and feathered along his legs. Floppy ears as mobile as flags made him seem very expressive. In fact, it looked like the dog was grinning as he sat and looked up at his owner.

"Good work, mate." The man knelt—she did not deliberately notice the shadow of a cleft as his shorts pulled tight low over his butt, but it was impossible not to—and stroked his dog with a big, matching smile.

Mac approached, intending to sound grateful for his intervention, but her treacherous gaze kept threatening to slip sideways to where that shadow deepened. She was not going to be caught checking out a man's ass. So not.

"Thank you." Eye slippage annoyed her into a pissy conclusion. "But you should have kept your dog on its leash. It's the law."

He looked up, giving her a surprisingly cool look from tropical blue eyes. "Jackeroo grew up on our cattle and sheep station near Canberra. Herding animals is in his DNA."

Remembering that she had a job to finish, Mac grabbed a slip leash from her pocket and looped it over Wookie's head before answering. "Yes, well, it's illegal here to have a dog off the leash in public places."

The man scrunched up his face, still managing to pull off handsome. "Americans. Bet you carry around those little poo bags, too." He held up clamped fingers as if gripping something distasteful.

Mac refused to be drawn into smiling. "Yes. I do. It's the law."

He rose to his feet, making her feel as if she shrank a foot just watching him rise.

She had to try even harder not to smile. Charm, she'd learned long ago, wasn't all it was cracked up to be. "Anyway, thank you for helping me."

He laughed suddenly, a large masculine laugh that cut

right through her thanks. "That offer of breakfast still stands."

"No thanks." She glanced down as Wookie pawed at and then rubbed himself against her shirtfront, as if to make certain he was sharing with her all of the smelly glop that covered his fur. She couldn't wait to drop the dog off and take a shower. "I need to get this little guy back to his owners."

"As long as it's not because you stink. Though, to be honest, you do. Have a nice day, detective."

"Right. Well, bye."

Shaking her head, Mac turned toward the parking lot where she'd parked her Honda Civic. That's when she saw two young men in hoodies emerge from the tall shrubbery that separated the lot from the street and approach the nearby line of cars.

It took her a few seconds to realize that they were searching for a particular car; then they stopped and checked the license plate of her car. They moved along either side of the Honda, pulled baseball bats from under their hoodies, and began smashing windows.

"Hey! Stop! That's my car." Mac ran toward them, Wookie in her arms.

CHAPTER FOUR

Oliver watched in disbelief as the young woman who called herself a pet detective—whatever that was—ran toward the two thugs whaling on her car with baseball bats.

It wasn't any of his business what she did. Heck, the way she was yelling, she might even know them.

Of course, they were damaging her property.

His conscience gigged him but he stood his ground. If she didn't have any better sense than to walk up on a pair of thugs with baseball bats, was it his obligation to step in and save her ass?

Something heavy settled in his chest as he watched her waving her free arm in the air and yelling at them to stop. Neither asswipe bothered to turn or respond. She might have been squaring off against a pair of Rottweilers. If they did get nasty, she'd have about as much chance of survival as that Pom she carried.

She saves puppies, mate.

"Bloody hell."

Oliver pointed to his dog. "Stay." He dropped Jackeroo's leash and took purposeful strides to wade into a fight he could not walk away from.

He'd waited a beat too long. Even as he fell into a trot he saw her grab the arm of the man nearest her and yank. "Stop. Stop that!"

Hoodie number one swung around, yelling, "Get off me, bitch." He stiff-armed her with his free hand, palm to her chest.

She staggered back two stuttering steps before she lost her balance and landed, hard, on the pavement.

Wookie, ejected from her arms on impact, erupted in an indignant flurry of barks, snapping at the assailant's ankles, taking the man by surprise.

The moment gave Oliver the distraction he needed to surprise her assailant from behind.

He grabbed the guy by the back of his jacket and spun him around. Simultaneously, he grabbed the bat and jerked.

Caught off guard, his opponent stumbled forward. Oliver met him with a sharp left jab to the face. Never his best punch, since he was right-handed. But it was enough to stagger the guy backward into the side of the car and make him release the bat in stunned surprise.

Oliver took the bat and heaved it as far away as possible. It sailed over the row of shrubbery and fell with hard rattling sounds on the sidewalk on the far side.

He was vaguely aware of people running toward them from the beach, whether out of a desire to help, or simply to watch the battle. But he couldn't wait to find out.

He pointed the second miscreant. "Clear out. Now."

"What the fuck? You want some of me, too?" The second hoodie grinned evilly as he rounded the car hood, swinging his bat repeatedly with both hands, as if he were practicing a bleachers-clearing home run.

Even though it was balmy, both men had laced their hoodies tight around their faces in disguise, making them look like twin Kennys from *South Park*. It also limited their field of vision, Oliver realized with a smile.

He didn't fool himself into thinking that because the second guy was short and much slighter of frame, he would be easy to shut down. Judging by the pimples visible on his nose and chin, he was seventeen or eighteen, only half Oliver's thirty-four years. But he had cunning on his side.

Oliver ducked back as the kid swung the bat in an arc through the space where his head had been a second before. Then he lunged forward, shoving the teen's wrists with his right hand to continue the momentum that twisted him at the waist, and shoved the heel of his left hand up into his chin. He heard the teen's teeth click together as his head snapped back. Oliver followed with a headbutt that buckled the kid's knees and he slipped toward the pavement, bat loose and rolling away.

A woman's cry behind him warned him of the first hoodie's recovery.

Oliver ducked as he turned but the fist thrown his way still caught him on the bony ridge above his eye. He saw stars as white-hot pain radiated through his skull. He knew the skin had split before blood ran into his eye. Tired of playing fair, and not willing to take any more abuse, he aimed a kick at the guy's crotch.

With a girlish yelp of agony, he went down.

"Oh no you don't! Come here."

Oliver swung around to find that the pet detective was on her feet again and trying to scoop up the Pom, who seemed determined to evade capture a second time. He whistled to Jack, who came instantly alert to the ancient command to herd, and moved in on the little dog in crouch mode.

The Pom stopped short, barking and quivering but offering no more resistance to the woman, who grabbed his trailing leash.

A tingling sensation made Oliver whip around. The home-run king was still on the ground, cupping his nuts and moaning so pitifully Oliver almost felt sorry for him. But not enough to keep him from scooping up the abandoned bat. He waved the tip of it under his opponent's nose. "Are we having fun yet?"

The teen groaned and kicked out weakly. "Get off me."

"You're a fuckin' maniac!" His fellow hoodie had staggered to his feet but he backed up as Oliver turned toward him. He glanced nervously at his companion. "Come on! We're done."

"I don't think so." Oliver grabbed the first guy by the elbow and jerked him to his feet. "The police are going to want to talk to you lot."

"No." Oliver turned his head in the direction of the voiced objection.

The Pet Detective had come up beside him. Her eyes were still big with shock but her voice was steady. "Let them go. It doesn't matter."

Taking that as his cue, the first hoodie jerked free of Oliver's grasp and ran.

Cupping his family jewels in both hands, his accomplice limped his way through the hedges and back onto the street, where a car was waiting to whisk them both away.

Oliver waited until they had disappeared before he

turned to the woman he'd been defending. "What the hell was that all about?"

"I—ah." She was saved from finishing by a sheriff's department cruiser pulling into the parking lot.

Deputy Sheriff Sam Lockhart shook his head as he looked over the damage to Macayla's Honda, which included broken windows, two blown tires, and fenders bent into freeform art shapes. The City of St. Pete Beach was a barrier island community whose law enforcement jurisdiction fell under the Pinellas County Sheriff's Office.

Though Sam wasn't the only officer on the scene, Macayla was grateful that Lockhart had taken the lead. He and she were friends. Had been since high school. The two other deputies who'd answered the call were interviewing the hotel employee who'd called 911, and a couple of tourists who'd taken video of the altercation with their phones.

As he approached Macayla, she prepared herself for his interrogation. Just because they were friends didn't mean he wasn't going to give her the third degree. Long and lean, with freckled skin and a somber long face that made him seem older than his twenty-seven years, Sam was a law enforcement officer, first and last. Friendship wouldn't patch over the incident. But that didn't mean she couldn't get around him.

She mentally straightened up as his basset hound gaze settled on her. "You won't be able to drive away from the scene of the crime this time, Macayla."

"This time?"

Both she and Sam glanced at the man who, to be honest, had probably saved her bacon twice in the past thirty minutes. He was standing a few feet away, legs braced and arms crossed over that magnificent chest. Behind his back, two teenage girls were checking him out. He'd already identified himself to Lockhart as Oliver Kelly of Canberra, Australia—*nailed it.*

Right now he was staring at Macayla as if she'd just kicked him in the shin. "You've been attacked before?"

"Not me personally." Not that it was any of his business. She had been avoiding thinking about the events that had taken place three weeks earlier. Now she was going to have to redouble her efforts.

"Excuse me." She moved past Lockhart to reach through the shattered driver's-side window and extract her purse.

Lockhart put out a hand to stop her. "You can't do that, Mac. You're tampering with evidence. Nothing can be moved until the crime unit is done."

Mac reluctantly withdrew her hand. "Believe me, they never touched the inside of my car. They were only interested in the outside." She avoided another survey of her beyond-damaged Honda. It hurt too much. "You want fingerprints, try the hood or the passenger-side door one of them slid down after being struck."

Lockhart glanced at Oliver. "That would be your doing?"

The big man nodded. "He swung a bat at me first. I tend to take a thing like that personally."

Lockhart nodded. "I'm getting a picture. What prompted you to come to Miss Burkett's aid?"

"An overdeveloped sense of chivalry." Oliver adjusted the single-use ice pack the officer had given him for his bleeding eye. "Two on one didn't seem like a fair fight."

Macayla rolled her eyes. "I could have handled that."

He grinned. "That was obvious from the way you were holding down the pavement when I stepped in."

Lockhart's attention swung back to her. "You were attacked?"

Mac shrugged. "I tripped."

"You were stiff-armed onto your back, the most vulnerable position there is."

Lockhart looked from one to the other with a thinning of his lips. "You two known each other long?"

"No—five minutes." Their answers collided.

"We're strangers," Macayla added for clarification.

Lockhart turned his attention to Oliver again. "Where were you when you noticed the disagreement?"

"It wasn't a disagreement," Mac cut in. "I had been chatting with Mr. Kelly about his dog." She pointed to Jackeroo, who stood patiently by his handler. "That's when two guys jumped through the bushes with bats and began caving in my vehicle."

Lockhart kept his gaze on Oliver as he asked, "Why your car, Mac?"

She shrugged. "Who knows? But they did pick it out. I saw them looking at license plates of other cars before they decided to destroy mine."

"So they knew whose car they were after?"

"They knew which car they were looking for. There is a distinction."

"So, which is it? They wanted to destroy *that* car. Or they wanted to destroy *your* car, Mac?"

"How should I know?" Mac ducked the officer's narrowing gaze and her savior's skeptical stare by setting Wookie on the grass, but held on to the temporary leash she'd dropped over his head. It was clear from his struggling that her rescued pup needed to pee.

Lockhart paused a second before saying a little too casually, "Too bad a big fella like you couldn't have detained at least one of them until we arrived."

Oliver didn't so much as glance at Mac, but she could feel the heat of the debate going on inside him from five feet away. Finally, all he said was, "Yeah. Too bad."

Lockhart watched him a beat longer. Then he turned back to Mac. "Got any guesses as to why someone would want to decommission your ride?"

Mac rolled a shoulder. "Because it's an eyesore?"

He shook his head. "You always had attitude, Mac. But this is serious. Attacks like this are usually meant as a warning. You owe anyone money? Missed a payment of some kind?" The look she gave him curdled the remains of his breakfast yogurt in his stomach. "Don't suppose you recognized either of the attackers?"

"Not really." From the corner of her eye she saw the Aussie's gaze narrow and knew he didn't believe her. After all, she'd asked him to let the attackers go. Why the hell should he care, anyway?

"Want to take a guess?"

"I'd rather not."

Lockhart stepped in close to her, cutting off Oliver from her view as his voice dropped to a near whisper. "This wouldn't have anything to do with your reporting a shooting over on the mainland three weeks ago?"

"Not now," Mac said under her breath.

"Yes, now." Lockhart's cop face dropped into place as he pointed toward his cruiser. "If you'll just step over there for a minute, Miss Burkett." Clearly he wanted to discuss this further, in private.

Reluctantly, Mac complied, but only because she didn't want to make any more of a spectacle of herself than she already had. Jefferina preached that keeping a low profile was rule one in the PI handbook. Or maybe it was number two, after, "Be safe."

When she reached the deputy's cruiser she spun around. "Okay, Sam. What do you want?"

"I want you to tell me what's going on. Weren't you told to keep a low profile until the St. Petersburg police investigation is done? Which, in my estimate of the events this morning, you're doing everything but."

"I was only doing my job this morning, luring a dog out from under a dumpster. That's not exactly high-profile stuff."

Lockhart glanced at Wookie, who was trying to hump his leg. "Geez. Curb your beast, Mac." He gently shucked him off with the calf of his other leg.

Mac reined in the little stinky ball of terror. "So, what's going on with the case, Sam? It never even made the papers. It's been three weeks and nobody has told me squat."

"That's because there's nothing to tell."

"Come on, Sam. It's me. You must have heard something via the grapevine." She'd learned from Jefferina that first responders gossiped among themselves like sorority sisters at a sleepover.

He scratched behind one ear. "I can tell you this much. They don't have a body. No suspicious gunshot wounds were reported by any emergency room in the area that night. None of the residents on the block would admit hearing the verbal altercation or a truck peeling out, let alone gunshots. Word is, without your video, the department wouldn't have taken you seriously."

"What about the call to nine-one-one?"

"It came from a burner phone. The neighborhood is full of pay-as-you-go phones." He gave her a sudden sharp look. "Could the attack this morning be tied to the shooting you say you witnessed?"

Mac took a deep breath to suppress the shock of nerves

erupting behind his reminder of how close she had come to being a second victim of the crime they discussed. "I don't see how. The—ah, shooter never saw me. The sound of the police sirens approaching made him change his mind about investigating the shadows I was hiding in. I'm still not certain if he knew I was there. Maybe he was just being paranoid."

"It takes steady nerves to shoot a man and then search for witnesses, instead of hightailing it away from the scene of the crime. That points to a cold-blooded type. Professional."

"Hit man?" She resisted the very idea. "What about the video I took? Wouldn't it be helpful in identifying the men?"

"It might be. If there was a suspect. St. Petersburg police have been tight-mouthed about there even being video. No one's seen it." He gazed at her hopefully. "What's on it?"

"Can't say."

The police had been quite clear about her *not* discussing the footage. To her dismay, it wasn't as sensational as she was sure it would be when she'd taken it. She hadn't caught the shots being fired. All she'd captured were shaky infrared images of two people moving behind the truck and then one man striking the other in the head with a bright object before flipping him into the back. There was a brief pan to her feet, reddish toes glowing inside her boots.

"I heard from a buddy in the department that they found some blood on the driveway. But without a body to match it to or witnesses to the shooting, there is no crime. The police have back-burnered the investigation until further evidence appears."

"But—"

"No buts. My advice, let it alone."

She let his advice sink in. Even for her, the events of that night three weeks ago were fast becoming more like a bad dream, without sharp edges or focus.

"There is some good news on another front. Only you didn't hear it from me."

Mac nodded. Sam was practically a one-man BuzzFeed.

"The necropsy report on the dogs you found? They were identified as the missing greyhounds."

In the uproar of the aftermath of the shooting, it had taken the police a while to home in on the reason she gave for being in the neighborhood in the first place. She was following a tip about the missing racing dogs. The source of the stench in the neighborhood was traced to the house in whose bushes she had been hiding when the shooting took place.

"What happened to them?"

"They'd been poisoned and left to rot. Vet said it looked like a last-minute job. A smarter criminal would have simply buried them in the yard with no one ever the wiser."

Mac swallowed convulsively as his words drew a picture she didn't want in her head. "Who would do that?"

"The prevailing theory is that the pair were taken for ransom." He stared at her before adding, "The owners refused to pay."

Mac frowned. She hadn't spoken to the greyhounds' owners. When Jefferina passed the job on to her, she'd never said anything about a ransom. Only that it was police business. "How much was the ransom?"

"Small, what we call a scrap metal crime."

"What does that mean?"

"It means the payoff from a crime is equal to what a petty criminal can make from fencing stolen scrap metal.

A couple of hundred dollars, at most. It's a petty crime that often stays under the police radar."

"Why?"

"Because pet owners just want their animals back safely, and quickly. The ransoms often aren't much more than people offer as reward for the return of a lost pet. So they just pay up and contact the police afterward."

"But the greyhounds were winners. They'd earned big purses. Why wouldn't the owners pay a ransom to get them back?"

Lockhart shrugged. "Not everyone has your tender spot for animals. Many breeders consider racing dogs a disposable commodity. They're uninsurable because they suffer so many injuries on and off the track. And there's plenty more in the kennels where they came from."

Macayla thought that over. Dog racing had a dubious and increasingly unfavorable image among many people in the United States. She was strongly in that category. Each year, nationwide, thousands of dogs were killed or injured in the sport. In Florida alone a racing greyhound died, on average, once every three days.

"If you're right, then why did the owners go to the police? And then go to the additional trouble of hiring me to find them?"

"Maybe they wanted the thieves caught before they could do it again." Sam smiled finally, and it turned his somber face boyish. "Despite the outcome, I think you do good work, Macayla."

Uh-oh. The only time Sam called her by her full name was when he was feeling sentimental toward her. She and Sam had dated exactly one month, in eleventh grade, and decided they were better friends. That stuck. At least for her. "How's Shay?"

His smile held. "Fine. We're talking about setting a date."

Mac socked him in the arm. "Go on, you dog! Congratulations."

Sam's ear tips pinkened. "Not now, Mac. Official business."

"Right." Mac picked up Wookie, unconsciously wrinkling her nose against the stench. "I need to get my quarry back to his family. If that's all right."

"Unless we get some new information . . ." He shrugged.

"I'm free to go about my life. Yay, me." She sounded much more confident than she felt. But bravado was all she had at the moment. "Thanks, Sam." She put a hand on his arm for emphasis.

Lockhart looked from her hand back over his shoulder. "That the new boyfriend?" He glanced past her to where the other two deputies and Oliver Kelly were observing them with interest.

Mac snorted. "Mr. Down Under? So not my type. Though I suppose I do have to thank him for stepping in."

"Yeah. I don't want to think what might have happened if you'd had to defend yourself alone."

The look of concern on Sam's face prompted her to be more honest than she had been. "Okay. I may have an idea who's behind this prank."

"Prank? They totaled your car."

"I know." Without an automobile, she didn't have the means to do her job. "But if I'm right, the instigator will want to make things right. Without police involvement."

Lockhart was scowling again. "Don't be stupid, Mac. If you're in some kind of trouble, you need to get in front of this. Talk to me. I can help."

"I'm not in trouble. If I need help, you'll be the first person I call. I promise." Mac made a production of crossing her heart with a finger.

He just shook his head. "Stubborn."

He added a few more notes to his notepad and then said, "We're done. You can take your things out of the vehicle when the crime unit is done. Meanwhile, I'll call a tow."

Mac shook her head. "I can't afford that."

He grinned. "I thought the doggy PI business was booming."

"Not new-car booming."

He nodded. "The tow is on the city." He looked down in distaste at the barking bit-of-fluff dog Mac held. "Ask Franklin to reimburse you for services. You were on the job."

"Toss in your cleaning bill, as well. As hazard pay."

Mac cut her eyes toward the source of that masculine comment.

Oliver had approached them. He stood a few feet away with his feet braced and his powerful forearms crossed, watching her. So far, he hadn't interfered with her version of the story. But she could tell by the stiff set of his shoulders that he was pissed about something. Probably his eye hurt like hell. Still oozing blood, it had puffed up until it was almost closed, but he had refused the offer by Lockhart to call the EMTs.

"See you later, Mac." He nodded at Oliver. "Sir."

Mac offered Sam a finger wave. "Thanks for being here."

Rather than try to dodge him, she turned to Oliver. "You're free to go now. Thanks again."

He didn't bat an eyelash. "Do you have any idea who did this, or why?"

"Not really." As close to an outright lie as she could tell with him staring her in the face. "And, really, this is none of your business."

"You could have said that before I took a punch."

"I didn't ask for your help." The way he looked at her,

all wounded-warrior offended, made her immediately ashamed. "Look. I appreciated your help. Really." She laid a hand on his arm without thinking about it. "And I'm sorry about your eye. You should get that looked at."

He grimaced as he touched it. "I'll manage. What are you going to do about transportation?"

Mac gave her car a sad glance. "Call a friend to come get me." She looked down at the animal wiggling in her arms. "I have to get this little guy back to his owners before I take care of anything else."

Oliver told himself that she was right. None of this was his business. Still he heard himself saying, "I can drop you off with the dog. And maybe I should get my eye looked at. It hurts like bloody hell."

Mac frowned. "I know a doctor who won't charge you, since it's me bringing you in."

She expected him to refuse, since he was good and pissed off. So it stunned her when he suddenly grinned and said, "Sounds like a plan."

CHAPTER FIVE

Oliver waited until they were in the stream of traffic before he glanced over at his companion. She was sitting straight up in her seat, having spread newspapers beneath her before she sat down. He was certain the car rental people would be grateful. They'd had to open all the windows to dispel the *eau de dumpster* that permeated both Wookie and her. It helped. A little. She still looked like a homeless person, except for the blotch of color in her hair revealed by her missing cap.

There was a thick streak of turquoise blue running diagonally from her hairline into the thick darkness of her waves where the streaks tailed off, like a comet. That kind of thing usually went along with a nose ring, gloppy mascara, and all-black attire. And plenty of attitude. Check *yes* on the last item.

At the moment, however, she seemed awfully subdued. Staring dead ahead, as if he'd steered them into five lanes of oncoming traffic, she stroked Wookie so hard the poor little pup would be bald if she kept it up. Her other hand gripped the door handle for dear life. Yep. Definitely a bit of shock setting in. Except for giving the occasional direction, she hadn't offered a word of conversation.

"You okay?"

She glanced at him, her rich caramel-colored eyes a little too wide for natural expression. "Of course. Why?"

He could think of about half a dozen reasons, starting with the fact that she was scared shitless, though he didn't know why. The freckles splashed across her nose and cheeks were standing in stark relief. But he'd had plenty of experience with people who'd suffered a shock. "You haven't told me your name. I'm Oliver Kelly."

She flashed a very fake smile. "Mac."

"Just Mac?"

She rolled a shoulder.

"Transgendering, are we?" She shot him a hostile sideways glance. "Just checking. What with the grunge clothing and turquoise hair dye, it's tough to tell who you're trying to attract."

"Not trying at all. This?" She swept a hand down her front. "Fashion statement."

He grinned. "What about the repell-y attraction vibe going on between us?"

She turned her look fully on him. "There's no attraction."

"Whatever you say." At least she was talking. "How did those asswipes know where to find your car?"

She repositioned Wookie, who was getting over his ordeal and becoming curious about the dog in the backseat. Jackeroo was watching the Pom with quiet intensity. "Lucky guess?"

"You told the deputy they knew which car they were looking for."

"Did I?"

Hard-ass. But so was he. "Those boys went all Beyoncé *Lemonade* on your car for a reason. That means you have an enemy. Had that occurred to you?"

Macayla didn't glance at him. She'd been thinking of little else. But she wasn't going to confide in a stranger. "You ask a lot of questions."

"You're trying to avoid them all."

She gave a little shake of her head. "This is not your problem."

"Tell that to my face."

She glanced back at him, really taking inventory this time. He was looking at her with his one good eye. The left was puffed closed. It dawned her that she should probably have offered to drive. A second glance at the hard set of his jaw beneath his beard told her that probably wouldn't have been a good move. He was trying to be a gentleman. Or maybe he was just the alpha-male sort who needed to be in charge at all times. Or she was just being difficult. Though she had no idea why.

To be fair, most people would have done what the other bystanders did. Call the cops and meanwhile take a lot of cell phone video of the violence they wanted no part of. "Why did you get involved in the fight?"

He was scowling when he glanced back from the road ahead. "You needed help. I was there."

"Is that the only reason?"

He gave her a curious look as he turned the corner. "You mean no other guy you know would have stepped in? Or do you think I just like a fight?"

She gave him a pissy look. She could feel it on her face.

He laughed. "Now, my brothers Rafe and Tommy would have rushed in for the sheer hell of it. Get a few beers down them and they go all aggro, spoiling for a fight. Started more than a few at the local pub in their younger years."

"What about you?"

He grinned. "I'm too vain to want to mess this up." He ran his palm under his chin as if presenting his face as exhibit number one.

Mac shook her head but smiled. She believed him. He had a lot to protect. Those cheekbones. That chiseled mouth. She noticed that his bun had come down in the altercation. Hair flowed onto his shoulders in the tawny shades of a lion's mane. As she watched, he ran a hand through it, fingers curled into a rake that lifted and settled the hair back from his face.

He caught sight of himself in the rearview mirror. "Aw, crap. I'm ruined."

"I wouldn't worry about that." Mac's dry tone brought his attention back to her.

"Sorry?"

"I mean, I understand your face"—as well as other parts of his ridiculously toned body—"is your fortune. But with a body like yours, most patrons won't notice a black eye." Her gaze slid over him to emphasize her point.

She didn't mean for it to snag on any particular part of him, like the hard curve of his shoulder nearest her. But once she began, the inventory took on a life of its own. He'd covered up his perfectly impressive chest by donning his hoodie. It looked as if he'd tucked a boulder in each shoulder seam. She'd already seen the abs, and the slim hips, and the tight curve of his ass. And the colorful shoulder tattoos. But it was the way he looked at her, like she had his full and complete interest. What woman could resist all that turquoise scrutiny?

"See something you like?"

What could she say? "Nice bod. Not that I'm interested."

"You totally are." He grinned and her toes curled inside her boots. There was a dimple hiding in his beard. A damn dimple!

Mac gave in to embarrassed laughter. "Okay. So you're a lot of hot. You expect ogling, I guess. Being in your line of work."

He frowned in puzzlement. "What are you talking about?"

"The Thunder from Down Under male revue. Your accent gave you away. There're billboards around advertising that you guys are in town. I've never been to a show, but I hear it's . . ." Suddenly she realized she couldn't repeat without blushing what she'd heard about all-male revues from her friends.

"A fun evening?" He was grinning wide, a twinkling of amusement deep in his gaze. "You should come to a show."

"Not my thing."

His amusement increased. "Too sexy?"

"Too sleazy."

His expression turned chill. "You just insulted my job."

Mac felt herself blush but didn't apologize. After all, this was a man who bared his ass for dollar bills. Still, she couldn't blame him for drumming up business. "Being nice to women comes naturally for you."

"Yes. My mum taught me well."

"She approves of what you do for a living?"

"Absolutely. My whole family's proud of the business I'm in."

"Hm."

"That was an insulting *hm*."

"Not my business. Here we are. Turn in here."

When they had found a space in the parking lot of Gulfstream Veterinary Hospital, Oliver rolled his head toward her. "The vet. You brought me to see a vet?"

She smirked. "It's not for you. It's for Wookie. I need to be certain he isn't suffering from any cuts or bruising from his ordeal before I take him to his owners."

"A bath and flea dip would be more in order."

Mac couldn't disagree. She had meant to make a joke of bringing Oliver to be treated by a veterinarian but his poor eye looked like raw meat. And that was no laughing matter. "The doctor I'm sending you to works in the Emerga-Care center just there." She pointed to a building across the street. "Ask for Dr. Alicia. Tell her I sent you and to put it on my tab."

"You have a tab at an emergency clinic?"

"I can get a bit scraped up chasing animals. I found Dr. Alicia's Rottweiler weeks after he'd escaped from her parents' care while she was on vacation. She was so grateful that she offered to take care of any injuries I might get, if they can be handled in the office."

Oliver was impressed. "She must really like her dog."

"Doesn't everybody?" Mac grabbed her purse, which Sam had handed off to her as her car was towed away. "Thanks for the ride." She reached back to give Jackeroo's head a scratch. "See you around. Or, no, I guess I won't."

Hand braced on the wheel, Oliver leaned toward the passenger side. He smelled good, of sunshine and warm skin. His smile could sell . . . anything. "That could change. Dinner?"

"Sorry. But I can't." Mac looked down, seeking less heat than his gaze. "I've got business. And my dogs. And things."

"I make you nervous."

She chanced a glance. "I imagine you make many women nervous." And hot and horny, et cetera.

Slow grin. "Sure you won't come by and catch my act?"

"No. Thanks. But no." Mac averted her eyes before they

could dip lower than his chin. No need to tease herself over what could not be. She preferred men who kept their pants on in public.

She slid out of her seat, Wookie in her arms. "You've been really helpful. Thanks again for the lift. And I am really sorry about your face."

"No worries."

He watched her walk away, unable to take his eyes off her. It wasn't as though she was spectacularly gorgeous. Cute. Or that he thought she was swaying her hips in a particularly provocative way for his benefit. She was half bent over that smelly Pom, whispering things too low for him to understand. Clearly her attention was on the dog. No, he watched her because he had the feeling that much more was going on in the pint-sized package than he knew. Perhaps more than she realized. The deputy had been concerned.

Oliver snorted as he reached to put his car in gear. Deputy Got the Hots for Mac had radiated territorial vibes that even Jackeroo had picked up on.

"If I put my mind to it, it wouldn't even be a contest." He cast that opinion over his shoulder to Jack, who leaned in and licked his chin.

Not that he was interested in seducing Mac— Shit. He hadn't gotten her full name.

He put the car back in park. He'd never come away with less than a name if he was interested in a woman. Not that he was interested in her, that way. But something was going on that made one side of her mouth pull down at the corner when she thought no one was watching her.

She was hiding something. It was there in the strain in her voice. By the absence of emotion, it was something big. He'd heard that lack of animation in a tone of voice many times, as people searched for a missing relative in the aftermath of an earthquake or a flood. Not yet willing to accept a horrible truth, they keep their voices quiet and their eyes open a little too wide in the hope of being wrong. Getting on with the horror of the searching, because if they stopped they'd be overwhelmed by their grief.

In response to that thought something heavy settled in his chest for a second time that morning.

Not his problem.

She kept saying that, as though he was a nuisance. Or she'd had way too much experience with people not being there for her when she most needed them. She could just be a giant pain in the ass—eye.

Oliver reached up to check his wound in the rearview mirror. But damn, he'd bled for her. He'd earned the right to at least her full name.

And that was the other thing. He knew for a fact that she'd ducked the question about recognizing the guys who'd busted up her car. One possible reason was that she was afraid of them. Another was that she was protecting them.

Oliver got out and opened the back door, dangling a leash.

Jackeroo, who made no move to exit the seat, watched him with lowered head.

"I know. You can smell a vet's office a mile away. But this trip's not for you. So buck up, mate. I'm the one going to visit the doc."

He glanced across the street toward the clinic, whose sign included a Red Cross symbol, and then back at the vet's entrance through which Mac and Wookie were disappearing. He should be able to keep an eye on the vet's while he got his eye looked after. Mac might think it was over but his curiosity was up. His brothers might prefer a fight. He loved mysteries.

CHAPTER SIX

"Thanks, Doc Webber. I owe you. Bye."

Mac backed out through the door into the vet's waiting room, using her hip to hold it open because her arms were full of Pomeranian, a plastic bag containing her filthy clothing, and her purse. Wookie smelled of the herbal peppermint shampoo she'd borrowed from the vet's on-site grooming center. While Mac's main job consisted of pet detective, she also taught dog behavior classes out of Dr. Webber's veterinary office, and occasionally sat in to do some grooming if they needed an extra pair of hands.

Transformed from a stray, Wookie looked dog-show-ready, groomed and blow-dried to pampered pet perfection. He seemed to know he looked, and smelled, good. His head was held high, ears forward, and he kept flicking his furry tail as if to draw attention to himself.

"There he is! Wookie!" A woman in floral stretch capris and a rose sequined T-shirt shot out of one of the plastic chairs in the waiting room and came toward Mac.

"Come to Mommy, sweetums!" She clapped her hands twice and then held out her arms.

Wookie erupted in high squeaky barks as he launched himself from Mac's into his owner's arms. She immediately buried her face in his immaculate fur as she hugged him to her. "You smell wonderful."

She glanced up at Mac with tears in her eyes. "I never thought— Well, you did it. You found him. Where?"

"Not far from where he disappeared. St. Petersburg Beach."

"He's okay, isn't he?"

Mac nodded. "I had the vet check him over. No serious problems, though we did have to trim him up a bit to get some of the goop out of his fur. He was flea-dipped and checked for injuries. Since we don't know what he ate while he was missing, you might want your vet to check for digestive tract parasites. The desk will have the details for you." She pointed to reception only to realize that there was no one behind the desk.

"You're a genius! What do I owe you?"

"Check with Tampa/St. Pete Recon. They'll have a tally for you."

"And that's what we call a didgeridoo."

Mac recognized the reason for the appreciative female laughter that followed that rough masculine exclamation even before she turned and looked down the long length of the waiting room filled with animals and their owners. Near the main door stood the epitome of male sex on two legs, Oliver Kelly. Just looking at him made her want to suck her stomach in.

He was chatting with several women who'd formed a semicircle around him. They didn't seem to realize, or care, that they had been loosely laced together below the knees by the intertwined leashes of their meandering pets.

Whatever they were chatting about seemed to be the most absorbing topic ever.

He looked up, saw her, and a smile broke over his face. That smile curled up like a soft warm kitten and nestled in her middle. He followed it up with, "There you are." He said it as if he'd found a prize.

Immediately four female heads twisted her way to see whom he had greeted so warmly.

Why that recognition from him made her feel special she didn't want to think about. Any tall, gorgeously built male with a killer smile would have had the same effect on her, she was sure. Pretty sure. She hadn't had a lot of experience with men who could set fire to a room simply by walking into it.

He said something low she didn't catch to his ad hoc harem, and then he was striding toward her, his gaze sweeping over her in a way that made her very conscious of being female. "You changed."

Mac shrugged. She didn't share Wookie's sartorial perfection. She'd had to make do with a quick shower in the vet's lavatory and a change into a pair of jean shorts and a gauzy crop top borrowed from Karen in reception. The top was made for a willowy woman with small breasts, like Karen. Macayla was very much on the other end of the spectrum and usually wore a bra everywhere but in bed. However, beggars didn't get to be choosy. Her bra, as smelly as the rest of her clothing, was in the bag she carried.

It was a fact that didn't go unnoticed by him. It wasn't a pervy stare, but Oliver's sea-blue gaze got stuck a second too long in the region of her chest for her to miss that he had registered the non-bra issue. "You clean up nicely."

"It wasn't much of a reach to improve from horror. But thanks. How's your eye?"

"All patched up." He touched the place that had been raw and oozing blood an hour ago. Now it was a clean two-inch-long seam neatly held closed by almost invisible Steri-Strips. "Doc glued me shut. She says I have free clinic privileges as long as I'm in town."

Mac didn't doubt it. As she suspected, now that his injury was tended to, the bruised purple eye didn't detract one bit from his manly appeal. In fact, it made him a little more appealing. He practically oozed sex. No wonder he stripped for a living. It wasn't much of a leap to imagine his G-string bulging with dollar bills. Not to mention— No! So not going there.

She gave herself a mental shake as Karen, the receptionist, walked up.

Karen touched Oliver's arm lightly, drawing his attention. "Your poor eye. St. Pete's usually a very friendly place. Love to show you around sometime. If only to make up for the poor impression you got of us this morning."

She sent an accusatory glance at Mac, as if she knew Mac was personally responsible for his "poor eye." "Glad the clothes mostly fit, Mac."

Mac grimaced a smile. "Yeah." Mostly. "Thanks."

"You take care." After a last pat on his biceps, Karen moved toward reception where Wookie's owner stood waiting for service.

Oliver grinned at Mac. "Nice girl. Friend of yours?"

"Yeah." Except for the territorial daggers she was aiming Mac's way at the moment, they were good friends who shared a love of animals.

She watched as Oliver reached up and gathered his hair off his shoulders into a bun he slipped through a tie; with a twist of his wrist, the sexy mess was done. As his hands moved lower one touched his wound, and he winced.

Mac winced, too, in sympathy. What was it about

women and injured men? Because, dammit, she was feeling that protective tug, too. She had to hold back the question, *Do you need anything? Ice? Water? Coffee? A shoulder to lean your battered head on?*

Oh no. The man tested positive for awesome. Now she'd caught the virus.

Shifting her gaze away from his injury, she noticed another change in him.

He wore a T-shirt with the slogan GOT STRESS? PISS ON IT AND WALK AWAY. On the back was an illustration of a dog watering a hydrant. It was one of several novelty tees the vet's office sold. "Nice shirt."

He patted the front. "My hoodie had blood on it. Karen gave this to me." He waved at the young woman now behind reception.

Gave it to him. Yep, a man in distress definitely brought out the nurturer in women.

But she had a life, thank you very much.

Mac hoisted up her bag. "Glad you're okay. Got to go."

She really didn't expect him to follow her. It was Jackeroo who, though leashed to a chair near the door, came to his feet and stepped into her path, tail wagging in greeting. *Ah.* She couldn't pass up the opportunity to love on the animal.

She squatted down and ran a hand through his fur. "Hey, Jackeroo. Just wanted to thank you for your help with Wookie. Good dog. You saved my bacon."

The dog barked brightly and licked her face. She wasn't sure which word he was responding to, but she was pretty certain it was *bacon*.

"Don't I rate a reward? I got injured on the job."

Mac scanned up the long way past hairy legs and neon-yellow board shorts, to the bearded man staring down at her. And said the first words that came to mind.

"Jackeroo's full of sand and needs a bath. I can take care of that."

Before she could change her mind, she had scooped up the Australian shepherd and was carrying him into the back.

Half an hour later she returned, sweaty-faced and with pieces of her messy French braid sticking to her forehead and cheeks. Jackeroo was on a lead, practically prancing with pride. His coat, once stiff with seawater and encrusted with sand, was once again free flowing and silky.

Oliver put away the cell phone he'd been using and came forward. "Is that Jack? Is that my Jackeroo?" he cried in a falsetto tone that brought glances of surprise from other clients his way. "It is. Come here, you big beautiful pup!"

Jackeroo responded like a puppy, leaping up into the arms of his owner and poking him repeatedly in the chin with his nose.

Holding fifty pounds of body-wagging dog, Oliver looked down at her and said, "What do I owe you?"

"It's on the house."

Mac glanced back over her shoulder at Karen behind the counter, who shrugged and continued to make eyes at Oliver.

Whatever.

Mac turned back. "So, both handler and dog are back in prime shape. I'm glad everything worked out. And now I think it's time we ended this on a high note."

She moved quickly out the front door, leaving behind what she could swear was a trail of sighs. Let him entertain someone else for a while. She was halfway across the parking lot before she realized she had nowhere to go until she made a call or two.

She whipped her phone from her pocket. Before she could push in a number a long arm with a hand attached reached over her shoulder and plucked the phone from her grasp. She spun around in exasperation.

"I don't have time for games," she said.

"Me either." Oliver took a step toward her. He was so close she could see the green shoals in his sea-blue irises. So close she had to tilt her head back to keep from staring at his shirt, or his Adam's apple, or his red-gold beard. She wasn't even surprised when he dropped a hand on her shoulder to steady her when she started to overbalance. And then very gently lifted a stray finger of hair back from her brow with the crook of one finger. "It's been real. But there's something I need to know before I walk away."

Had he moved in even closer? She could swear there was an invisible cord drawing her in toward his body. She stiffened her spine. "What is that?"

"Your name."

"I told you."

"Your whole name."

Deep sigh. "Macayla Evangeline Burkett."

"That's a lot of name, Macayla Evangeline Burkett." He grinned.

"Everyone shortens it to Mac."

"You might be small but like you, your name's got curves in all the right places. Macayla. Gives the tongue a workout."

He was flirting! She didn't know why his being so close made her nervous. But something about this man seemed wrong for her world flow.

Suddenly his gaze was serious. The warm blue sea turning a chill iceberg green. "You were attacked today."

"That's not news to me."

"It might not be safe for you to be running around in the open until the authorities find out why."

"I disagree. It was my car, not me, that was attacked."

"It could be that accosting your car was a way to lure you out into the open."

"I was already in the open. Chasing a dog, remember? Why not just find me at the dumpsters the way you did?" She flinched at the mental image of two men with baseball bats cornering her by the dumpsters. "Anyway, that's not why they were there."

"How can you be so sure?"

"I think I know who's responsible."

"Did you tell that to the deputy?"

"I didn't want to falsely accuse anyone."

"So what now? You're going to wait until they make a second visit so you can make a positive ID?"

"You're annoying, you know that?"

He grinned. "Ta. But seriously, Macayla. Those weren't amateurs. They'd had some experience with violence."

That was the same conclusion Sam had come to. Mac willed that thought away. If her theory was the right one, it was amateur night. And she so needed it to be the work of an amateur in the art of intimidation. "I need to talk to someone."

"Who would that be?"

"The person I think was behind the attack."

He studied her for a long moment, assessing the truth of her answer. He wanted to ask her a few more questions, but he didn't. He heaved a sigh. "I'll take you."

"Aren't you in town for a job? Don't you need to practice or something?"

Grinning like a madman, Oliver pulled up his shirt and did a hip roll and pelvis thrust then python-rolled abdominal muscles in a move that a *Magic Mike* star might envy. "Some of us are just naturally gifted."

Mac did a palm plant on her forehead. *Note to self: Stop encouraging this man.* He was beyond embarrassing.

If possible, he drew in a little closer, his warm minty breath caressing her forehead with his words. "Look at it this way. I have a car. You don't. I have time. You need a lift. I'll drive you to see this person. It never hurts to have a bodyguard around for these kinds of discussions. I'm already battle-tested." He pointed to his bandaged eye.

He knew how to get to her. She really did want to follow up on her hunch before she faced her boss Jefferina with the tale of her morning. And she was unlikely to make a creditable entrance if she arrived alone on a bus.

"Okay. But just this one stop. Then we're done."

He grinned. "We'll see. Where are we going?"

"To talk to my number one fan." So not!

CHAPTER SEVEN

It was a nice neighborhood full of small neat houses with trimmed lawns and tamed shrubs. A few even had window boxes sprouting colorful flowers. But one house, on the corner, looked as if the Gingerbread Man had turned Goth. The house was white with black wooden shutters and a porch that ran across the front. The paint looked so fresh it seemed to have not fully dried, as if daring the Florida sun to crisp, flake, or bake its austere perfection. Even so, it didn't look like the home of someone who cared about curbside appeal. Not a single flower, shrub, lawn ornament, or anything else decorative marred the two green felt squares of grass bisected by a narrow concrete sidewalk that led to the front door. The grass was edged to perfection. Too much perfection. It was as if it had been trimmed by the Grim Reaper to knife-edge precision.

Lining the front of the yard like a miniature picket fence was a series of signs that read: KEEP OFF THE GRASS. CURB YOUR ANIMALS. THIS GRASS HAS BEEN TREATED. NO PETS. NO TRESPASSING. NO CHILDREN.

A small elderly man stood on the porch, his eyes searching up and down the street. Narrow of face and body, he was a string bean with hips so slim that not even a belt could keep his pants up. He wore suspenders over his T-shirt. With a bald knob head that seemed too large for his scrawny neck, he looked a lot like Barney Fife. But at heart, he was a bully with delusions of grandeur, mostly about his rights as a citizen and homeowner. His name was Joel Massey.

"That's the guy you think is responsible for the damage to your car?" Oliver leaned across the steering wheel for a better view. "He doesn't look like he could stand up in a stiff wind."

Mac nodded. "You'd think that. But he's got a mean streak a yard wide that holds him up."

Oliver's expression brightened. "You've had dealings with the man?"

"Twice, so far, this month. He's the neighborhood asshat."

"What did he do?"

"See those signs?"

Oliver glanced at the signs with a frown. "Okay. Tell me what I'm missing."

"It began when a neighbor of his hired Tampa/St. Pete Recon to recover her missing cat. I did some neighborhood reconnaissance and learned that Massey hated pets. So then I did a bit of snooping."

"You mean trespassing."

She sent a sly glance his way. "It's called following a tip. I discovered Massey had my client's cat, plus a dozen other missing neighborhood cats and dogs, locked up in a storage shed in his backyard. They were filthy, hungry, and dehydrated. He'd covered up the stench by tossing in bags of cat litter periodically. I called the police. He told them that he was only looking after strays he'd found in his yard. Doing his own animal rescue."

"The police didn't arrest him?"

Mac shook her head tightly, getting angry all over again. "They couldn't prove he stole the animals. Only that he detained them. The owners admitted that their pets were off leash at the times of their disappearance. Massey was only fined for having more animals than city ordinance allows without having a license to run an animal shelter."

"And he blamed you for the fine?"

"You got it. So then last week several animals on the block developed sores on their paws and the neighbors weren't sure why so they called me."

"Why not the police?"

Mac shrugged as she watched Massey survey the block like a sentry on duty. "I could smell the reason for the problem half a block away. Massey had dumped cans of cayenne pepper all over his yard to try to keep animals off his grass."

"He's got a right fetish about his grass."

"You could say that. Massey claimed that neighbors were deliberately bringing their animals to decorate his yard with feces and urine out of jealousy. He now had proof in that the animals could only have suffered chili burns if they'd trespassed on his grass yard."

"He's a wanker. But a clever one."

"Yeah. He's a real peach."

Oliver eyed her thoughtfully. "You really don't like him."

"I'm worried about what happens next. He's escalating. He's lucky a child didn't get into the cayenne before he was reported. The police fined him and told him a third call out would result in him being charged with creating a public nuisance, which can carry a jail sentence."

Oliver wagged his head. "You think damaging your car was his way of getting revenge for the second police visit?"

"That's what I want to ask him."

She reached for the door handle but Oliver reached across her and grabbed the doorframe. "You aren't seriously going to confront the nutter?"

"It's broad daylight. I'm just going to talk from the sidewalk."

"Then I'm coming with you." The stubborn jut of his chin said there'd be no persuading him out of it. "He's a whack job, as you say. That doesn't mean he's not dangerous."

"Fine. Just let me handle this."

Mac felt a little self-conscious as she approached Massey's yard. She wanted to hunch her shoulders as a trickle of sweat from the humidity of the warm day skied down her spine. The weather report on the car radio said that the low in the mid-Gulf had become a tropical depression. It was predicted to become a full tropical storm later in the week as it bobbed in the warm waters like a cork in a hot bath. Possible landfall was still a huge fan-shaped pattern from Louisiana to the middle of western Florida. At the moment, it was a sticky sun-drenched day in St. Petersburg.

Of course, her discomfort might come from the fact she was wearing shorts and a crop top, braless. Not at all her style. Men had radar for such things. Massey watched her approach with narrowed eyes and a permanent smirk that had nothing to do with humor. She could develop a serious rash from that stare.

When he didn't speak, she stopped three steps from his porch. "Morning, Mr. Massey."

He snickered. "What brings you around these parts, Pet Dick?"

Mac ignored the insult. Making fun of her job kept half the town snickering. "I'm here about a car."

"None for sale on this street."

"It's the one I was driving until two thugs with baseball bats made it impossible."

"That so?" Despite his efforts, a huge smile blossomed into a lipless gap in Massey's face. "Getting so a body can't stand in his own yard and feel safe."

"You weren't standing your ground last month, Mr. Massey. You willfully covered your yard with pepper in order to cause injury and damage."

"It's my right to do with my yard as I see fit. It's in the Constitution. A man's home is his castle."

"Reckless endangerment is against the law. You knew it would injure your neighbors' pets."

"What pets would that be? The ones that the neighbors won't keep off my property?" He pointed to the front of his yard where those signs were impossible to miss. "I did the animals a favor. Do you see any loose animals on my street? Do you see piles of dog shit on my yard, or any yard on this street? No, you don't. That's thanks to me."

"Then you should consider that your civil protest was worth the fines."

His face puckered up like he'd tasted something nasty. "You didn't have to turn me in, but you did. Those fines are on your head."

"So you thought you'd hire someone to take it out on my car?"

"Don't know what you mean." But he couldn't keep a second smile from his lips. It dried up almost instantly. "Who's that with you?"

Mac felt Oliver move in behind her, as if he was provoked by Massey's words when she wasn't. She'd never had a bodyguard before. It felt weird. Still, her show.

"Can you think of anyone else who'd want to damage my property, Mr. Massey?"

"I couldn't say. But I'm sure I'm not the only person you've persecuted with your weird ideas about animal rights." He crossed his arms over his bony chest. "So how do you like it when people trespass on your property?"

"You didn't trespass, Mr. Massey. You destroyed."

"Don't dramatize, Miss Burkett. A broken windshield—if that's what happened, since I don't know for sure—isn't much. A pebble from an eighteen-wheeler could have caused that same damage."

"It wasn't a truck. It was your grandson, Woody. I recognized him in his car parked in the street." It was a total lie but she thought it was worth a gamble. "He and his friend didn't just break my windshield. They totaled my car."

He scowled. "That wouldn'ta been Woody. Even if he got it into his head to do some blame fool thing, he wouldn'ta done more damage than to make a point."

"Is that what you told him?"

He jutted out his chin, bony shoulders dragging upward. "Don't know what you're talking about."

"Why don't we ask him?" Mac pointed to the skinny teen pushing through Massey's screen door. "Hello, Woody."

A younger, healthier version of his grandfather with a shaved head, gauges in his ears, and a mismatch of tats showing behind his white T-shirt sleeves, Woody paused with a piece of pizza halfway to his mouth. "Who're you?"

"The owner of the car you and a friend beat up this morning."

Woody shrugged and pushed on through the doorway. "Don't know nothing about that."

"I've got proof it was you."

"That's not possible." He exchanged glances with his grandfather before blurting out, "I farmed it out."

"You what?" Massey swung around on his grandson.

Woody froze like he'd been busted with a bag of weed and a joint between his lips, while his half-eaten pizza slice drooped off the end of his fingers. "You offered me fifty dollars. I had a date so I gave a twenty to a friend to do—something." He smirked at Mac. "Whatever happened, I'm innocent." Mac smiled. Just as she'd figured.

"You retard!" Massey swung around on his grandson and waved a gnarled fist. "They totaled that damn car."

Woody's pale eyes bugged out a bit as he did a theatrical backstep, the cheese on his pizza sliding off unnoticed onto the porch. "That wasn't me."

Massey turned back to Mac, his expression realigning into lines of combat. "What are you going to do? Call the cops, little girl?"

Mac was beyond baiting. "I need transportation in order to do my job, Mr. Massey. Solve that problem for me and we're good." She glanced at Woody. "As long as it doesn't happen again."

Scowling, Massy turned to his grandson. "You got your car keys on you?"

Woody nodded and pulled them out of a pocket. "You want me to take her home?"

The older man snatched the keys out of his grandson's palm. "No, you're loaning her your car until such time as you make reparations."

Woody gaped. "My car? You can't give her my car!"

"Last time I checked the registration was still in my name. That's a lesson for you, boy. You could've been fifty dollars richer and kept your car, you done as you were told."

Massey turned to Mac and held out the keys. "I apologize

for my dumbass grandson. Shoulda known if I'd wanted something done to do it myself. Not that I'm admitting to nothing. Your word against ours. Still, you've got wheels now. What you gonna do?"

Stunned by the offer, Mac hesitated to reach for the keys.

Seeing his moment, Oliver intervened. He grabbed the keys and pulled her aside at the same time so that his body was between her and pretty much the rest of the world, since he topped her by more than a foot. "Let the kid keep his ride. You don't want to be caught taking a bribe if things get ugly. Better yet, let me explain to him how it's going to be."

Seeing protest bunch up in her eyes like storm clouds, he didn't wait for a reply.

He turned and approached the kid.

Woody was leaning against a porch post opposite his grandfather, munching the remainder of his bald-crust pizza. But as the six-foot-four Aussie approached he straightened up, his eyes growing wide.

Oliver marched up the first two steps, enough to give him most of his height advantage. Yet he spoke very softly as he dangled the keys before the young man's face. "I'm giving you a chance to earn back your car. In return, you're going to make Ms. Burkett's well-being your number one priority."

The kid shrugged and reached for the keys. "I done nothing to her."

"Wrong answer." Oliver snatched back the keys. "I'm the guy who took down your homies. They tell you about the fight?"

The kid backed up a step, indicating he'd heard something. "They said they were attacked by a bunch of guys."

"I'm the bunch." Oliver grinned evilly. "And they had

bats. You getting a visual? Good. If Ms. Burkett gets so much as a fleabite after this, you deal with me."

The younger man scowled, too nervous to reach for the keys a second time. "They weren't supposed to total her car."

"Oversight of employees is a bitch. That's why I don't delegate." Oliver jangled the keys in front of the boy's nose. "You hear anything on the streets connected to Ms. Burkett, you tell her. Immediately."

Woody glanced at his grandfather, who was watching him with a sneer of distaste. That hostility gave him a spurt of courage. "What's with the funny accent? You don't sound like a cop. You one of them rent-a-cops from the mall?"

Oliver grinned. "Let's say I'm private security."

He saw the younger man pale a little before he shut down his fear. "You work for her? That pet dick? Pet dick. I got a dick she can pet." He snickered, overcome by adolescent male humor despite the circumstances.

Oliver took a step closer, leaning down into Woody's face until his head was craned as far back as possible on his neck. "You don't get to think nasty thoughts about Ms. Burkett. Not even in your dreams. So clear your lame brain of porno ideas." He thumped the younger man on the forehead.

"Yeah. Whatever."

Oliver backed up a step. "Ms. Burkett wants to save you jail time. So we're going to play this her way. Don't make me wish I'd overruled her. Because if I come back I won't be bothered by rules of law." He touched his bandaged eye. "Ask your mates."

"Yeah. Okay."

Oliver dropped the keys back in the boy's hand. "Fair dinkum."

Massey waited until Oliver had retreated to Mac's side before he spoke.

"You come all high and mighty with me, Ms. Burkett. But I heard about you."

Mac knew better than to take the bait. Absolutely knew better. "Like what?"

"Dognapping, Ms. Burkett." Massey nodded. "You hire street people to steal dogs and then you show up at the owner's home, offering your services as a pet detective. If they pay, you bring the pets back, pretending like you found them when you're responsible for them being stolen in the first place."

Mac rolled her eyes. "You need to stop smoking your grass clippings, Mr. Massey."

Mac felt a tug at her elbow. She looked up into sea-blue eyes. "We're done here."

Mac gnawed her lip as she followed Oliver back to his car. That was twice that he'd stepped in without her asking for his help. When he wanted, the man beside her could switch out the flagrant man-slut attitude for a kind of scary-quiet alpha confidence. Woody hadn't been the only one to feel the danger vibes coming off Oliver. He'd been deadly serious, and meant every word he said.

She was beginning to suspect there was more to Oliver Kelly than met the eye. How much more, she wasn't certain she wanted to know.

She was even less certain of her reaction to him. Because deep down, she was feeling an awareness of him that bordered on attraction.

She glanced up sideways to find him watching her with a speculative gaze. Check. Speculative on Oliver Kelly was pretty spectacular. Suddenly the sidewalk went all melty soft from the heat.

Ridiculous. She didn't need Sex-On-Two-Legs in her life. She had enough to deal with.

Once inside the car, she gave up trying to guess what motivated Oliver Kelly. No matter his intention, she needed to set him straight on a few things. "I appreciate you trying to help but there were better ways. Intimidation of a minor? Way to go. Now I don't have a ride, and I've made an enemy."

"You're kidding, right?" Oliver pulled away from the curb. "The kid adores you. Hell, he wants to do you."

"Did not need that information."

"No, it's good. It means he'll do anything for you. You didn't call the cops on him. He'll brag about that to his friends. How you're all up in his shit with any excuse."

Mac grimaced. "Oh joy."

Oliver grinned and nodded. "In addition he gets to lie and say he saved their butts by dealing with me, the guy who kicked their butts. Finally, Woody needs to turn all that adolescent sex drive for you into something he can boast about. In trying to look out for you, he'll be proving his manliness to himself." He winked. "No worries."

"Awesome. Except for the part where I don't have a car." She made driving motions with both hands.

"No plan's perfect. Where to next? I'm getting into this protector stuff."

Mac turned to tell him exactly how much she didn't need a protector but found herself drinking in his expression. It took her breath away. Despite his no-worries tone, concern and interest were doing a tango in the twin Caribbean pools of his eyes.

Having him look at her with such concern was having a strange effect on her. She wanted to confess that she had no idea what came next. That not having a car was tantamount to losing her job. That she was worried about making her rent. But it wasn't his concern. Nothing that had happened since he'd stepped into the shadows where the hotel dumpsters stood had been his concern. Yet here he was, staring down at her with those incredible eyes and an expression that said he was seeing more than she allowed most people in her life.

He's passing through. He's got a lot of women to entertain before he goes. He's an actor or dancer. Whatever. Part of his job was to make it believable that every and any woman he looked at was the most desirable thing on the planet.

Shaking her head, Mac unfastened her seat belt and opened the passenger door as he stopped for a light.

"Hey." He reached for her but she slipped out too quickly. "Where are you going?"

"I'm going to work." She slammed the door and broke into a run.

She made it to the corner just in time to catch the bus about to pull away.

Oliver looked down at Jack, who hopped into the front seat she'd vacated. "Think we handled that well."

Jack tilted his head to one side.

"Yeah." He'd pretty much bungled the whole morning. He was usually much smoother with women. Hell. Women loved him. He didn't have to try. Of course, he hadn't much practice with dumpster-divers.

A car behind him blared its horn.

"Yeah. Yeah. Keep your knickers on, darlin'."

He drove through the intersection, realizing he wasn't going to see the pet detective again. Ever. Not that it was a big deal. She was a big girl. She was accustomed to taking care of herself. He wasn't looking for a nice lady friend. Now, some down-and-dirty sex, that was more like it.

He looked up ahead and spotted a billboard with eight shirtless men, oiled and tanned and ripped to perfection. No need to read the words. Macayla Evangeline Burkett thought he looked like that? *All right!*

He sat up straight, sucked in his gut, and began pumping his pecs to the imaginary rhythm heard only inside his head.

A long wolf whistle jerked his head toward the car that had pulled up beside him at the next stoplight. Three Latino men in work clothes and hard hats sat in the back of a pickup, waving coquettishly and blowing kisses.

He laughed and offered them his Aussie middle-finger wave as he pulled away, feeling a lot lighter in spirit.

It must have been the threat of the speaking engagement hanging over his head that had been messing with his mind when he encountered Macayla. That, and the encounter with Massey and his dickhead grandson had punched a hole in his usually sunny mood.

"Pet my dick." He snickered, overcome by the same adolescent humor as Woody. But it lasted only seconds before he was scowling again.

Jesus. He was completely off balance. He hadn't done his weights. Missed his martial arts workout. Hadn't even had breakfast.

He glanced at Jackeroo. "One bark for egg-white omelet. Two barks for pancakes and ham."

Jack barked twice. Who said dogs didn't understand words?

CHAPTER EIGHT

Macayla knew the exact second it went wrong. The court-room had been filled with the hum of voices—not un-usual before the bailiff called the room to order with the appearance of the judge. In that moment, only she saw the man enter the child custody hearing room of the Tallahas-see courthouse, the beginnings of his smile telegraphing his intent.

He came straight toward her and her partner Katie, a mixed Lab, who was a courthouse facility dog. They were sitting off to one side, waiting with this man's ten-year-old daughter until it was time for her to testify against him in a domestic abuse case.

That little puff of air. It escaped between his fleshy lips like the sigh from the neck of a balloon.

And then she was looking down the barrel of a pistol. Everything after that disappeared behind the metallic glare of that hollow eye.

No time to scream.

There was only the impulse to throw herself over the

child hugging her dog. To shield, protect, block whatever came next.

She didn't feel her body moving. Only dimly registered the flash. Barely heard the shot.

Pain. Searing through skin. Tearing into muscle. Cracking bone. The stunning sensation of fire, inside, stopping her breath.

Macayla opened her eyes, staring at nothing until her vision adjusted and she realized she was looking at the ceiling of her bungalow on 49th Street in Gulfport, Florida. She didn't need to glance at the clock. She knew what time it was: five forty-seven a.m. She woke every morning at the same time. Every time.

It had been nearly six months since she'd woken scrambling into reality from that particular nightmare, a year since the actual event.

She should feel grateful for the half-year reprieve. Except that it had been replaced three weeks ago by a different specter, of an infrared image stalking her with a flame-barreled gun. Now the uglier memory had reinserted itself into her life. Two experiences blending together in horrifying detail.

She felt a bit sick, like she'd been too long in the Florida sun in a small boat, on a rocking sea.

She put a hand to her mouth and levered herself upright. "Not going to hurl. So not going to do that."

Her voice sounded dry in the silence, like the heaves would be if they defied her and came anyway. "It's just a dream. Just a friggin' dream!"

Maybe. But nothing about the dream, or her reaction to it, had altered in any way during the past year. The same flop sweat as before made the sheets stick to her torso and legs like Saran Wrap. The same sick pounding of her heart remained long after her eyes were wide open to reality.

Months of counseling had helped. She no longer felt the guilt of not shouting out in warning. She was a hero. Everyone said so. Because the child's life had been saved by her.

But she'd lost Katie.

Macayla opened her mouth as wide as she could, until she felt her jaws would crack. She'd learned that trick in middle school. Opening your mouth really wide pinched the tear ducts shut. An important bit of knowledge for a girl navigating seventh grade. And now.

Not thinking about Katie.

Not owning a dog or cat helped. Sticking to helping others hold on to their precious pets. That was enough for her.

Her gaze lit automatically on the lead-glass dolphin night-light plugged into the wall a few feet away. The cheerful blue-and-white creature was in midflight, tail arched to complete a backflip over a curl of silver surf. She'd bought it in a baby store to keep her company at night. Something to focus on when life threatened to overwhelm her. How shameful was that?

She'd once heard a TED Talk where people heralded as heroes tried to make sense of the impulse to risk everything for a stranger. They all said the same thing.

"It seemed the right thing to do. I didn't really think about it."

Didn't think.

Those two words still haunted her, a year later. That was her greatest failing. When something or someone was in trouble, she often didn't stop to think. Like yesterday. First when the Pom nearly ran into the street, and then later when she saw those guys destroying her car, she'd acted without stopping to think. If she'd thought twice about her actions, she could have kept Oliver from getting into a fight. For her.

That thought brought her up short. Oliver had fought for her. And been injured, though he'd clearly won that battle.

She couldn't help smiling at the memory of him grinning like a kid, with blood running down his face. She'd been both horrified and a bit turned on.

"You hypocrite." The words hung in the silence.

Some women thought men getting in a fight for or over them was sexy. The idea had never appealed. She didn't want anyone in jeopardy for her. Why should she feel a surge of lust for a man who was a stranger, just because he'd bested two other guys?

Okay, not just because of that. Oliver Kelly was something else. Funny, irreverent, and caring. He'd offered to buy her a meal when he thought she was a street person foraging for food. Not your average guy. More than charming.

He had a very nice smile. She liked nice smiles.

Maybe she should have been nicer.

Make that definitely.

So maybe she'd go to see his male revue after all.

Feeling a little less shaky, she palmed her cell phone off the nearby table to check the time. "Crap!" It was now after six a.m. She was supposed to report to Jefferina Franklin, who'd been on a stakeout overnight. They were meeting in twenty minutes. The PI business had a lot in common with shift work. Assignments often meant working at night and sleeping as one could find time during the day.

Mac peeled herself free of damp sheets and swung both

tan legs over the side of the bed. The painful catch in her lower left side caught her by surprise.

She stood up gingerly and felt along her left side below her ribs. Something must have gotten wrenched when she was stiff-armed to the ground the day before. She'd been so pumped with adrenaline, it hadn't registered. The soreness was a reminder that, though it had been a year, she had not gotten away without her own scars, emotional and physical.

Hit man.

Sam's words drifted into the sun-drenched bedroom like an unseen specter.

Mac shivered and reached for the T-shirt she'd peeled off during the night. The police didn't believe she'd witnessed a crime? Yet she had video proof of the altercation. What did they think happened?

Professional hit.

That sounded like something from a thriller. She was just a pet detective. She'd just been in the wrong—no, the right place, at the wrong time. Still, it wasn't her problem. There'd been nothing in the media about the crime—no, non-crime. Nothing to connect her to what she'd witnessed. Or her discovery of the greyhounds. She'd never even met the greyhound owners. Jefferina had been the contact. Whatever had occurred had nothing to do with her. She was safe. Right. Safe.

Mac occupied one of the pair of chairs that flanked her boss's desk. She'd just finished recounting the details of her rescue the day before. Debriefing, Jefferina called these verbal reports.

Jefferina Franklin, owner of Tampa/St. Pete Recon, sat behind her desk at the offices located just off Beach

Boulevard in Gulfport. She wore a crisp collared white
shirt, open at the throat, a khaki jacket with matching
slacks, and moto boots with buckle and zipper details. She
had a face that could best be described as majestic, high
planes of forehead and juts of cheekbone wrapped in rich
brown skin. Today her crisp dark hair was pulled back in a
neat chignon, her only concession to the pre-storm humidity blowing in off the bay a couple of blocks away.

As for her expression, it said *cop-calm but ready for
anything*, an unusual mind-set for the office when it was
just the two of them. Mac just had no idea what had put
her boss on guard. But she knew to tread lightly.

Finally Jefferina spoke. "The Pomeranian owner wasn't
happy about the vet bill you stuck her with. She called to
say she has her own vet and would have taken Wookie in
herself."

Mac seldom had to defend herself. Something definitely
didn't feel right.

"Wookie had been on the streets for days. He smelled
awful and his fur was a mess. His owner would have been
horrified if I'd brought him to her looking like that."

"That's what I said, more or less." Even Jefferina's smile
had an edge. "I told her we saved her the pain and guilt of
seeing what happens to a pet with a less-than-vigilant parent. She wasn't too happy to hear my opinion."

Mac could believe it. She was feeling a bit defensive at
the moment, and her boss was defending her. "Does this
mean I'm stuck with the vet bill?"

"Not a chance. But from now on take photos of the beasts
in the condition and location in which you find them."
Jefferina wasn't a dog or cat person. She didn't dislike them,
but her allergies made them a misery to be around. That's
why Mac never brought her rescues into the office.

"Guess there won't be any repeat business there."

"We'll see. The owner admitted that Wookie's a runner. Usually gets away in the neighborhood and is soon apprehended. This is the first time she's needed to call in professional help."

Mac eased back into her chair. If Jefferina was defending her, she'd done a good job. Now was the time to introduce the next issue.

She quickly related what had happened to her car, omitting her run-in with Massey because it had amounted to nothing useful. She ended with, "My collision coverage doesn't cover attacks with a baseball bat, so I'll be riding the bus every day for a while. Under the circumstances, I need to ask for an advance on the wage I'm due Friday."

Jefferina frowned at the request. She pinched pennies until they squealed. "Business has been a little slow. I made a few calls last night to clients with outstanding bills. Told them to settle their accounts or they'll be hearing from my attorney shortly."

"I understand." Mac swallowed her disappointment. She'd learned since working here that, like attorneys, PIs often had trouble collecting their fees.

"Deadbeats," Jefferina continued, as if picking up on Mac's thoughts. "Lucky for you, pet recovery clients pay promptly. The Pomeranian's owner paid in cash." She pulled out her wallet and counted out five twenty-dollar bills for Mac. "Will that hold you until Friday?"

Macayla nodded. "Thanks."

"There's something else we need to discuss." Jefferina played with one of the studs in her ear. They were diamonds. "What do you know about a petnapping operation in the area?"

"Nothing worth repeating." When her boss continued

to stare at her, Mac relented. "I heard from a policeman yesterday that there have been some dognappings in the area. He called them scrap metal crimes."

"Anything else?"

Mac shook her head, still unwilling to bring Massey into this. That was her fight.

"Because I got a call this morning from the St. Petersburg police. They find it odd, in retrospect, that you found the bodies of those racers when they couldn't."

"They're just jealous I did their job for them." Mac smiled to lighten the moment, but Jefferina didn't return it. Something was going on here. Something she needed to get the right end of. "What, exactly, did they say?"

"It's more accurate to say they were fishing. They've heard rumors on the street about those dognappings—that someone calling herself a pet detective is behind the animal thefts. She hires a local hoodlum to steal the animal then hits up the owners with promises to find the lost pet, for a fee." Jefferina lifted a dark impenetrable stare to Macayla. "This wouldn't have anything to do with you, would it?"

Mac felt as if a bucket of ice water had been upended over her head. "You think I'd do something like that? Steal animals in order to make money?"

"Would you?"

Jefferina asked the question so matter-of-factly that it took a second for the hair to rise on the back of Mac's neck. "You know me. I've worked for you for nearly a year. What does your gut tell you?"

Jefferina shrugged. "I was a cop. I don't have hunches. I go on facts. And you've been less than open with me in the past."

The temperature in the room fell to Arctic levels, causing a shiver to pass through Mac, but she didn't give in to her anxiety. "What are you talking about?"

"I ran a background check on you before I hired you. I do that for everyone, employee or client. You never told me you worked for child advocacy in Tallahassee. Or that you are a licensed counselor who worked with a courthouse facility dog for three years before you abruptly quit."

Mac held back her flash of temper. "So?"

"You weren't honest and I find that troubling."

"The past wasn't relevant."

"The past is always relevant. You could be making good money in your former occupation. Yet you choose to leave it behind and work several part-time minimum-wage jobs just to keep a roof over your head."

"That's not a crime."

"No. But here's another way to look at it. You just asked me for an advance. That means extra cash would come in handy for you. And you weren't open about your private life, or your work history. Two red flags that you're hiding something."

"If you know my history, you know I've never done anything illegal."

"In my line of work you quickly learn that anybody is capable of almost anything, given the right motivation or stress factors."

Her mention of stress made Mac stiffen. "Do the police think I had something to do with the disappearance of those greyhounds? Or is it you?"

Jefferina shrugged. "Convenient, is how the lead detective put it. And the business about the shooting that same night? You're the sole witness."

She remembered Sam saying the same thing.

Mac reached for her purse, angrier than she could remember being in maybe ever. "Is this where I confess? Because I've got to tell you, this is where I would confess, if I was guilty. But I'm not."

She put the money she pulled out of her purse back on the desk. "You can send my severance check when you collect the full amount you owe me."

Jefferina looked slowly from the bills back to Mac. "Unless you are working a side angle, you're going to need that."

Mac said nothing as she held her boss's hard gaze. But there was no guessing what was going on behind her black-berry eyes. "Either you trust me or you don't, Jefferina. I can't work for someone who's suspicious of me."

"Did I say I didn't trust you?"

"You said I wasn't honest with you."

"You weren't. And I don't like that. But maybe you can make me understand it."

Mac took a beat. This was the last conversation she wanted to have with anyone, ever. "You read the media accounts of what happened in Tallahassee. It was awful, all the way through. Worse of all, I got tagged as the hero of the hour. Everywhere I went that's all people wanted to talk about."

Jefferina sat back. "You make that sound bad. Who wouldn't want to be known as a hero?"

Mac flinched. "Anyone who's been one."

She could feel the solid weight of her boss's gaze on her but she was done explaining, even if she knew she'd said precious little.

Finally, Jefferina stood up, her jacket flaring just enough for Mac to notice the weapon she carried. "I could use an extra pair of eyes in the field today." She looked Mac up and down. "We have just enough time to drop by your place so you can change."

"I meant what I said. Either you trust me or you don't."

Jefferina sighed. "I run a business that requires discretion and sensitivity, with sometimes paranoid clients. That's why I do background checks. I wouldn't have hired you in the first place if I didn't think I could trust you. That doesn't mean I won't continue to ask the hard questions from time to time. It's who I am."

Macayla supposed that that was as close to a vote of confidence as she was going to get from her boss. "I don't know how to prove myself to you."

Jefferina smirked. "Continue doing good work and bringing in fees."

"What about what the police say?"

Now she smiled. "The police are only as good as their efforts. Somebody might be running around stealing dogs but, so far, it's all speculation. When they find that person, you'll be busy doing something else, for me. You ready to work now?"

Mac nodded. "I'm ready to work."

They were seated in Jefferina's Jeep Wrangler before she spoke again. "About what happened to your car. You might as well be prepared. The sheriff's department and the St. Petersburg police are looking at it as a possible squabble among thieves. That you didn't pay off your dog-nappers, and so they took revenge."

"Isn't that a big gigantic stretch?"

"They're holding back the details, Mac. I don't know what else they have. This is where I say, be careful."

Mac stared straight out the window, feeling anger curl through her like heat off the tarmac.

"You need to get in front of this, Macayla. If anything else suspicious occurs you want to tell me first."

That was the second time in the last twenty-four hours someone had offered to be her confessor. Sam. Now Jefferina.

She was a suspect. At least a person of interest for the St. Petersburg police. Had been for, what? Weeks? Ever since the greyhounds disappeared?

Mac turned slowly to meet her boss's gaze. "I'm not guilty. Of any of this."

Jefferina nodded. "I believe you."

Mac felt the squeeze on her heart relax. "What changed your mind?"

"Call it a gut feeling." Her boss gave her a wide smile.

"You don't believe in hunches."

"Almost never," Jefferina agreed. "So let's go with the novelty of this one for now."

CHAPTER NINE

"What kind of case is this?"

"Philandering spouse. Our target is named Daryl Holmes. In from Cleveland for a pharmaceutical convention. He's staying here." Jefferina pointed to the middle hotel in a picture she'd brought up on her cell phone of St. Pete Beach hotels. She could have turned and pointed to the hotel because it was directly behind them. But Jefferina was careful about the small things. "I saw Holmes arrive last night. With three other guys and two women from his company. According to the wife, the lover is his boss. Magda Lawson." She flipped to a polished professional photo of an attractive woman. "Tall, leggy, lots of blond hair." She sniffed dismissively. "Not my type."

Macayla smiled. Jefferina's type was small, curvy, and Latina. Her partner, Julia, was a Salma Hayek look-alike.

Jefferina bought up another photo. "This is Mr. Holmes." It showed a man in suit and tie who looked like any of a thousand other middle-aged Midwesterners with a slightly receding hairline.

Mac shook her head. "Not a lot of help."

Jefferina gave her a look. "The mole?"

She leaned in as Jefferina made the photo larger. Sure enough, the man had a small dark mole on his neck above his collar. "Huh." All she had to do was get close enough to her subject to see a mole. Not a particularly appetizing thought.

Jefferina put her phone away. "I'll troll the beach and pool areas, see if I can get any juicy gossip from the staff. Call me if anything significant happens. Otherwise we're on duty until three p.m."

Macayla really hated this part of the private eye business. Tracking cheating spouses and significant others seemed smarmy. But it paid the bills, her boss assured her. And she owed Jefferina.

Macayla hitched her large logo-bearing beach tote onto her shoulder and tipped her large sunglasses forward over her eyes as she approached the beach entrance to the hotel. She hoped she looked like a tourist. And that none of the service people she knew casually would recognize her, especially after the fiasco with her car the day before.

The lobby was open to the Gulf breeze, but air-conditioned air met her with a heavy chill as she walked midday through the main lobby. She marched up to a bell-boy she didn't recognize and asked for directions to the conference floor.

"Which one? We're hosting several."

"Pharmaceutical."

He pointed her to a bank of elevators. "Mezzanine."

The elevator she took was crowded with people wearing conference badges on lanyards. But they weren't what she was expecting. Both the men and women seemed to be wearing a themed uniform: polo shirts in shades of beige, brown, green, yellow, or white with logos stenciled over the heart, as well as cargos or khakis with tactical boots.

When the doors slid open, Mac had to step out to let those in the rear out. As people moved past her she noticed that a few wore T-shirts with sayings like MWA: MALINOIS WITH ATTITUDE and TRUST THE DOG. Others simply had POLICE K-9 UNIT, SHERIFF K-9 UNIT, or the name of a volunteer SAR K-9 group emblazoned on the back.

Looking around, she spied a large long banner hung over a pair of doors at the center of the hallway. It read INTERNATIONAL PROFESSIONAL SAR K-9 HANDLERS CONFERENCE.

Mac turned quickly back to the bank of elevators, but the doors had closed. Damn. She moved quickly to the next one as it chimed its arrival on the floor.

When the elevator doors opened, a bellhop stepped out carrying a three-foot-long billboard prominently displaying the face of a man impossible to forget. The beard. The hair, pulled back this once for a more business-like look. And those eyes: blue-green pools between thickets of dark lashes.

"Excuse me." She stepped in front of the bellboy as he was about to move past her. "May I?" She scanned the words stenciled above and below the photo.

Annual Awards Banquet
Featured Speaker: Oliver Kelly
Co-founder of Bolt Action Rescue K-9 Services
(BARKS)
Honolulu, U.S.A./Canberra, Australia

"You dog!" she muttered under her breath and stepped into the elevator.

Even she had heard of BARKS. They'd played a part

in nearly every headline-making story of disaster around the world for the past five years. She'd even seen pictures of the owner. She remembered the TV interview, not because it was about earthquake relief in Nepal, but because of the gorgeous, tall, dark-haired SAR leader from BARKS. Definitely not Oliver Kelly.

No, Oliver Kelly was a wiseass. He'd let her believe he was a stripper. What a joke on her. He was a K-9 handler. And not just any handler. To be a banquet speaker, he probably had more credentials and more honors than she, a pet detective, would ever earn.

He must have had a good laugh watching her crawl around in the sand trying to lure a lapdog out from under smelly garbage bins when he led life-and-death search-and-rescue missions for a living.

She felt her face catch fire and whipped around to examine herself in the elevator mirror. She expected to see embarrassment or fury. But what she saw surprised her.

Her coloring was high, but her eyes were shining and her mouth was trembling with a smile. She'd scorned her own interest—okay, attraction to him—because she'd thought he was a boastful, egotistical slacker accustomed to getting by on his looks and potential sexual charm. She'd never given him a chance.

Maybe she hadn't been fair.

Maybe she owed him an apology.

Maybe Oliver Kelly was more than a pretty face. That meant he had to be taken seriously. And if she did so, it might turn out that he was pretty damn awesome.

Ugh! She'd done what she disliked in others. She'd been blinded by her preconceived notions and had behaved badly toward a man who had only been trying to help her. One who'd put his physical well-being at risk for her.

She hadn't wanted to admit what tingled through her body as proof. She was very attracted to him.

And also running scared.

A man like Oliver Kelly would never need to spend a night alone. He was gorgeous, a celeb, and probably wealthy. Either way she added it up, she didn't see how she'd ever fit in his world.

"Excuse me. Coming or going?"

A man in a magenta shirt was staring at her. How long had she been holding the elevator doors open while her thoughts had been a million miles away, on Island Oliver?

She hurried through the doors onto a floor filled with a much larger press of people exuding the air of anticipated business deals.

Mac did a mental adjustment as the pair of men nearest gave her outfit the once-over. Everything else on her mind vanished as she gave them the mole check in return. Jefferina expected her to be on the job for the next few hours. And she needed the money.

Three and a half hours later, Mac stood at the back of a sea of people waiting for the bank of elevators that were always full when they stopped at this floor. At the end of her first stakeout, she'd learned three things.

There's nothing more boring for an outsider than an industry conference that involves highly specialized subjects such as *Innovative Research, Manufacturing Parameters, Clinical Strategies, Risk Management and Consequences*, or *Regulatory Challenges in Drug Design and Discovery Involving Parenterals.*

Sure, there was serious business going on behind the closed doors with workshop titles longer than some song lyrics. But out in the corridors, it was a hotbed of social interaction that made Happy Hour at Hooters look like slack time. Lots of too-bright laughter, arm touching, one-arm hugging, and suggestive kidding filled the space with sound and movement.

Thankfully, Daryl Holmes wasn't difficult to find. A quick perusal of the schedule and there was his name, listed as co-presenting something called Novelties in Pre-Filled Syringe Products. She'd slipped into the session and waited until the speakers were introduced, thereby identifying her target—no mole gazing required. Once he was spotted, she'd slipped out to play video games on her phone while she waited for the workshop to be over.

When he emerged, she approached him to offer her own congratulations for a speech she hadn't listened to.

He'd seemed glad to have someone, anyone, to chat with. He'd even invited her to join him for the luncheon.

By the end of the meal she was pretty certain the only thing straying in his marriage was his wife's imagination. He'd sounded and acted in every way like a married man. There'd been pictures of his two children produced and then photos of their dog Sofie, a gregarious-looking mutt who loved Slip 'n Slides as much as his kids.

"I don't think he's cheating on his wife," she'd reported by phone to Jefferina from a stall in the ladies' room at the end of her allotted time. "He doesn't seem to have the imagination or energy."

"I agree. Ms. Lawson definitely has her sights on someone else. I've been watching them flirt for the past hour poolside. If she flips her hair one more time I may have to go over there and slap her on behalf of grown-up women everywhere. We're done here. Need a lift?"

"No, I'm going to sit on the beach a while and enjoy the view." Mac had tucked a swimsuit and a towel into her bag to make her cover story as a hotel guest more believable.

"Good for you. You need a life, Mac."

It was true. For all the time she'd spent at the beach since moving back ten months before, she might as well have lived a hundred miles inland.

Now that she'd had time to think about it, she didn't have a single legitimate reason to seek out Oliver Kelly. What was she going to say—*Hi, I'd like to talk you now that I know you're someone important*?

That phrase had both fan-girl and stalker-y elements all over it. No, she'd had her chance. Time to absorb some healthy vitamin D.

Five long minutes after standing in line, she was finally at the front when the elevator doors opened. It was already nearly full of conferees wearing badges for the K-9 SAR conference. Mac wedged herself in, trying to ignore the tall man next to her who boldly looked down her front. Being short had a few disadvantages.

"Hey, you. Up here." When he jerked his gaze up from her bosom to her face she said, "Do you know Oliver Kelly?"

A grin split his face. "Sure. Well, I mean, we all know him. BARKS is a legend among SAR handlers. I've seen him in action. He's great, isn't he?"

Murmurs of admiration filled the elevator as it stopped at the first mezzanine. Mac backed up to allow everyone else to exit. *A legend?*

As the doors were closing, she suddenly changed her mind and popped out of the elevator and into the sea of search-and-rescue conferees.

Oliver stood at the podium in the empty ballroom, white-knuckling the sides as if he thought it might heave up and toss him off. He felt besieged. Sweat dotted his brow. His shoulders were hunched against imminent attack. His brows rode so low his eyes were hidden beneath the fur-rowed ridge. Was he Captain Ahab who'd sighted Moby Dick?

He looked across the sea of white-linen-covered tables and empty chairs as it dawned on him who the great white whale was. Once this space filled to capacity tonight, he would be the one harpooned by fear. Mute, furious, and without defense.

"Shit." He swallowed, blinking furiously. He'd been in tight spots plenty of times, environs that threatened his and Jackeroo's lives. He'd come up against the possibility of real bullets and natural threats of many kinds. This large banquet space should not frighten a grown man. That's why he'd come here to face his demons. But the watery gut feeling flowing through him couldn't be conquered.

Everything he thought he knew about himself was on the line. And he didn't have a clue how to conquer his im-minent sense of failure.

He'd pulled people out of raging rivers.

He and Jackeroo had recently found a young girl who'd been buried in a mudslide, digging her out just seconds be-fore she smothered.

He'd even shot enemy insurgents who were killing first-aid workers in an encampment for survivors of disaster. He was strong, resourceful, the person other SAR team members leaned on in times of crisis. Why, then, was sweat pouring into his eyes as his fingers dug into the wood of the podium?

The pulse pounding in his temples was pure fight or flight. There was still time to get the hell out of here. There were planes leaving town before seven p.m. No one would question it. There were a dozen good reasons why he might be instantly called away. His and Jackeroo's skills needed somewhere else.

Should he do that? Desert his duty? Humiliated. Desperate. A coward.

"Hi."

He startled and blinked. He hadn't paid any attention to the figure who'd slipped in a side door near the podium, thinking it was a server checking the room. Now he saw that the person who had come in stood staring at him. She was a looker, petite but in high-heeled sandals that made the most of her muscled tan legs. And even the loose top didn't deceive a man of his experience. She had a rack worth gazing at. It was when he reached her face that he got a tiny jolt of surprise.

"Macayla." He blinked again, to clear his thoughts. "Is something wrong?"

"No." She looked embarrassed. "I was just in the hotel, for another reason, when I saw a poster with your face on it out in the hall."

She smiled at him. Something in his middle jumped. She had the nicest smile. Why didn't she smile more often? "I'm impressed, Mr. Kelly. You're the conference banquet speaker."

He winced at her words, reminded of how undeserving he was at the moment of her admiration. His stomach heaved again, and not in any good way. And then he was moving, fast, away from the podium and toward her.

He scooped a hand under her elbow to propel her along with him as he marched down the main aisle toward the nearest exit.

"Come on. I need to get out of here. Now."

CHAPTER TEN

Mac didn't argue. Clearly his sunny attitude had changed since the day before. Something was driving this man hard. Plenty of time to find out what when he stopped moving.

As it was, it took her full concentration to keep up with his wide long-legged stride while she walked double-time in her heels.

They stepped into the first available elevator, occupied by several men and women who greeted Oliver by name.

He gave them a general chin-up greeting but didn't speak. The blue-eyed thunder of his eyes shut down the inclination anyone might have to become chatty.

Mac assumed they'd be headed down to the lobby, maybe the bar. He radiated the jittery intensity of someone in need of a good stiff drink. Instead the elevator rose, taking them toward the room floors.

He had his key out and all but burst through the doors on the fourth floor as they parted, only glancing back at her so that she would know that she was to follow him.

She heard the chuckles that accompanied a man's voice saying, "Somebody's about to be a lucky girl."

Macayla shook it off. Oliver was moving at high speed and she couldn't change an impression of someone who didn't matter.

The moment they were inside a room at the end of the hall, he whipped out his phone, pressed a number, and began stalking across the room as he waited for someone to answer. When that someone did, he didn't start with hello.

"I can't do this. I won't do this. Call it the fuck off."

He punched the END CALL button and slipped the phone back into his rear pocket before he stalked over the windows and shoved open the curtains on French doors.

The room was suddenly flooded with the clear hard light of warm-water shores. The sky was metallic blue streaked with thin clouds. The water below was a deeper shade of blue, curling into foam on a powdery beach that looked like white sugar.

Uncertain if she was still welcome, Mac remained by door. But she helped herself to the sight of him.

Against that backdrop of sea and sky, Oliver reminded her again of Thor: strong, majestic, his thick mane swirled around his shoulders like some ancient mantle of authority. His beard a striking emblem of maleness. But there was wariness in the tension holding his body taut as a guitar string. He was a man, after all. A worried, angry man.

Her gaze strayed across his shoulders to where his sage-gray polo shirt pulled tight over the contours of his back, swelled by toned muscle. She remembered how his body looked under that shirt. The compact swells of muscle over his stomach and ribs. As for his ass in those knee-length patrol shorts, well. For the first time in a long time she really wanted to reach out and touch.

As he swung around, having suddenly remembered she

was in the room—had he heard her panting?—Mac jerked her gaze up to his face.

He stared at her with an expression that could have meant anything. It wasn't just his injured eye, less swollen but still turning blue, that made her sigh. The happy-go-lucky Aussie she'd spent the morning with the day before was gone. In his place was a man who looked mad and bad, and just a little dangerous.

"What can I do for you, Macayla?"

Good question. She wished she had a good answer. *I just wanted to see you again* sounded lame. Every other thought in her head was too racy for the situation. The situation, that is, where she wanted to touch and go on touching. Good grief. Once released, her hormones were trampling good sense. She needed to get out of here and regroup.

"You know, this doesn't seem like a good time. I can come back later . . ." She turned to leave.

"No. Stay."

It sounded more like a command to a canine but she decided to ignore his tone and hear that he wanted her company. She turned around, allowing him to see the questioning in her expression.

He swung out an arm. "Come in and get comfortable. I'll be right back."

He walked over to a door that led to the bathroom.

Mac glanced at the bed that filled the second half of the open area suite. Had he really meant to gesture toward it?

Oh my god. Did he assume, just like the guys in the elevator, that because she'd come to his room it was as good as an invitation into her pants?

Jackeroo bounded out of the bathroom and launched a wiggling body at his alpha.

A smile broke over Oliver's face as he squatted down and let Jack do a happy dance all around him, repeatedly leaping up to lick his handler's face. "Sorry to lock you up, Jack old boy. But you will nip at the maids' heels."

After a few more gyrations around Oliver, Jackeroo took off across the room to greet Mac. Surprisingly, he didn't bark in greeting. But he nosed up under the hand that hung freely by her side, giving her permission to pet him.

Mac went down on a knee and scratched him behind first one ear and then the other. "Hello, Jackeroo. What a good boy."

Jackeroo appeared pleased by her greeting and sneaked in under her arm to lick her chin. He got a good bit of her mouth with that lick, too.

Reaching up to wipe her mouth free of doggy kisses, she looked across at Oliver, who watched them interact. "Why didn't Jackeroo bark in greeting when you entered? He had to know it was you."

"He's trained not to bark in unfamiliar surroundings until I signal that it's okay. We've been in some places where a barking dog is like a beacon, sometimes to the wrong people." He frowned. "Why are you still over by the door?"

She decided not to give the real answer but rose to her feet. "Can you do that? Teach a dog not to bark even when alone?"

He raised an eyebrow at her. Right. She'd just been witness to a demonstration of his abilities. Speaking of which, "You could have told me you weren't a stripper."

A half-wattage smile appeared on his mouth. Even 50 percent was enough for her to feel the burn of being the center of his attention. "It was more fun letting you think I was a man slut. You seemed to get really worked up about the idea."

She was not worked up. Okay, maybe a little. "I just don't like to see anyone waste their lives. Men or women."

She saw his expression sharpen with interest. "Not every stripper is a loser. I have a friend who danced her way through college and came out debt-free."

"And did she have a problem being taken seriously later?"

He frowned slightly in memory. "Fair point."

"I take it you were practicing your speech just now in the ballroom."

"No." He looked away from her. "I'm not giving a bloody speech."

The anger in his voice took her by surprise, as did the strangely troubled look he redirected her way. Everything about him, from the slightly widened gaze to the sudden movements and excessive energy, hinted at anxiety. She'd learned most of what she knew about animal behavior by helping out Saturdays at an animal shelter from the time she was ten years old. And, later, a vet's office. In her experience, the symptoms and signs of stress in animals could be found in humans too. Those signs in animals were due to protective instincts and could lead to aggression if not handled correctly. Not that she expected Oliver to be dangerous. Only that he probably wasn't going to share with her what was wrong.

Like most men, he didn't seem to have any trouble getting in touch with his inner gladiator. But he wasn't going to open up just because she was here.

If you wanted an animal's trust, you first had to make certain the animal felt safe. That's what all the sniffing and retreating and re-approaching between dogs was all about. *Do I know you? Are you safe? Will you hurt me? Can we be friends?*

She wasn't certain what she and Oliver were. A few intense hours together didn't exactly qualify as a fast friendship. But the grip he'd had on her elbow as he'd all but dragged her up here with him was proof enough that, at the moment, she was the port in a storm he needed.

Macayla smiled. She shouldn't be so happy about that but, for now, she let herself feel the warm cozy feeling that came with being needed by this supremely capable man.

That didn't mean she wasn't going to meekly follow his lead. She was done with taking orders. And she was never going to find out what was wrong as long as he was in combat mode.

She dropped her purse on the credenza by the door, then walked over and pulled out the chair from in front of the desk and swiveled it around. "Sit down." She, too, had a handler's voice.

He stood there, looking wary. "Why?"

"Do you care? Or are you afraid of me?" She bent both arms to make a muscle in each biceps, though they were hidden by the loose sleeves of her shirt.

Again his half-wattage smile had the power to make her tummy dance.

He sat down but glanced at her over his shoulder as he did so. "Just don't braid my hair."

"Shit. I wanted to practice my Dutch braid technique."

He snorted and leaned back.

CHAPTER ELEVEN

Mac slid her hands under the fall of his hair, liking the silky weight of it on her skin. There were women who would maim for this much body and shine. In fact, she had to resist the urge to run her fingers through it.

His body tensed as her hands settled instead on the ridges of his shoulders, but she pretended not to notice. She was busy dealing with the sensations running up her arms on contact. Touching him was like touching a cord with a powerful current running through it. She wasn't shocked, but it was impossible to pull away. She hadn't considered how touching him would affect her. But it was too late to pull back now.

She began to apply pressure to muscles that felt like cement. It was going to take some time to warm them up through the fabric of his shirt.

"What are you doing?" His voice was pitched low, as if he wasn't sure he wanted to speak.

"Guess." She held her hands in place a moment, deepening the pressure as she inhaled slowly. She felt him breathe deeper in response. Good. At least he was paying attention. He moved his legs to sit more fully upright in the chair as her hands moved to the slope between his neck and shoulders and she began a slow circular motion with her palms. But her thumbs kept getting caught in the collar of his shirt, interrupting what was supposed to be smooth soothing motion. Giving up for the moment, she moved lower, applying pressure to the muscles of his upper back along either side of his spine, and then a little more. But she wasn't certain it was working. The heat coming through his shirt was minimal. At least he hadn't slid away.

"Wait." Again he used that impatient, male, imperative tone.

Her hands paused in their movement as she held her breath. She'd relaxed into the moment too soon.

He leaned forward, rising back off the chair. Turning toward her, he gripped the back of his shirt by the collar and pulled it over his head.

Mac didn't have to wonder where to look first. She simply took in every inch of him at once.

He was big, with perfectly toned muscle swells and cuts and valleys covered by warm human skin. But she quickly skimmed that magnificent chest, seen once before. This time, she curiously eyed the tattoo that rode the swell of his right biceps from shoulder to elbow. It was an Aboriginal design of a kangaroo made up of small geometric designs and stripes in strong earth colors of red, yellow, white, and black.

As he turned at the waist to toss his shirt on the bed, Mac got another surprise.

Two other tattoos decorated him. A pair of boomerangs followed the natural contours of his back, curving from either side of his spine up over his deltoids and onto the turn of his shoulders. They were designed to look like wood but were individually decorated using the same color palette as the kangaroo. However, these designs were made up of dozens of small dots forming circles and wavy lines. Along each centerline, the dots created an animal. One was a snake, the other a turtle. His tats were so finely detailed they could have had a place in a museum. Except that the owner carried them on his skin.

She pointed to the kangaroo. "It's beautiful."

"Ta." He lifted his arm to glance at his tat. "The details make it special."

She nodded. He was beautiful. But she wasn't going to say that.

"Massages work better on bare skin." He gave her a dark look, daring her to disagree.

"Okay."

He sat back down. This time he spread his legs in a more relaxed manner.

It took her a second to work up the courage to touch all that exposed skin. What had started out as a simple offer of relaxation had become a full-contact skin-on-skin exercise. She slipped her hands back under his hair. As she did, he reached back and gathered his hair in both hands, pulled it up off his neck, and smoothed it out a few times before slipping it though an elastic band. He twisted the end a couple of times and pushed it through a second time. The man bun in ten seconds.

"Better?"

She nodded, though he couldn't see it because he hadn't looked back.

The exposed column of his neck looked suddenly vulnerable. She had the sudden silly impulse to lean forward and place a kiss at the base. Instead she slipped her hands back into place and made slow pressure circles with her thumbs. This time the dense smooth skin of his shoulders warmed quickly to her touch.

After a few seconds more, he took a deep breath and gave up what she sensed was the struggle not to enjoy what she was doing.

"You do this a lot?"

"Yes."

"Lucky guy."

She smiled above his head. "I actually do male and female. After we've become close friends."

He started in surprise under her hands. "Really?"

"Yep." She knew what he was thinking, dirty-minded souls that men are. Time for the punch line. "I'm one of the best dog masseuses in all of Tampa/St. Pete."

He laughed then, the humor startled out of him.

"Sit still. I'm not done."

He did as he was told, for three seconds, before reaching back to lightly touch the back of one of her hands with his fingers. "You've got great hands."

"I can't afford to get many complaints. Dogs bite." She felt his shoulder shake in silent humor this time. Good. Now it was time to find out what the real problem was.

She placed a thumb on either side of his neck, using an up-and-down motion with carefully measured pressure until she felt the muscles beneath his warmed skin begin to soften. "Want to tell me what's wrong?"

"No." When she didn't respond, he heaved a sigh. "I don't give speeches."

She almost laughed, thinking he was joking. But the strain in his voice told her he was serious. He was afraid of public speaking! She couldn't quite imagine him afraid of anything.

"Aren't you the guy who took on two thugs with baseball bats single-handedly? You were like Batman without the armor."

"You *were* impressed." He twisted his head around to flash her a sexy grin that made her toes curl, despite the sweat that had popped out on her forehead as she worked.

"Yes, I was impressed. And angry because I was scared for you. You didn't know me. You didn't have to do that."

"Yeah, I did. And I'm trained for that. But giving a speech?" He shivered, a big manly quake that was all wrong, and somehow endearing. "That's why I'm backing out."

She returned to massaging his neck, enjoying the heat that rose into her palms from his skin. She knew that stage fright was a phobia for many people. "Okay. Let's think about this. There are lots of ways to get over stage fright."

"I'm not frightened." He swiveled hard in the chair and glared at her, all manly offense. "I just can't—don't want to do it. It's not my job. Kye should be here. He always plays front man. That's our agreement."

Her palms tingled from their contact but he was no longer in a position for her to continue so she crossed her arms under her breasts. "Kye is your business partner?"

"Yeah. Kye McGarren."

"Is he good at speaking?"

"The best." He smiled in a way that told her Kye was his friend and probably the person he most admired in the world. "He's this cool Hawaiian. The Rock as a surfer dude. He can be something of a goof. But he can talk to anyone about anything. Men like him. Women love him." He cut his gaze to her.

If he thought she was going to hand him a big old softball of *You're sexy, too*, he was in for a disappointment. He didn't need any encouragement. "Why isn't he here?"

Oliver grunted and leaned forward, signaling Jackeroo to his side. "He decided to go and get engaged without telling me. Now he's staying in Hawaii to be with her."

"The nerve of some people."

He glanced up to catch her expression, but Mac didn't crack a smile.

"You've told me about Kye's strengths with an audience, friendliness and humor. Why not play to your strengths? Which are?" She pretended to think hard. "Ah. American women love an Australian accent."

"This is mostly a roomful of big hairy guys."

She loved his accent. *Beeg 'airy guys.* "What else?"

He winked. "Good in the sack."

"That might not impress *all* the big hairy guys."

He snorted in laughter. "I can belch 'Waltzing Matilda.' "

"Again, *hm*. But you know your audience."

"That's just it. I can handle a hazing. But looking a complete bloody fool in front of everyone?" He lifted a shoulder.

She couldn't make fun of that. She had a lot of heavy lifting yet to do. "Men admire that Aussie in-your-face spirit. You're all madmen, right? Playing some kind of football without helmets."

He brightened a bit. "Footy. Australian rules."

"That's it. I watched a game once. It seems like a mash-up of soccer with an American football, and lots of brawny men in tight shorts banging into one another. I liked the shorts." She offered him a sly smile. "You play?"

He just grinned.

"So. You put on your game face and go get 'em."

He opened his mouth like he was going to say something. But he didn't.

"Did they give you a subject?" He just stared at her.

Her attention shifted to Jackeroo, now sitting beside

him. "Okay. That means you can talk about whatever you want. You and Jackeroo have worked all over the world for BARKS. What do you see as the number one mistake SAR handlers make?"

He sent her a grudging look. "The handlers get caught up in the search, and don't properly or continually access their animals. Or they let ego and competitiveness with other handlers get in the way of safety precautions. BARKS lost two great dogs last year, one to heat prostration and another who fell off a cliff. Both times the handler's fault."

She made a circle motion for him to turn the chair back around. His skin was warmer now when she touched him. She smoothed her palms along his shoulders, indulging in the pleasure of touching. "How can that happen when they were trained professionals?"

"People get sloppy. Slack up on discipline. The dogs are only as good as their handlers. If the handler doesn't assess the situation properly before starting out, he or she can come up short on equipment needs. Something as simple as lack of water can be a killer under the right circumstances."

She pressed more deeply now, using her thumbs to find the kinks in his muscles and slowly working to loosen them. He didn't sigh but she felt him easing into her massage, no longer resisting her hands. "Talk to me about the dogs. What mistakes do they make?"

"They don't. SAR dogs are amazing. They know their stuff and are eager to please. But they aren't aware of the dangers of a landslide or of floodwaters, the way a human is. It's a handler's topmost job to protect his or her canine partner. Even if it means pulling the team from a search, or refusing to take part because the conditions aren't right."

"That's a pretty passionate speech. Tomorrow you'll have a roomful of people interested in what you have to say. That's your chance to tell them what you think and how you go about assessing a situation. Give them real-world examples."

He shrugged, momentarily capturing her hands in the valley between his shoulders and neck. "God. That feels good."

Mac didn't answer, working her thumbs along the column of his neck until she was pretty sure he was about to purr. Or maybe she was about to purr, because touching him made her want to touch more. It would be so easy to slide her hands forward over his pecs— Uh-uh. So not going there. She was trying to earn his trust, not get in his pants.

"Where was your last search-and-rescue assignment?"

"I'd rather talk about something else." Definitely a sore spot there.

"Okay. Tell me about Jackeroo."

"Best dog in the world. My best friend, really." The heavy muscles of his upper back began to loosen beneath her firm pressure.

"Best friends? But he can't hold a conversation. Isn't he more like a tool, being trained to do a job?"

"Tool? Fuck no. He's smarter and got better instincts than most of the humans in the field."

"Is that one reason you make such a good SAR K-9 team?"

"It's the only reason. We can practically hear each other thinking on the job." Oliver patted his thigh and Jackeroo set his chin there, bright eyes full of adoration.

Oliver ruffled his fur. "Jack's always with me. More than my family. More than my friends. We rely on each other from first eyeball in the morning to last eye shut at night. I trust him with my life. He trusts me with his."

"You're a pack."

"Exactly. Once, we were moving through rubble in a village devastated by an earthquake when Jack suddenly stopped and whimpered. Then he began jerking wildly at the leash, nearly pulled me off my feet. We scrambled off that pile, me cursing up a bluey. Two minutes later an aftershock nearly as large as the original quake struck. If we'd been atop that pile I'd most likely be dead."

Mac worked a few minutes in silence while he continued to talk about his experiences. It felt like a great victory that he was talking to her about things that mattered to him. He was a natural storyteller. That didn't mean she could think of a way to lessen his fear of public speaking. It wasn't her business, of course, but it seemed a shame when his stories were totally interesting and lively.

Finally, he reached up with both hands and lay them over hers. "You've got to be tired."

Strangely enough, she wasn't. She could have gone on touching him for a lot longer. But he was signaling to her, *Enough.*

She backed up as he swung around to face her. He was actually smiling. "God. You've got to be sick of my yammering."

"No, it was really interesting. You have everything you need to give a speech. Great stories. Exciting escapes."

His grin reduced to sour-pickle status. "I can chat. That's different."

"You absolutely can do it. If you're worried that you'll forget something, write down the things you just told me and read the speech."

His expression lost all friendliness. It ran quickly through defiance and anger to end at pain. "I can't."

"What do you mean? Of course you can."

He jerked his head in a single negative as he looked away.

"Now you're being childish. Anyone can read a speech."

"Not me."

When he looked up, it was to slam her with an expression that felt like a fist.

"I can't read."

CHAPTER TWELVE

"I can't read."

His expression emptied of emotion as he repeated himself. "At least not well enough to give a speech in front of a crowd. I'm dyslexic."

He jerked his head back like a boxer greeting his opponent then doubled down on a grim squinty stare. "Not so impressed now, are you?"

"It's not about being impressed," Mac snapped.

"Sure it is. That's why I'm here." He held up and spread his arms as if holding up a banner. "Oliver Kelly. Co-owner of BARKS, successful business entrepreneur and well-regarded SAR K-9 handler." His hands dropped to his sides. "Only they wouldn't have invited a wanker to speak if they knew the truth. I'm bloody stupid."

"People with dyslexia are *not* stupid." Mac was a little surprised by the anger in her voice, but she didn't pause. "You've got a learning disability. Everyone knows that's not the same thing."

He lowered his head like a fighter absorbing a blow. "Not everyone."

That gave her pause. He was Australian. But every country was aware of this learning problem for kids. She'd recently run across a blog about a new clinic-based program opening in Nepal. There were many new helpful approaches to dealing with dyslexia being developed all the time.

Yet the frustration, anger, and pain pouring out of Oliver was real. It came at her like a tidal wave, leaving her shaken. He'd not been one of the lucky ones.

Jackeroo, too, reacted to the pheromones pouring off his handler. He erupted in barks and leaped on him, trying to draw his attention for comfort.

Oliver shushed him with a single hand movement. The dog immediately sat. But he never took his eyes off his handler, riveted to his human's every move.

For better or worse Oliver's attention was on Mac, and he looked ready for anything.

She gave a palm-up gesture. "Look. I didn't mean to upset you. It's none of my business."

"You made it your business, didn't you?"

The accusation stung. "By trying to help, maybe."

"It's not your job to rescue every damn stray you come across."

"Stray? I've never met anyone less helpless in my life."

He grunted. "You don't know me."

Macayla subsided on the edge of the bed, her full concentration on the man in front of her. He was right. She'd been so busy being intimidated by his sexiness that she'd nearly missed knowing the man. "Talk to me."

He rubbed the scruff of beard along either side of his chin, obviously debating whether to answer. She couldn't blame him. They were strangers. Would probably never see each other after this day ended.

Perhaps he was thinking that, too, because he gave a little nod and sat back in the chair. Was it wrong that she wished he'd put his shirt back on? Irrelevant, but she'd concentrate better.

"I grew up on a station fifty miles from a real school. My brothers and I attended what they call School of the Air. I was behind from the first. My parents tried but for me, reading was like learning to write with only thumbs. I was terrible. After the doctor's assessment of dyslexia, my father said it didn't matter about my getting an education. I'd run the station when I was older."

"That was well meant, I'm sure."

"No. He said I'd run it. He didn't say I'd own it. I couldn't read contracts or keep the ledgers. I could run the operation with our cattle and sheep. My younger brothers would inherit the station."

She could see what it was costing him to admit to what he saw as a deficiency in his father's eyes. "My mother wanted to ship me off to Sydney to a boarding school that said they could help. But Da said it wasn't a good use of money."

"What did you do?"

"Took off as soon as I was able. Joined the army at sixteen and half. Dad signed the papers. Bit of luck there." He smiled. "Turns out I'm not quite as stupid as everyone thought. I could memorize anything after a few times of someone reading it to me. I was able to join the special operations command and work with dogs, as I'd always been good at training our sheepdogs. Dogs don't seem to care that I can't read worth a fuck. I'm good to them and they are good to me. Two dumb animals. A natural fit."

Mac knew better than to play into his self-pity. He would not thank her for it. Best to keep him talking. "Why didn't you make the army your career?"

He reached down and stroked Jackeroo. "I got some special help in the service. Enough to read simple stuff, when I'm on my own. But after I'd done my stint, I wanted to see something more of the world. I traveled around looking for the type of job I thought I could handle, and met Kye. We worked SAR for other companies for a few years and then decided we could do better on our own. Here we are."

"Impressive story. Maybe you should share that in your speech."

He scowled at her. "You need to give that up."

"Then how about telling the crowd that there are ways around obstacles if you keep looking for solutions? Look where you are. Partner of an internationally recognized company. You told me yesterday your parents are proud of you. Or was that just about the stripper thing?"

"No. It's real. The family moron made good. But I won't talk about myself like I'm a poster child for some cause."

"Fine. Then just talk off the cuff, like you're doing with me."

His blue gaze swam with doubts. "What if I freeze up like a bloody Popsicle? What if I hurl all over the podium?"

She couldn't answer those questions with empty reassurances. She wanted to reach out and touch. But she held back.

He was silent a long time, as if he had retreated to another time and place. Finally, he looked up, his distant gaze returning slowly to the confines of the room. "Wish you could give the speech. You're good at this."

"Almost everyone is good at talking about things they're passionate about."

"What are you passionate about, Macayla?"

"Finding missing pets." But the way he looked at her he knew he was asking a more personal question.

"What's your pet's name?"

Mac blinked. "What?"

"You don't have one, do you? Why?"

Mac wet her lips. How did this conversation turn into one about her? "I'm too busy. I can't chase dogs and cats all day with a pet on board. I'd have to leave it home alone all day. That wouldn't be fair to the animal."

He stood up and came slowly toward her. "You could have a cat or a gerbil. Or a goldfish."

Mac suddenly felt very nervous. "Yes. I suppose. I hadn't thought about that."

"Liar." He stopped before her, looking down into her face. "You're not a coward, are you, Macayla?"

She loved the way he said her name, every time. But he was scaring her all the same.

"I watched you yesterday. And while what you did and said sometimes didn't make sense to me, you have a reason for everything you do. So there's a reason, not the logical one you just gave me, why you don't have a pet."

"What difference does it make to you?"

He reached out and touched her face, fingers skimming her cheek. "You know what I thought the first time I saw you?"

Mac smirked. "Bag lady."

"The loneliest person I'd come across outside a crisis zone."

Mac backed up, feeling as if he'd touched some intimate part of her. "That's a bit dramatic. And sad."

"Sad. Yeah."

"Oh no you don't. You don't get to turn the tables on me, to make me feel vulnerable just because I learned your secret. I'm not going to betray you to anyone. You don't have to threaten me."

He looked puzzled. "How would owning a dog threaten you?"

Mac bit her lip. She needed to turn this around. Fast. "You want a secret from me? Fine." She looked him in the eye. "I've wanted to kiss you since the first moment I saw you. Wanted to climb right up that magnificent body of yours, wraps my legs around your hips, and kiss you until I was drunk with your taste. Enough truth?"

She expected him to make a joke, or at least laugh. He'd done that a lot in the hours she'd known him. But he was staring at her now with all the amazed intensity of a man who had just struck gold.

Feeling suddenly exposed and desperate to escape his scrutiny, she backed up a step and reached for her purse. "I've got stuff to do."

As she turned toward the door, he wrapped a hand around her upper arm to halt her exit. She swung back and glared at him, not sure if she'd made things better, or worse.

He was smiling. "That's not news to me. We're both grown and know how to read the signals of the opposite sex. So you know I've wanted to kiss you, too."

Well, actually, she hadn't. She'd been so absorbed in the novelty of her own responses that she'd completely overlooked that possibility.

He tugged her arm. "Come on, Macayla. Let's do it. It's just a kiss."

She sensed a trap in there somewhere, but she couldn't resist the invitation. Probably just what she needed to get her *atta girl* up and running again. So far, it had been a tough two days.

He slipped her beach tote off her shoulder, moving slowly as he kept his eyes on her. "I like your hair down."

"I like yours, too."

A smile jerked up one corner of his mouth as he reached up a hand and pulled off the elastic band that held his bun in place. He shook his head once as the cascade of hair slipped free, and it fell in a perfect tumble onto his shoulders. The man had serious hair moves. Anyone who watched shows about Vikings, or pirates, or historic Scotsmen knew that there was nothing but testosterone pride in his display.

It was only natural that her gaze strayed away from his face to his biceps, where the Aboriginal kangaroo stood proudly. Did he have other tattoos? From what she could see on view they'd have to be hidden behind his trousers. *Uh-oh.* Better not to speculate at this moment about what his pants contained.

It was more of an issue as she glanced back and up at his mouth, framed by his mustache and short beard. She'd never kissed a man with a beard.

Mac swallowed the excitement she felt building inside her. She'd kissed dozens of men. Had several boyfriends. But the past six months had been a deliberately chosen dry spell. She'd been too busy to think about romance. At the moment it was front and center and all-consuming. But it wasn't a good idea.

"Not a good idea."

"Why? Because I'm defective?"

Mac hadn't realized she spoken until she heard his reply. The look on his face didn't help the situation one bit.

She rolled a shoulder in annoyance. "I liked you better when you didn't try to get by on pity."

"You think I want you to kiss me out of pity?" He

smiled then, and she felt as if he'd handed her a prize. Her only reaction to that smile was lust, pure and urgent.

She leaned up on tiptoe and balanced her hands on his bare chest. There was only one problem. He was a foot taller than she, and even in four-inch heels she couldn't close the distance.

She pretend-scowled up at him. "I could use a little help here."

He picked her up with ease, hands at her waist as he hauled her up onto his chest. The fierce strength and sheer size of him made her feel small. Growing up, she hated reminders of how diminutive she was. In high school, boys were always trying to show off by picking her up to prove how strong they were. Several got a sharp elbow in the ribs for their efforts.

But with Oliver it felt amazing. He scooped her up hard against him, all the heat of his bare chest radiating through her blouse into her skin. "This enough help?"

"Show-off." She wrapped her arms around his neck and pulled his head down.

He had a good mouth, wide and full, but not too wide or too full. And he knew how to use it. His kissed her softly at first, just a touching of lips that did not ask anything. But she felt a zing through her body as his beard grazed her face.

Kissing Oliver Kelly for the first time was easy and friendly. And just provocative enough for her to want to linger, learn more, feel more.

It happened by degrees. Her hands turned from holding on to his neck for support to gripping him as she sought fuller, deeper kisses. She felt him slide a hand lower and scoop it under her butt to hold her more firmly to him. So, naturally, she brought her legs up, straddling his waist. Kisses were like that, at least kisses with Oliver were. She couldn't put a finger on another makeout session quite like this one.

That was it. Kissing Oliver was like an old-fashioned makeout session where both parties knew nothing more was going to happen.

Even if she was locking her ankles behind his back like he was the pole and she was the dancer.

Mixed images. But he did that to her. Sweet and sinful man.

A groan escaped beneath her mouth and then he gripped her tighter, two hands palming her butt. She heard herself sigh, falling, slow-spiraling, ever more deeply into the sensation of his mouth moving on hers. The stroke of his tongue on hers excited and weakened her. Very soon they were no longer sighing but murmuring with the urgent sounds of two people ready to connect.

She grabbed fistfuls of his hair. He swung her around and up against the wall, using his weight to pin her there while one freed hand went roaming. First, his hand went under her shirt at the back, where he dragged his fingers up the side of her torso from her waist to the edge of her bra. He nudged it up, fingers seeking her warm round flesh. But the band was too tight.

Mac lifted her mouth from his to suggest that he undo it, but he was ahead of her. He'd shifted her weight back onto his chest while his hand skimmed up her waist to find the hooks. She wasn't sure how he did it but they all came free at the same time.

"God. You feel beautiful."

Feel beautiful. She'd never heard that phrase before. But then she was yanked away from thought as he rolled a nipple between his fingers. "I want to taste you, Macayla. Everywhere."

"*Uh-huh*," or sounds to that effect, was all she could

muster. Not particularly sexy foreplay. But her eyes were
rolling back in her head in ecstasy. Just from the action of
his hand at her breast. Not a lick. Or a suck. Just his magic
Aussie fingers teasing and pulling and rubbing her to
mindless lustiness.

"You're so easy, Macayla."

She tried to surface through the waves of lust beating
on the shore of her desire. Wasn't sure *that* was a compliment. *Easy* often had bad connotations where women were
concerned.

"You like my touch. Your body is so open and warm
and responsive."

You have no idea, she thought. He was still delving into
her bra, as if there were goodies he hadn't yet sampled. Oh
yeah. Her right breast. Found it.

She was melting, sliding into the warm sexual pool of
desire. Would he be shocked when he eventually found the
love sea below?

She giggled. Oh my god. She giggled.

"What?"

She leaned her head against his chest, groping for
words. "You're bad for me."

"I'm damn good for you. We needed this."

We. At least he hadn't said *you* need this.

"Macayla?" He was breathing hard against her ear, his
beard like a muffler against her neck.

"Hm?" She made the sound against his mouth when his
returned to kiss her, and got a little buzz effect that went
to her head like champagne.

"We'd have more fun horizontal." His voice was no
more than a growl.

What happened to just kissing? They were quickly
moving past it—

"Oh!" He'd slid a hand under the edge of her lace shorts

and skimmed his thumb over the seat of her panties. Not much that she could say in protest. Not when she had her legs wrapped around his waist like a pretzel.

"Can we at least be in a position where I have use of both hands? You'll like me having both hands available."

"Okay." She shivered in anticipation. He was bad. Or that good. Maybe both.

The thumb moved, this time with deliberate intent to skim her most sensitive parts. Definitely, he was that good.

What was she thinking? This wasn't what she'd come for. Or stayed for. But it was, at this moment, all that she wanted.

She unlocked her ankles and slid down his body. He lowered her slowly, letting her feel every solid warm inch of them touching through their clothing. Her clothing. He was bare to the waist. Feeling a little dizzy when her feet hit the ground, she pressed her face into his arm, meeting his kangaroo eye-to-eye.

"Hi." She slid a finger down that curved surface as she traced that animal spirit. Just a second, in just second she'd have her equilibrium back.

But he was back-walking her toward the bed and she was two-stepping her way with him. Her knees hit the back of the mattress, and then he switched positions, sitting on the end of the bed and pulling her into his lap.

She saw his eyes as he lowered her onto his lap. His sea-blue eyes contained warm tropical currents that enveloped her. She was ready to ride those currents—no, him—as long and a hard as she could—

The jolt of an electrical current at her crotch sent her scrambling off his lap. She stared wide-eyed at his lap. "What was that?"

"Shit." Crazed by lust, Oliver gazed down as something buzzed his erection a second time.

Phone. On vibrate.

He snatched it out of his pocket, intending to hurl it across the room until he saw Kye's picture. He swiped to answer. "What the fuck?"

"Uh-huh. Uh-huh." He stood up. Raking a hand through his tousled mane he listened hard to his quietly angry friend telling him in short, terse sentences why Oliver was going to give a speech tonight. End of subject.

"Done." It was the only word Oliver spoke before hanging up. He took a quick breath before turning to Macayla. One look was enough to halt his thoughts. She looked beautiful. Disarranged by his hands and mouth, a job he badly wanted to finish. But he couldn't. He could see in her expression something that had always scared the shit out of him. In her gaze he saw tomorrow.

Yeah. She was that kind of woman. So not his type.

"Problem?" How pretty her voice sounded. It made him want to snag her by the waist and drag her back onto the bed to finish what they'd started. She wouldn't mind. He saw that much in the trusting smile she offered him.

And that's why he couldn't. At least, not with what he needed to ask her hanging over the moment.

"I want you to come with me tonight. Up on that stage."

Mac frowned. "I can't do that."

"It's the only way it will work." He came toward her, one hand out to touch her face. "You said it earlier. You ask me questions and I'll answer. But not on paper. I can only do this if I'm looking at you. Just you."

He could see her thinking about it. "But that wouldn't be a banquet speech. That would be an interview."

He grinned and hauled her in to hold her against him. "Your idea. Your fucking great idea."

Her arms tentatively slid around his waist. A sign

she was considering it. "What if the conference people say no?"

He looked down and brushed back that hair tangled in her lashes. "My show. They do it my way."

She bit her lip, the lush lower one he'd been sucking on earlier, and his dick twitched. "But everyone will wonder who I am. I have no credentials. No part in search and rescue. I'm a nobody."

"Oh, so you can self-shame but I'm not allowed to be stupid."

"I don't have anything nice to wear." Every woman's lament.

"Wear nothing. The men in the audience won't hear a thing I have to say. Hey, that's got possibilities."

"Not on your life." She pushed back out of his arms and he let her go. He'd done all he was going to do to coax her. "How formal is it?"

"You won't catch me in a tux, if that's what you're asking."

"You'd look good in a tux."

"I look good in anything. But you're saying yes, yes?" He grabbed her. "Crikey! We'll show them how it's done Aussie-style." He kissed her. "Then maybe I'll show you how other things are done Aussie-style."

Mac laughed. "What happened to your wounded ego?

"Oh, I know my worth. Where I fail and where I excel. Modesty was never an issue."

CHAPTER THIRTEEN

Once they were unmiked, Oliver practically pulled Mac off the stage behind a curtain that separated it from the banquet audience.

"Where did you learn to do that?" He was grinning like he'd won the lottery.

Macayla almost couldn't form words, she was smiling too hard. Now was not the time to tell him she'd once conducted interviews with often reluctant subjects on a daily basis. "I cued off things you said this afternoon. Was it really good?"

He grabbed her and kissed her, hard and swiftly. "You're a mad genius."

And that was all he got to say because he was being rushed by members of the audience, who'd followed them backstage, along with a reporter and a couple of cameramen. Nearly everyone else had their cell phones out taking shots.

Macayla stepped back out of their path because there

was no doubt that this was Oliver's moment. And she wanted him to enjoy every minute of it.

There had been a second there at the beginning, as they stepped onstage to begin the interview, when he'd looked like a fish jerked out of water onto the beach. He was on the verge of panic—though she suspected only she knew it. She'd talked him into this, she'd reminded herself. She couldn't now let him make a fool of himself.

The inspiration to ask him first about his boast that he could belch "Waltzing Matilda" had turned out to be a brilliant strategy. Once the audience laughed at his typically Aussie response, "When I'm proper pissed, yeah," he settled, and the rest of the interview went off flawlessly.

Though she received several compliments from those pressing around Oliver, thankfully, no one detained her long. Just as well because she didn't want to answer any personal questions. This was Oliver's night.

Finally, as the crowd around him thinned, Oliver waved her forward.

She arrived at the edge of the throng to hear a man say, "I have to admit, Kelly, after meeting you at last year's conference, I'd written you off as a pretty face. But hearing you tonight, talking with such passion and commitment, I'm impressed. You have a rare capacity for capturing the complexities and nuances of SAR work and making them easily understood."

"I wouldn't know about that. I just work hard and believe in what I do. Talk is cheap. The field is where the real work gets done."

"True as that may be, every cause needs a charismatic spokesperson. I'm chairman of a philanthropic agency that's looking into ways to better serve disaster-stricken communities. I believe you have something to contribute. Call me." He handed Oliver his card.

Oliver eyed the man. "I have strong opinions. You won't like many of them."

The older man shrugged. "We like to think we welcome all views." He shifted his gaze to Macayla. "And you, young lady. Good job tonight. I'm Jarvis Henley."

He held out his hand, smiling at her as if he knew her. Macayla noticed that he wore an expensive linen suit with an open-collar pale-blue shirt. Silver hair pomaded to perfection topped a tanned and weathered face. Everything about him said *Florida money*. "And this is my wife, Sara."

A tall, elegant woman with a spiky silver pixie haircut stood beside Henley. Nearly as tall as her husband, she wore a tailored blue shirt and linen trousers that reflected her husband's attire. She, too, exuded money, from her perfect minimal makeup to the simple silver chain around her long neck from which hung a pendant of a greyhound.

She smiled at Mac, a friendly but assessing expression on her face. "I know who she is, Jarvis."

Macayla held in her breath. *Damn*. Nearly a year had passed since anyone had said some version of *I know you* in that slightly amazed tone. Her former professional life was about to be exposed.

"You're Tampa/St. Pete's Pet Detective."

Macayla let out her breath in a rush. "Yes, I am." Safe.

"Is that so?" Henley gave Macayla a second, longer look. "Sounds like interesting work." His voice was still friendly, but something in his gaze made the hair lift on her arms. "Had any interesting adventures lately?"

"Ah, no." She must have stiffened at the question because Oliver's arm, slung loosely about her shoulders, tightened protectively.

"I need a drink." He looked down at her. "Ready, Macayla?"

She nodded and tried to shrug off the sense that something was wrong. It had to be the shock of thinking that she was about to be outed in public that had her nerves all jangling. That and the high of having pulled off a success with Oliver. She just needed a little space and quiet. Crowds had always made her slightly uncomfortable.

Henley set a hand on Oliver's shoulder as he turned away. "I'd like to get a picture with you and your lady."

"Not me." Macayla stepped back as two cameramen came forward at the invitation and took several photos of Henley, his wife, and a slightly frowning Oliver. His gaze was homed in on her, and she knew he was wondering why she'd opted out of the photos. She supposed she had a lot of things to tell him about herself, if and when the time seemed right.

When they were done, Henley slapped Oliver on the back. "I expect a call soon, Kelly."

Oliver shrugged. "Your funeral. Ta." He took Mac's hand and pulled her with him toward the closest ballroom exit.

She fell into step beside him. "*Um*. That was rude."

Oliver shook his head. "I know his type. Big contributor to the cause who doesn't give a toss about the realities of what we do. They get their jollies listening to stories of suffering and deprivation, lob money at us, and then go home to their Jacuzzis and steak dinners and martinis."

"I like martinis. When I can afford them."

One side of Oliver's mouth jerked up. "You *earned* a martini. Let's hit the beach bar. I feel stifled in here."

"What about the rest of the awards banquet?" She didn't want to stay another second but felt obligated to point out, "You're the guest of honor. Shouldn't you be present until the end?"

Oliver stared at her in a way that heated her up from the inside. "Is this what you really want?"

What she really wanted? That would be to climb on top of him and go for a long, sweaty, dirty ride. *So* not the time to think of that! She touched his arm. "It's your night. Your call."

His face lit up. "Beer and martini coming up."

For reasons she could not explain, Macayla looked back as they were about to exit the ballroom. Jarvis Henley and his wife were still standing nearby. Something struck her as familiar, and not because they had just met.

An unease slithered out of her subconscious, teetered on the brink of knowing, as the man met her gaze. Chandelier light glinted off the expensive watch on his wrist as he raised his hand, arm bent at the elbow. Three fingers curled back and his thumb cocked as he pointed his forefinger straight at her and smiled.

I know that gesture.

The thought struck cobra-sharp, injecting her with blade-sharp terror.

Oliver, who paused as she jerked away from him, turned back. "What's wrong?"

She shook her head. Her insides had gone liquid with fear. "I—nothing. You're right. Let's go. Now!"

She turned and hurried past him, stumbling blindly into those who were in her path.

"Sorry. Sorry. Sorry." The word, repeated over and over, was all that kept her from screaming.

Inside her head, she was still looking down the barrel of a gun meant for her.

CHAPTER FOURTEEN

Macayla moved so quickly, Oliver thought she might get away before he could stop her. He didn't know what had panicked her, but he'd seen that wide-eyed contracted-pupils stare often enough on the job to know that kind of reaction couldn't be faked. Something had spooked her. Frightened her to the core.

He found her across the hallway, pumping the elevator button as if she were giving it CPR. "Macayla!"

She swung around at the sound of his voice, her gaze still startled, moving past him as if she expected to be followed.

He moved in close to her so that she couldn't see past him, demanding her full attention. "What just happened back there?"

"It's nothing. A stupid mistake." She shook her head, refusing to meet his gaze. "I just need to get some air." She turned at the sound of the elevator and pushed through the doors before they'd fully opened.

As he went after her, she moved to the back of the space, head lowered.

Not about to let it go—he'd seen that wary expression before she could mask it—he moved in again, enough to make it impossible for her to ignore his presence, not enough to worry her.

"It's okay, whatever it is." He kept his voice low, not wanting to add energy to the situation. "Macayla?" His hands settled on her shoulders to turn her to face him. Then with a finger he lifted her chin. "You need to talk to me."

"Not here." She gazed up from beneath lowered brows as several other guests from the banquet joined them on the elevator, all talking at once.

"I thought that would never be over."

"Amen to that. Where's the bar?"

"Going down."

"By the way, great job, Kelly."

"Great performance from both of you."

One of the men sporting an NYC SAR logo stepped almost between Oliver and Macayla, grinning crookedly. "You're coming down to the bar, of course, Kelly. Beers are on me."

A woman on his right threaded her arm through Oliver's as she gave Macayla a *sorry* smile. "You don't mind, do you? He promised us, 'Waltzing Matilda.' "

Macayla glanced up at him. What he saw in her expression stopped his inclination to accept the invitation, for both of them. "Ta. I need to walk my dog, Jackeroo. He's been cooped up in my room all evening."

"Then after." The woman squeezed his arm. "You promise?"

Oliver nodded vaguely as the crowd walked off the elevator onto the main floor, where the bar was located.

"We'll be waiting." The woman reluctantly let go of Oliver's arm, the last to leave.

When the elevator closed, only Macayla and Oliver remained. He smiled at her. "Alone at last. Can you talk to me now?"

She lifted her head and let out a shaky breath. "It was nothing. Adrenaline overload being up in front of that crowd." She tried to smile at him. "I freaked."

"You don't freak. I've seen you in action. You run toward trouble. It's one of my favorite things about you."

He moved to put his arm around her, but she shied away. "Look, it's been nice. But you have things to do. So do I. Thanks for a nice time."

He frowned. "I thought the nice time was just beginning."

She looked up, eyes flashing. "Am I on your list of things to do? Walk the dog. Screw the girl. Then spend the night belching in the bar with your adoring fans?"

Oliver frowned. Macayla had run through several touchy moods in the short time he'd known her: preoccupied, annoyed, introverted, even snarky. But bitchy didn't sound right coming from her.

The elevator came to an abrupt stop, again at the ballroom level. As the doors opened on a waiting crowd Oliver stepped into the breach and held up a hand toward those who surged forward. "Sorry. Illness on board. Take the next car."

He pushed the CLOSE DOORS button and the LOBBY button before turning back to Macayla. "What's going on, Macayla? And don't make it about us. I saw your face at the table. Something happened that scared the shit out of you."

She glanced up at the camera mounted in the corner. "I can't talk here."

"Okay." Oliver was all too aware of security in the modern world. If she was worried about being overheard then something important was going on.

When the elevator opened on the main floor, he saw her hesitate. "Thanks for wanting to help. But I'm really tired. Can we talk tomorrow?"

Oliver stuck a booted foot in opening to keep the doors from closing. "You don't need to be alone right now."

She made the little frown face that pursed her lips and drew tiny lines between her brows. He'd seen that before, and thought it made her look like an annoyed kitten. One with sharp claws. "Fine."

Macayla ducked under his arm into the hallway to the lobby. She heard a roar of greeting from the bar but turned and walked quickly in the opposite direction.

Now that she was over the shock, embarrassment was overtaking every other emotion. She couldn't adequately explain to herself what had occurred in the banquet hall. She knew how it would sound if she tried to explain it to Oliver.

Jarvis Henley pointed a finger at me and that reminded me of the gun pointed at me three weeks ago when I thought I was going to die. Or maybe it was the previous time. You see, I've been shot at before.

That explanation sounded bat shit crazy even to her. That couldn't be what happened. But it was.

And now her nerves were ruining her chances of spending the night with a man she wanted very much to be with.

She almost glanced back, wanting to see Oliver's confident smile, but not quite ready. He was elated by the evening's outcome. And had every right to be. He had conquered a huge fear. How could she spoil his triumph with her crazy stories?

No, better not to involve him. After all, he would be leaving shortly.

That brought her up sharply at the hotel's main doors with a strange little stab of pain in her middle. He was here for a conference that ended tonight.

She turned to find him right behind her. "When do you leave town?"

Something came and went in his expression. "I have a flight tomorrow. But that can easily be changed. I made the arrangements before we met."

"A day or two isn't going to make any difference. Will it?"

He scowled. "What are you asking me?"

What was she asking? "Nothing. I'm asking nothing of you."

He took a beat during which he took her hand and threaded his fingers through hers. "Macayla. We made a good team tonight, yeah?"

"Yes. You were great." His happiness was infectious. "I knew you would be."

"*We* were great. Because you had faith in me." His smile had a new, softer edge to the cocky self-assuredness. "I think we should celebrate. Just you and me."

The way he said those final words spun her world gently. She couldn't lie that she had been waiting for a chance to get back in his arms but now that it was here, she was caught between it and the jangle of nerves stilling revving her anxiety. When he looked at her the way he did now, her insides heated up. He wanted her. She wanted him. Simple. Easy. All she had to do was say . . . "Yes."

She thought he would lead her back to the elevators so that they could go to his room but he bypassed them and headed down a hallway toward the back of the hotel. "Where are we going?"

"Somewhere we can be alone."

He led her out across the back patio and down the shallow stairs onto the beach. Nearby tiki torches lit up an area with firepots and Adirondack chairs where hotel guests sat drinking and making s'mores. She was surprised to see that the beach beyond was not shrouded in darkness. The banquet had seemed to last forever. However, nightfall had not quite claimed the view.

The sun was already a memory. Yet a thin wash of colors lit the horizon in palest shades of orange, yellow, and aqua before abruptly turning sapphire. In that darkness hung a sliver of moon. Above it Venus glinted liked a diamond solitaire.

"Hold up." He stopped and pointed to his boots. "Bare feet from here."

He rolled up his pant legs to the knee before unlacing and shucking off his boots; he stuffed each with a peeled-off sock. Then he tied the laces together and slung them over a shoulder.

Meanwhile Macayla unbuckled and slipped out of her sandals. The sand was still warm from the sun. But as her feet sank down into the shifting surface, the soles of her feet found cooler layers beneath.

"Come on."

They moved onto the smoothed sand, emptied of beach chairs and canopies, to where the surf curled silver at the edge of an ink-dark sea. He took her hand and they wandered off toward the darker end of the beach, away from the cluster of hotels. Neither of them said anything. It wasn't necessary.

As the night closed in around them, Oliver's hand on hers was warm and strong, something solid to hold on to. Macayla lifted her face to the sky, feeling the foreboding easing away from her. The wind ruffled her hair as the gentle lapping sounds of water against the sand consumed her. She'd always loved the sea best at night, or after a storm, when sky and water merged and the sands were nearly empty but for a few brave souls.

After a few minutes more, the back-and-forth slide of surf seemed to feed a different kind of restlessness. She was on a beach with a man she was very much attracted to. It felt like more than that. He'd shared things about himself few other people knew, none in his present life. He'd trusted her with what he saw as his greatest vulnerability. Not that she saw it that way. She thought he'd done a remarkable job of making a place for himself in the world, against the odds of family expectations. And perhaps his own. She was proud of him, and very touched that he felt safe with her. And now she wanted to share more, in a very personal and intimate way.

There'd be plenty of time tomorrow and the day after that to drive herself crazy with nightmares and useless speculation. They might only have tonight.

She glanced sideways at Oliver and wondered if he knew what was happening.

As if he'd heard her thoughts, Oliver paused and turned to her.

She felt a pang of regret as he saw the solemn lines of his face outlined in the dark. He wasn't smiling. It must be time to turn around. She searched her mind for something to say, how to be okay with regret.

"Macayla." He said her name in a silky rough whisper, and then he kissed her. And it was just that simple. No words needed after all.

He kissed her. And then he kissed her some more, until she was sighing and lifting her hands to find his shoulders as he stroked her libido to life with his tongue. It's what she wanted, so very badly. Just this. Now.

When he lifted his head they were both breathing hard. His hands, having found their way into her clothes, rested warmly on her bare back.

"We should go back to your room." Her voice sounded as breathless and eager as she was.

Like the disappearing Cheshire Cat, the gleam of his teeth in the dark was the only indication of his smile. "Why waste the time?"

She glanced right and left along the quiet stretch of beach as his intention dawned on her. "We can't do that here."

"Don't tell me. There are rules against it. Haven't you ever wanted to say, *Screw the rules*?"

"Sure. But—"

He lay a finger against her mouth. "*Shh.* I've got better uses for your beautiful mouth."

When he finally moved back from her again it was to pull his shirt over his head and drop it by his boots in the sand. He looked up when she didn't follow suit. "It'll be more fun with your clothes off."

She began to laugh, caught up in the naughtiness of his suggestion. "Seriously. What if someone comes by?" She looked around for a secluded spot but found nothing, not even the shelter of sea grape vines. Nor were the dunes plumed with sea oats in the distance sufficiently tall. "We can't just lie down in the sand."

"No. We're going out there." He pointed at the gently rolling swells. "The tide turned recently. It will be calm for a while yet."

"You want to have sex in the surf."

He looked at her, one leg out of his pants, one leg still in. "Have you never?"

She took a breath. So many things, she'd never. But that wasn't the problem. "I have my purse, and my phone. What if someone steals them while we're in the water?"

"What's an adventure worth to you?" He stepped out of his pants. That left him in a pair of dark-blue boxer shorts that fit him in a way that revealed as much as they concealed. Was sex with him worth losing her purse? Maybe. Definitely, the possibilities revealed by his shorts were worth exploring.

"What if we get arrested?"

"I get deported and you get a fine. Okay?"

She stared at him a moment longer. Then shrugged off her jacket. "You're a bad influence, Oliver Kelly."

"Ta."

He ran toward the surf as she wriggled out of her dress. The feel of the wind against her body drew goose bumps.

Farther along the shore, fishermen sat on a jetty night fishing. The glow from their gas lantern was the only spot of light on the dark pier. Though they were more than half a mile away, their friendly voices carried clearly over the water.

As she stepped out of her dress more stars winked into being, and a meteor streaked overhead. A long-legged heron croaked from some unmapped quadrant of the dark sky.

The water lapped cool against her body but his hands were warm as he drew her in. His mouth was cool lips and warm tongue. She clung to him, letting the waves ride over and around them.

They were standing in what was waist-high water for him. Chest-high for her.

He pushed his shorts to his knees. "Climb on board."

She shook her head. "I'm not sure about this."

"You're right." He hooked a finger in her panties and

tugged at them as though she hadn't spoken. "These have to come off first."

His laughter was so infectious she felt her anxieties ebbing. "You're dangerous."

He ducked under the water and stripped her panties down her legs. She lifted one foot and then the other, palms on his back to keep her balance. The cool currents of water felt chill against her overheated flesh.

When he came up, he had her lacy boy shorts hooked around one finger. She reached for them but he took them and pulled them, waist first, down over her head until it looked like she wore a lace cap.

He chuckled. "Now you won't lose them."

One big callused hand slid over her bare butt and she shivered. The fingers of his other hand trailed down her belly. And then he was diving underneath the waves again.

She gasped as the rasp of his beard followed his path of his fingers and then the hot length of his tongue slid over her skin and in between her thighs. He nudged her legs apart until she stood wide-legged in the sand. And then with his hand on her bare bottom, his lifted her off the seafloor.

"Float, Macayla."

She stretched out her arms in the water, feeling the bounce and roll of the water beneath her.

"Breathe. You can't float if you aren't breathing."

Macayla nodded though it didn't translate to a response when she was on her back in the night sea. After a heartbeat or two, she opened her eyes. Far above her dozens of stars seemed to have caught fire as sharp pinpricks of light. And then she forgot about everything.

Oliver wedged his head between her thighs and drew

her to his mouth. The touch of his tongue, hot after the cool touch of the sea, made her gasp and flail a bit.

His hands tightened on her backside, holding her steady.

"Relax," he said in a whisper that came from between her thighs. "I've got you."

Macayla smiled. He had her. Understatement of the year.

He rubbed his chin along the sensitive skin of her inner thighs as he kissed his way back to the apex. Then once again, the heat of his breath made her shudder as he drew her bud into his mouth and gently sucked.

"Oh. My. God."

Macayla's world careened away. She was floating, drifting, about to fly away until his hands found her waist and pressed her back into the bottom.

She grabbed him, dug her nails into his shoulders as she scrambled to hang on to the one solid thing in this liquid world.

When she was steady, he released her and ducked under for a second. When he surfaced, he was halfway back to the beach. She watched in confusion as he climbed the sand and picked up his trousers. And then she smiled in understanding as his hand went to his pocket, his wallet.

Even so, she gasped as he shucked out of his boxers. His audacity took her breath away. And then he was stalking back toward the water. Naked.

He dived into the water like a dolphin. He was a much stronger swimmer than she was. Obviously, he spent a lot more time at the beach than she did. When he emerged from the dark water beside her, his muscular torso gleamed wetly in the moonlight. He tossed his head, salt water flying from the ends of his hair as if he were the ancient god of the oceans, Poseidon himself.

He pulled her to him, one arm across her back, and other lower down to fit her body so snugly to his that there could be no doubt about how engaged he was in the moment.

"Had enough?"

She blinked water out of her eyes. "Not nearly."

"Good." He smiled at her, though she could only surmise that smile because it was tucked into the darkness of his beard. He leaned in, his cool wet lips against her ear. "I'm going to fuck you right here, in front of the whole world. If that's what you want."

"I do."

"The magic words."

She shivered again and it wasn't the Gulf or the breeze or the temperature. It was the overwhelming sensations pouring through her as his erection nudged her cleft, inches from where she longed for him to be.

He began working her bra. "Wait." She reached up and felt for her panties. They were still on her head. "I don't think I can manage any more garment accessories."

"Can't have everything, I guess." He sounded regretful. That didn't keep him from exploring. He lifted her up by the waist, easy to do in buoyant water, and pulled her to him to tongue her nipples through the lace of her bra, then gently bit each hardened bud. The sensation was too much. It buckled her knees. But he seemed to anticipate that, and held her upright.

Finally he ran a finger round one swollen nipple. "Save something for next time."

Macayla felt something being pressed into her palm. "You do the honors?"

She nodded, feeling her cheeks heat. Why was she embarrassed by a condom when he'd just been giving her the ride of her life on the tip of his tongue? She took open the packet and carefully extracted the contents.

Frowning, she looked up. "How do I?"

He released her and lay back in the water, his lower body floating up as his legs framed her shoulders.

She smiled. Had to admire his lack of modesty. Bobbing just inches from her eyes was a very impressive hard-on, a tent pole in the moonlight. Fingers trembling, she rolled on the condom, taking a moment to enjoy the length and heat of him.

"Playing with fire." He wrapped his hand over hers and stood upright again. "You hold this, I'll do the rest."

And then he was lifting her, hands on the back of her thighs to part and pull her legs around him. She quivered as his erection touched between her thighs. He groaned low in answer and adjusted the angle of her hips. And then, with his hot gusty breath on her chilled face, he thrust into her, going to the hilt in one sure stroke.

She clung to him, a little tired of fighting the gentle push–pull of the currents. But he began to move, pulling out only to push in again in sure hard strokes that took possession of her in a way she could only smile about. She wanted to help, but in this situation he had total control of the delicious sensation of their union. The feel of him moving beneath her hands, the bunch and glide of his muscles as he arched into her, his hands hauling her in and down to meet his thrusts.

Everything in her tightened, the tension building until she was breathing openmouthed, her head thrown back to the sky. But her eyes were squeezed shut to better feel the exquisite friction of their connection.

It happened so quickly. One moment she was a coiled spring. The next she was spinning apart. She thought she saw a shooting star arch above them, or maybe it was just those exploding contractions felt behind closed lids.

"Damn, Macayla. You're killing me."

He pulled her close, one hand coming up to press her upper body against his as the other dug into her butt cheeks while he thrust into her with an urgency beyond gentle or kind, just primitive and orgasmic.

CHAPTER FIFTEEN

Macayla didn't realize they were moving until they had waded in close to shore. In fact, she couldn't quite recall anything beyond the heat in her lower belly and the whisking sensation where the breeze touched her damp body in touch-tender spots. She felt tumbled by the surf, tossed by the swells, pounding by a rhythm as ancient as the tide. And it all felt pretty damn wonderful.

Her body quivered as she glanced at Oliver, who held her strongly by the waist as he half carried her to shore. She would have walked it by herself, but she felt a little smug about the possessive feel of his arm. She doubted much engaged this man's emotions for long. But, for tonight, he belonged to her.

She stood ankle-deep in water when she realized he hadn't been right about one thing. The tide. It had risen while they were out in the depths. For how long, she had no idea; they'd been in the water much longer than she realized. While they'd been swimming and kissing and touching in the aftermath of sex, little by little the sneaky tide had been encroaching on their things in the sand.

She saw two young women who'd been walking along the beach carrying an electric lantern stop and turn to stare as they came out of the surf.

Not the least bit intimidated by an audience, Oliver marched up the beach, revealing all that nature had given him. Nature had been ridiculously generous. He gave them a salute. "Next show eleven thirty. Room for all." Then he grabbed his pants from the wet sand and put them on.

Mac heard their giggles as the women turned and hurried away.

She came more slowly out of the surf, less sure about her ability to be so at ease in her undies—panties back on but made nearly transparent by being wet. Even in the darkness, the breeze was stronger now.

Oliver came toward her and pulled his polo over her head. She didn't argue though she did wonder. "What will you wear?"

"Not your dress." He turned and picked it up. "It's sopping wet from a sinkhole. Come on, let's go get you dry."

She looked down at herself. His polo was long enough to cover her to midthigh. She grabbed her purse and jacket, glad to see that neither was wet.

"Don't know about you but I'm starving. Fancy crab cakes and a beer?"

"Sounds awesome. But no one will serve us dressed like this."

He pointed up the beach to Grabby Bill's Seafood. "They will. Out on the deck."

"Okay." She tried to squeeze some salt water from her hair. "But people are going to wonder what we've been doing."

He grinned and leaned forward to kiss her. "They'll know what we've been up to. Do you really care?"

She shook her head and pulled his face to hers again for another kiss.

He rubbed his beard along her jawline. "That's good enough for me."

She wondered what he meant but she didn't have time to think about it. He had grabbed her hand and was pulling her along in his wake.

A cell phone played the sax intro for "Who Can It Be Now." Tip-off, even as she was dragged to wakefulness, that the call wasn't for her. One moment she was entangled with a big, hard, warm body. The next she was marooned on her side of the bed, feeling the chill of separation.

The other side of the bed dipped, then she heard a masculine voice say, "Yeah?"

Smiling, she turned toward him and wrapped an arm about his waist. She met nothing but wonderful almost hot skin. He was like a furnace, heating up everything he touched. Mostly her.

"How bad? Yeah. I can make the flight. No, I'll make my way to you. Where will we set up base? Yeah. I'll call when we land. Ta."

Oliver reached over and turned on the light before reclining back on the bed. That gave Macayla an unobstructed view of all she'd felt and tasted but not really seen the night before. He was worth looking at in the light.

Stretched out before her was the definition of *male in his prime*. Six-pack, check. Ripped and ridged torso and arms, check. Heavy corded thighs and firm swells of calves, yep. As for the eager-to-please erection, *oh my*.

Her most vulnerable lady parts stirred with a reminder

of how well his parts and hers had fit together not once but twice during the night.

He touched a finger to her brow and used his finger to sweep away a curl that fallen on her brow. "You okay?"

"Absolutely." Macayla rolled closer and propped her chin on his chest. "You're still looking good from my perspective. If you have the time."

He frowned down the length of his nose at her, but the finger sliding down her spine toward her hips said he was in no hurry. "You heard the call, yeah?"

"Sounded like work." She wiggled her backside as his finger slid into the shallow before her cleft.

"It was work. I have to pack and leave. Now." He gently cupped one buttock.

She knew that. She'd known it the same instant he had. But when he said the words it hurt all the same. Because she wasn't ready. And he was leaving. As she had known all along that he would. But later, much later would have been better.

"Okay." She said the word very carefully, not glancing up to meet his gaze. "This has been—something."

He was silent a moment. "Yeah. Something. I don't know—" He shook himself. "I need to move. Sorry." He reached down and gently lifted her from him and sat up. His expression said a lot of things but he said none of them. "I'm really sorry. But lives depend on me hauling ass out of here." He stood up.

That's when she saw it. It was a tattoo of a koala bear, clinging to a tree, positioned on his lower right side, beside his groin. Unlike the works of art on his arm and back, this was brightly colored and cartoony. The fuzzy little guy was holding a beer with a flower tucked behind one ear. And his eyes were slightly crossed.

Macayla sat up in bed. "What's that?" She bit her lip and pointed.

Oliver rolled his eyes. "The last time I did something really stupid."

"Is it drunk?"

"Or high on eucalyptus leaves, or both. He's an ugly blighter."

Macayla tried not to smile as she watched his naked butt walk away. The tattoo really was an awful blotch on such a sexy male body. "If that's how you feel you should have it removed."

"No." He reached for his duffel bag and began shoving things in it. "I keep it to remind me that I have to live with the consequences of my actions."

"What actions?"

"I bet a guy I could . . . never mind. I was nineteen. I lost."

"This was the booby prize?"

"Yeah. I had to get a tattoo of his choosing."

"I suppose it could have been worse." The seriousness of the moment settled over her as he pulled out fresh clothing. "Where are you going?"

"Chile. Southern end. Earthquake. Seven point eight. There's going to be a lot of rubble to go through. If we get there in time, we'll be able to save some lives."

She saw the tension in his expression as he collected things to take into the bath, and remembered the stories he'd told earlier at the banquet about what his working life was like. They scared her and elated her, though she had no experience to put to her imagining. But he did this all the time. And he wasn't alone. He and many others like him went where the world was cracking open, or breaking apart, or drowning, to save lives. What would it be like to do that?

The ridiculous thought struck her that she'd like to go, too. To be useful as he was. But that was fantasy. Hadn't she learned that she couldn't trust herself? She'd fail as a SAR operative, just as she had at child advocacy. Because she didn't want to be responsible for anything as precious as a human life. And if she did fail, then she'd have even less of herself to put back together than before.

Oliver was a genuine hero because he went again and again. She'd been thrust into the melee of one of life's worst moments, and run away rather than risk facing a similar situation.

Something rose to the surface of her disturbed musings. A new possibility, and it wasn't at all to her credit. She'd convinced herself that it was the title of *hero* she'd been running from. Now she realized it might have been the title of *coward*. Once a hero, people would always expect her to put herself out there, do what needed to be done. Over and over again. She'd need to keep proving her worth. Only she hadn't done that. She'd acted without thinking. Because thinking made her shy away from the very idea of being courageous. She suspected she'd only been heroic because she didn't have time to think.

Oliver was showered and dressed by the time her thoughts returned to the moment. He sat back down beside her to lace up his boots. She wanted to throw her arms around him and hold on, urge him to take care and let her know when he got there, and how he was, and when he thought he'd be—back?

He wouldn't be back.

He'd come to St. Pete Beach for a convention. They'd hooked up. It had been beyond great. But it was over.

She swallowed back the sudden concern that welled up in her. They didn't know each other like that. This was a one-off, a fantastic one, but nothing more permanent than that. She knew it going in. They didn't have ties that made one worry about the other or want to console the steeling against horror she'd glimpsed for a second in his gaze. She didn't have that right.

So she said nothing about her concern for him, though it hurt her heart not to speak. She was going to be the perfect hookup. Cheerful and pleased, without recriminations. It was all she could offer this man going off to face death and destruction.

Macayla slipped off the bed, drawing his attention. "You're cute in the morning," he said. "All tousled and sleepy. But you don't need to get up. The room is yours until noon. Order in breakfast and put it on the tab."

She nodded, but she wouldn't do that. It felt wrong. "So, thanks for the evening."

He finished the final knot and came toward her, enfolding her nakedness into him. "This isn't how I wanted this morning to go. But I have the kind of job that doesn't allow me to make plans. I should have warned you ahead of time."

"I understand."

"You're good company. You know that? Nice to wake up to."

She smiled. "You just want more sex."

"Definitely. But today I wanted to just, I don't know. Hang out."

"That's a novelty for you, hanging out?"

"I shouldn't admit it. But yeah. I'm not much for watching the telly and munching on crisps after the main event."

"It's thank you, ma'am, and she's history?"

He frowned. "Not like that."

"Then how?" She kept her tone playful.

He frowned harder. "You're not making this easy."

"I'm not faulting you for who you are. It's just that I don't date men like you. So I don't know the routine."

"What's a man like me?"

"You could have any woman you want."

"I want you." His face caught fire with a grin so lewd she tightened her thighs in purely female response. His body arrogantly responded in a way that could not be misinterpreted.

"So I noticed."

Again he was silent. "Is there a man in your life?"

"Wow. Now you ask?" She hoped she sounded the right playful note.

"Is there?"

"No. Not at the moment."

"Good."

He kissed her softly and then more urgently until he groaned and backed away. "I hate my life sometimes. I have to go. There's a flight I have to arrange for, and Jackeroo needs to be walked first."

"I can do that while you finish making plans."

He looked at her in surprise. "You'd do that?"

She shrugged. "Since I'm awake."

"You're an unusual girl."

"You have no idea."

CHAPTER SIXTEEN

Keeping her quarry in sight, Macayla let out the neck loop of her slip lead until it was nice and big. She crouched down on the side of the highway just on the other side of the guardrail, making herself as small as possible, and swiveled her body sideways so that she didn't present an aggressive stance. A trainer once told her that, to a frightened dog, a human stranger with arms extended or held wide looked like a grizzly bear on his hind legs. She needed to look small and nonthreatening so that the poor animal would come close enough to sniff and realize she was sending out only friendly pheromones.

The Boxer was a beauty, with a golden coat and white stockings, spattered now with mud from his time on the loose. He'd been sighted by a jogger wandering along U.S. Highway 19 in Pinellas Park, near Gateway Center Boulevard. When she arrived he'd been in the median of a six-lane traffic area, probably trying to scent his way home. His owner said he'd been missing for two days.

Luckily the worst of the evening rush hour was over.

The early-evening sky was still bright enough for her to see clearly. With two truckers who stopped to help, she had been able to herd the dog across the road into a park-like area. She'd thanked them and said she had it from here. Too many captors might spook the Boxer, who had the look of a runner.

At the moment, the dog was standing in the grass by the concrete culvert that ran under the highway. With its neck stretched, head held high, and hind legs braced, it projected what Macayla thought of as a racehorse pose. Just from watching his graceful power, she would have guessed without being told by the owners that the Boxer was a prizewinning show dog.

She tossed a treat to land in the middle of the distance separating them.

"Okay. Big fella. It's okay." She kept her voice low and pitched deeper than normal in order not to fuel his agitation. Her tosses were slow and light. No sudden movements to frighten the dog.

He came forward to sniff the treat when a raccoon suddenly waddled out of the opening of the culvert. The Boxer stopped short and barked in surprise.

The raccoon, intent on reaching the treat, hissed and arched its back. The Boxer barked wildly as the raccoon approached, running back and forth. But the other animal kept coming until it made a sudden leap and slapped the dog on the nose using its razor-sharp claws. As the Boxer yelped and danced away, seeking shelter in the opening tunnel of the culvert, Macayla jumped up and threw a handful of shoulder gravel at the raccoon.

"Go! Shoo! Bad raccoon!"

The raccoon made a quick waddling turn to face her and rose up on its hind legs. With its signature face mask and razor-blade claws, it looked like a miniature bandito ready to rumble. Mac readied her loop in one hand as she reached for the pepper spray hanging from her utility belt with the other.

The Boxer, sensing an ally, came roaring out of the culvert barking loudly. The raccoon half turned, fur in full bristle, and hissed. The dog skidded to a stop, probably remembering the sting of the last attack. Macayla, with knees flexed, held her ground, not sure what to do next.

Great. What they had was a Mexican standoff, a confrontation between her, the Boxer, and the raccoon in which no party could attack or retreat without being exposed to danger from one of the others. Only one thing to do.

Macayla slowly moved her hand from the pepper spray to her phone and hit speed dial. She needed assistance. Animal control.

During the wait, they attracted a crowd of onlookers, parents out for an evening stroll with their kids, kids on bikes, others on skateboards, preteen girls in clutches so tight they seem to move in unison, like birds in flight. She warned them away, citing the danger of the raccoon, which drew more agitated with every additional witness. To her surprise and relief, the animal control truck arrived within five minutes.

To her lesser delight the man emerging from the truck was Gerald Boyd of the climbing-wall date. It *would* be Gerald.

Dressed in overalls that draped his rangy physique, he came toward her with a loose-limbed walk that betrayed his climbing interest. On any given weekend he could be found in Georgia or the Carolinas rock climbing. He paused on the roadside by the guardrail, a grin on his face.

"What's your problem, detective?"

"Wildlife interrupt-us."

"Come again?"

"I'm trying to rescue that Boxer." She pointed to the dog peering out from the culvert. "But he's being detained by a member of the Florida wildlife family. I tried to get a loop over it, but the beast bared its teeth and hissed at me."

"You got a damn strange job, Mac. Chasing pets."

"You chase bats, raccoons, and armadillos and you think my job is weird?"

"Let's see what we've got." He climbed over the rail to stand beside her and checked the scene with a big old grin on his face. "You want me to extract your varmint or your dog?"

"Extract the raccoon. I'll take it from there."

"Anything for the lady." Gerald went back to his truck, lifted off a canister with a short hose attached, and climbed back over the railing.

"Watch this." He flipped on the square light hanging from his belt, turned on the canister, and began yelling at the top of his lungs as he ran toward the raccoon.

The animal, taken by surprise, flipped around and waddle-ran as fast as its short legs could take it toward the trees fifteen yards away.

Macayla was impressed, thinking she should get a canister. "What did you spray on it?"

"Water. Most animals hate getting wet." Gerald held the hose up as if he were going to give her a squirt. "Shall we get your fleeing canine?"

"I got this. Watch and learn." Mac slipped down the shallow rise to the mouth of the culvert. "Come on, sweetie. Mac's got kibble and treats."

To her surprise the Boxer appeared at the opening, shaken but alert. He sniffed the air in her direction. Soon the dog came forward, clearly tired of the adventure. A bit of kibble eaten and Mac switched hands and slipped the loop carefully over the dog's head.

The moment the loop tightened a bit to feel like a leash, the Boxer heeled and trotted back to the guardrail at her side, as if it were the most ordinary thing.

Gerald nodded. "You got skills."

Mac grinned. "You know it."

"Wanna get a burger? I haven't had dinner yet."

Mac shook her head. "Thanks but I've got to deliver my catch to his rightful owner."

"How about later? Movie?"

"I'm kinda seeing someone."

He shrugged. "Your loss."

Mac swung away, rolling her eyes.

I'm seeing someone.

That thought made her amazingly happy, considering that he was thousands of miles and several time zones away. And not really hers at all. Even if he had shocked her by calling nearly every day.

"Hey."

Macayla groaned under her breath as she turned around. She'd almost gotten away.

Gerald was coming toward her. "You should know there's a wild rumor circulating about you."

"What kind of rumor?" Please don't let it be the one about how she got busy in the ocean with Poseidon in front of a beachfront full of hotels.

"It's says your pet detection business is shady."

She reached for her canister. "What do you mean shady?"

He backed up a step. "Don't kill the messenger. All's they said was some of them dogs you find are actually stolen. After the dogs are taken, you show up and offer to find them for a fee. See where I'm going?"

She did and she didn't like it. "Who told you that?"

"One of our other technicians. He heard it on the street."

"I hope you defended me."

He looked like a deer who'd spotted an oncoming car. "Sure. Sure I did."

"Thanks, Gerald." She walked away shaking her head.

She loaded the nervous Boxer into the dog crate wedged into the back of the car she'd borrowed from Jefferina's cousin. *Car* was a generous term. Two doors were wired shut. The shattered rear window looked like something a spider had spun from glass. The tires could have passed inspection in a billiard ball factory for smoothness.

"Not that I'm complaining," Mac said to the person on the other end of her phone conversation as she drove toward the home of the boxer's owners. "I'm mobile. That means I'm working. There's only so many Poodles you can groom before you start to question your value in the universe."

"You should have let me advance you the money." Oliver's voice caressed her ear even if the connection sounded remote. Chile was a long way away.

"Let's see. I screw a guy I've only known five minutes and then take money from him? I don't think so."

Oliver laughed. "When you put it like that."

They talked a few minutes more. She hadn't allowed herself to believe him when he'd said he'd be in touch after he left St. Pete. That would have been asking for heartbreak. But he had. It had been three days and he'd called every day. The first call surprised her. Most people stayed in touch by texting. But that wouldn't be easy for Oliver. As a result, she got the bonus of actually hearing his voice when they communicated. She could tell from his tone if he was tired, or worried, or feeling pretty good about how his job was going. All the intimate and immediate emotions missing in texts were there, in her ear, in real time. It was a rush.

She was careful to be cheerful and talk about nothing. She didn't ask if he was okay or how things were going, after the first call. He didn't want to talk about his work. She was his distraction from work. She got that. For now. When the job was over her usefulness as a distraction wouldn't be needed. So she made the most of now.

There was no reason for him to come back to Florida. She didn't even have money for a new used car, and her old one wasn't worth the cost of repairs. A trip to Hawaii, the place where his business was based, was out of the question. But it was fun to have him calling while it lasted.

She leaned forward, scanning the row of stucco houses with red tile roofs, looking for the address. "That's it. Arrived at my destination."

"Then I should let you go." Oliver's voice sounded oddly wistful. "If you had a better phone we could video chat. I miss looking at you."

"You'd only want to sext."

"Would you do that?"

"Dream on." She waited for the words she knew she would never say first. *I'm not looking for a relationship.*

He let out a little sigh. It shouldn't have affected her, but it did. A lot.

She exhaled. "I know it's hard to get through from where you are."

She could hear him thinking on the line before he spoke. "I'll call tomorrow."

"Awesome."

She put her phone away quickly, not letting herself think silly things like how she missed him. Or how much it meant that he was staying in touch. And especially how lonely she felt since he'd gone. It had been a long time since she'd allowed herself to need someone. Still, forty-eight hours wasn't enough to leave an indelible impression.

That's what she'd have told a girlfriend. If she had girl-friends.

Leaving her life in Tallahassee behind a year ago had left her alone in the world. What she wanted, at the time. But it did have a downside.

A few minutes later she was standing in the courtyard of a beautiful house in Pinellas Park. From the street the house seemed narrow and cloistered. Nothing special. But inside the heavy glass doors reinforced with lovely wrought-iron designs, the gardens of the courtyard were lush and filled with flowering tropicals. A maid—maid!—had let her in and asked her to wait for the owner here. The long front wall of the house was glass, looking out onto the courtyard with a small swimming pool with a wa-terfall at each end. Lanterns topped the surrounding high stucco walls. The bricked patio, plus the wrought-iron chairs, lounges, and tables, gave the space an Old World air. But the furnishings inside the house, seen through the glass walls, were sleek and modern, with lots of white and light woods and gleaming surfaces.

Finally, as the Boxer began to whimper with impa-tience, a woman appeared wearing skinny jeans, a lemon tank top, and stiletto sandals. Her hair was up in a messy ponytail, but Macayla knew how much effort went into that casual look. Every inch of her face was made up. She was wildly attractive and she knew it. At the moment, the skin around her eyes and mouth was drawn tight with suppressed emotion.

The Boxer went wild at the sight of her, barking and leaping explosively at the end of the leash.

"Arielle!" The women fell to her knees and threw her arms around the dog. The Boxer barked and licked her face, jumping even as she held on. She seemed not to mind that her pet nearly destroyed her careful, polished look. One point in her favor.

Finally she rose, but she didn't offer Macayla a smile, or even the usual thanks most pet owners offered. "I'm Ann Siler. You're the Pet Detective?"

Mac nodded. "I'm pleased to return your Boxer, Ms. Siler. He—she seems to be in good shape, except for a swipe on her nose from her run-in with a raccoon."

The woman's gaze widened, then she bent to check her dog's nose. "Was the raccoon rabid? Did you corner it for testing?"

"I called wildlife management. He didn't mention a problem." Rats. She hadn't thought about rabid animals. But the raccoon wasn't drooling or foaming at the mouth. "I would get her checked by your vet. She's been loose two days."

The woman straightened up. "She's been missing three days, and you know it."

"Okay." No need to argue with a client. "So then, I'm pleased to deliver a happy outcome for you. Good night."

"No. Wait." The woman kept glancing beyond Macayla so that it was all she could do not turn around and check to see what the woman was looking for.

"You want to be paid." She pulled several hundred-dollar bills from her pocket. "Is that enough? I don't want to have any more trouble."

Macayla didn't take the money. "You settle with my boss, not me."

"That isn't what I was told. The caller said to have the second payment ready on delivery. Obviously I don't want to prolong the association." She pressed the cash into Macayla's hands and quickly stepped back. A spasm crossed her face. "I'm sure you think of Arielle simply as a moneymaker, which she is since we show her. But she's family, too. She's my world. I don't know how you can live with yourself, taking money for causing so much pain."

Macayla blinked in surprise. This was the first time someone blamed her for taking money for her services. Guess there was a first time for everything. "I'm sure you won't have any more trouble. Just make certain she doesn't have time to dig out from under your fence again."

"You know that's not how she got away."

"Uh-huh." Mac back stepped, wanting nothing more than to get away from the distraught woman, fast.

"She was snatched from me. In broad daylight. In the park. He ripped her leash out of my hand." She opened her hand to reveal the red welt across her palm.

Suddenly the woman's anguish made sense. "You were attacked, too, not just your dog taken. Why didn't you call the police?"

The woman's face contorted in pain. "We were told not to."

"You were told? By the dognapper?"

She took a step toward Macayla, face flushing with anger. "Don't you toy with me. I've done as I was told. Now I hope that's the end of it. Because I know who you are now and I will call the police next time."

She remembered then what Gerald had said about the rumors about her. Shit.

Macayla tried to de-escalate the moment. "I don't know what you've heard but I'm not responsible for your dog being taken. My job is finding missing pets. You called us, remember?"

"That's right, deny it. As long as we are straight and I never see you again."

Whatever. She'd tried.

"Good night." Macayla turned away, getting more

ticked by the second. But more than anything she wanted to be out of this house. She needed to talk to Gerald, pin down the source of the rumor, and scotch it before it did any more damage to her reputation.

It was only as she reached the sidewalk that she noticed the first police car approaching. And then the second. They parked on an angle, ready to give chase if it was needed. There were no sirens but three officers exited their vehicles looking like they had business to conduct.

The oldest of the three, fiftyish, faded blond hair, approached slowly, hands resting on either side of his belt buckle. "Macayla Burkett?"

"Yes."

"We'd like you to come with us, please. We want to ask you some questions about dognapping."

CHAPTER SEVENTEEN

"You could help yourself here by cooperating. Get in front of this."

Macayla stared at her interrogator. Detective Sergeant Mullins looked and sounded just like Detective Andy Sipowicz in a cable rerun of *NYPD Blue*. The mustache, the longish receding hair, the paunch, the weary eyes, even his accent. He must have retired early and come down to Florida, as so many New Yorkers did. But he couldn't quit the force. The force was with him.

She strangled the urge to laugh. This was so not a funny situation. She had been brought in on suspicion of dog theft with "ransom money" in her pocket. Marked bills that the police had given Ms. Siler to give to the person who brought back her dognapped Boxer had her fingerprints on them.

"You hearing me, little girl?"

"Woman. I'm twenty-seven years old." She leveled an annoyed look at him. Hated it when her height, or lack thereof, was viewed as a supposed disadvantage by others.

"I've heard what you had to say. I'm innocent. I have nothing to add to that."

"That's not cooperating, which could be taken as an indication that you have something to hide."

She looked away from him, aware that she wasn't winning a friend or influencing this person standing in front of the desk she sat behind.

After being brought into the station, she had been made to wait for at least an hour in this small room with one tiny window at the top of the wall before anyone came in to say anything to her. During that time all the details of every police procedural she'd ever watched and read came back to her. How the police left a suspect—

Suspect! Dear god. She had been arrested as a suspect in the theft of dogs.

—to sit and think and worry and generally work herself up into a lather before someone came in and offered her a drink. She'd requested water. But she could only take a few sips. Her throat had seemed to swell shut.

Then more waiting. Now the waiting was over.

The questions came thick and fast with the arrival of Detective Sergeant Mullins.

How long had she been planning before she snatched Arielle? Or did she operate strictly by taking advantage of an opportunity that presented itself? What brought her to Tampa/St. Pete? Was she desperate for cash? Who did she owe money to? Had she been in debt as a gambler before? How long had the thugs who bat-slapped her car worked for her? What determined the amount she charged as a ransom?

She'd sat nearly mute under the barrage of this first round of questions, willing her heartbeat to slow. It felt, instead, as if she'd been running bleachers. Some of the questions were wild accusations. She wasn't a gambler. Never had been. Others were *When did you first get involved with a dognapping ring?* type questions. No way to answer without incriminating herself.

All of them were aimed at catching her in a lie.

Now Mullins was back. This time he took the chair across from her, slouching back as if he was tired and needed propping up. "If you give us the names of the people you work with, we might be able do a deal for you that will lessen your jail time."

Macayla began blinking hard. *Jail time.* No. She wasn't going to be stampeded into fear. "Pet theft is a misdemeanor, petty theft. There are exceptions, if the pet is a purebred breeding animal or a show animal. Livestock and racehorses are also exceptions."

"Oh, so you looked it up, did you?"

"I find lost pets for a living. Of course I'm familiar with the laws surrounding that activity."

"That makes you a pet detective. And you know that Boxer's a show dog. But why don't you tell me how you locate these animals you say you find?"

Macayla chewed her lip. Everything she said could and would be used against her in a court of law. But, for the moment, she couldn't see the harm in talking about her job. "I begin with where they went missing, check out the surrounding area, depending on how long an animal's been missing—most pets don't stray far. I can often coax them out of hiding with treats, water, or toys. That sort of thing."

"What if you don't find them there?"

"I have a network of people that I alert to be on the lookout for the missing animal."

"Want to give me a list of your network?"

Mac could have kicked herself for that comment. She wasn't being careful enough. "I don't want to get anyone hassled."

He smirked. "Why would they be hassled, as you call it, if they've done nothing illegal?"

Because she felt hassled and she hadn't done anything wrong. But she didn't want to give him the satisfaction of hearing that.

She clasped her hands so tightly in her lap the knuckles ached and met his gaze. Then she gave him the names of Sam Lockhart and Gerald Boyd. Both city employees in their respective towns, they would know how to conduct themselves. She thought of Cedric, homeless and wary of authority, who'd brought her the rumor about the greyhounds. The police picking him up could have awful consequences, with him possibly losing his dog Dougie. Not Cedric.

"Is that all?" Mullins didn't sound mollified.

"Outside of local police and animal control, it's an informal network. It's local contact type thing. Joggers and neighborhood watch people. Different with every location." Not a lie. But not the whole truth. "I sometimes find pets through a veterinarian's office or at shelters where they've been taken by concerned citizens who found them and didn't have a way to get in touch with the owner."

Mullins suddenly leaned forward, propping his forearms on the table. "Who's the muscle you hired to threaten Mr. Massey?"

They knew about Massey?

When she didn't reply, Mullins reached for a clipboard he'd set on the edge of the desk when he'd walked in. He flipped through a few pages.

"I've been checking you out, Ms. Burkett. St. Petersburg has a recent complaint filed against you. A Mr. Massey says you accosted him on his own porch, brought muscle with you. Giant guy with a foreign accent."

Mac was too surprised to shut down her reaction. She smiled.

"What's so funny?"

"Mr. Massey has a public nuisance sheet as long as your arm."

Mullins smiled. "Friend of yours, then."

She held on to her temper. This guy didn't like smart-mouths. "Mr. Massey's been fined for reckless endangerment to animals twice in the past month. That's due to me. Which I'm sure you know, too."

"I know you were involved in the theft of a pair of racing greyhounds that ended up dead."

Boy, he was playing the old switcheroo with her. Bricks coming from every direction.

"Not involved, hired to find them, through Tampa/St. Pete Recon, which I did. Check with my employer."

"How well do you know the breeders of the stolen racing dogs?"

"Not at all. Don't even know their names."

"Are you sure about that? Because I got a thousand-word photo that says different." Smiling, he pulled a sheet from the stack of clipped papers. It was a picture of Jarvis Henley and his wife talking with Oliver. In the shadowy foreground a figure had been circled in ink. It was Mac.

The detective laid out several more shots, all of them including her. In one she was shaking hands with Mrs. Henley. "Nice photos, huh?"

"Mr. Jarvis Henley owned the greyhounds I was hired to find?"

He frowned. "You want to play it that way, fine. I got more."

He pulled out another photo from the *St. Petersburg/*

Tampa Bay Times. It was one of her and Oliver on the stage together. "Seems like you've got connections to all the players." He tapped Oliver's photo. "Massey claims this is the fella who threatened him."

"No one threatened Mr. Massey." His grandson, possibly, but this was a don't-volunteer-squat situation. "That gentleman was the banquet speaker for the SAR conference. He's a search-and-rescue rock star who's since gone home."

"Drawn to the spotlight, are you?"

Mac didn't respond.

"Have it your way. St. Petersburg police are waiting their turn to speak to you."

"About Massey's complaint?"

"That and other things. You should know we've got some serious intercity cooperation going on here. Mr. Massey filed his claim after his grandson and two others were picked up on suspicion of felonies committed in the area in which five dogs have been snatched this week. He says your threats were an attempt to keep his grandson quiet about what he knew about your part in the thefts."

Mac let the crazy wash over her. Too many things were coming at her thick and fast. "I'm done talking about this."

"Then let's talk about you, Ms. Burkett. I thought your name was familiar. Macayla Burkett is famous in Florida."

Macayla flinched. Here it came, the reason she'd left Tallahassee.

"You were a Trauma Services Child Specialist with Children's Advocacy Services in Tallahassee. You also worked with a therapy dog. The case was pretty sensational. Made all the media including national. Six-year-old girl with disabilities who'd been the victim of an abusive parent attacked . . ."

Macayla stopped listening. She knew the story better than he ever would.

Jily, her mother called the defendant. Confined to a wheelchair, Jillian Catherine Neighbors was expected to call her father an abuser in a courtroom filled with adult strangers.

Jily didn't speak well. Her disabilities had robbed her of so much, and were sapping more. But Jily liked the big flop-eared Lab/retriever mutt named Katie whom she'd met at Macayla's office. Loved Katie so much that she would talk to Katie about anything.

Macayla had thought about offering her dog to Jily's mother. But she doubted the woman had time for a dog in her life, not with all they were already going through. Still, she'd made the decision that she and Katie would remain in Jily's life, afterward.

Katie.

Macayla breathed in slowly through her mouth. Katie was dead.

Suddenly the world she'd spent a year constructing shattered. Her nightmare had broken through and gone live.

The chill of the courtroom was back. The blank walls, the hushed silence as they sat in the rear. Waiting. Waiting for the unspeakable to play out.

The father entering the courthouse.

Their gazes locking at the exact same moment. And she knew.

How had he gotten the gun through security?

Too late for that. Jily's face was pressed into Katie's neck as she whispered secrets meant only for doggy ears, never aware of a thing. A blessing.

But six years of life was not enough. To give her a chance at more, Mac could only wager her twenty-six years.

Shots fired.

One life spared. One lost.

"Ms. Burkett? Ms. Burkett?"

Macayla snapped back, tasting salt on her tongue. When she focused on Detective Mullins she saw that he was holding out a tissue. He looked very unhappy. "I got that you saved the girl's life. That was a very brave thing to do."

"Was it bravery? I don't know."

He frowned, but went on doggedly. "How about this? You were celebrated as a hero for a while. Saw the footage of the CNN interview. That kind of attention can turn anyone's head. Then, like all good things, the spotlight moved on. You were last week's news. That has to have been hard for a young woman. You'd been shot protecting the girl. You could have died. You deserved the attention."

"That's disgusting."

"No. I can see it happening. In looking for ways to feed your need for the praise that made your sacrifice worthwhile, you started stealing dogs so that when you returned them you would be rewarded with the praise that you deserved."

She stared at him. He'd woven a perfectly plausible, if emotionally unstable, motive for why she might succumb to stealing dogs. Except for one thing. "I only find dogs after they've been lost or abandoned."

"Bet you thought of that, too. Dognappers often just abandon their victims if the owners won't pay the ransom. Convenient for you to show up, collect it another way."

"Coincidence. Not convenient." But he'd shaken her confidence at last. He'd fabricated a motive. Or someone had helped build a case against her. "Someone's trying to frame me."

Mullins sat back at the table, his expression suddenly

mellow. "Why would someone want to do that, Ms. Burkett?"

"I don't know."

"Who would want to frame you?"

"I don't know."

"What do you know?"

Not nearly enough to answer his questions. She drew in a long breath that sent a shudder through her entire body. But when she looked up at him, all of Macayla Burkett was in advocacy mode for herself. "Arrest me, or let me go. Either way, I want an attorney before I say another word."

"No need for that. You haven't been formally charged yet. You voluntarily gave us your fingerprints."

She shrugged. She was already in the state system. "I have nothing to hide. That doesn't mean I don't need protection."

"From what?"

From you and your theories. But she was done talking. Way past done.

Mac shook her head. Somewhere things had gone off the rails.

"Then stand up, because I am formally charging you with theft and extortion. I'll show you where you can make that call."

CHAPTER EIGHTEEN

"I'm pulling you off the streets until this is settled." Jefferina put her vehicle in gear and pulled out of the police station's parking lot. "Call it vacation time."

Macayla thought she had never seen anything as beautiful as the late morning sun after a night in jail and an early morning bail hearing.

She tried to take a deep breath but her throat was still fear-locked. Shallow breaths was all she was good for at the moment. "I can't afford a vacation. I've haven't earned this month's rent. And now I owe you bail money."

"Only if you don't show up for your court date. And we both know you will."

"Thanks again for doing that. I wouldn't have asked but I didn't have anyone else to call."

Jefferina glanced at her. "Why not, Mac? You could have friends. You just hold us at bay."

Us. Macayla didn't think in terms of having friends in the plural. She had acquaintances and colleagues, in a matter of speaking. But friends? Friends were people who took your side, even when you were in trouble. They tried to understand and help. Did her boss really consider herself Mac's friend? How could she be so dense as to not understand that?

Macayla felt instantly ashamed for not considering Jefferina a friend before now. Jefferina had given her a job when no one else had, even though she knew Mac had avoided the whole truth about her past. And when push came to shove, Jefferina had been her one call because there was no one else. A small mercy that she was very much grateful for.

The only other person she wanted to call was thousands of miles away, and besides, she didn't want to drag him further into her problems. According to Mullins, Oliver was already on his radar. Knowing her was something Oliver might come to regret now that she'd been arrested. She hoped it wouldn't come to that. She hoped he never learned about last night.

She glanced at Jefferina. "Why did you bail me out? I mean, you have more reason now than before to think I'm mixed up in some sort of criminal activity."

Jefferina drummed her fingers on her dashboard. "I never said I thought you were guilty of anything. I just needed to verify a few things. I've done some checking around."

"And?"

"I discovered in going over your receipts that you routinely undercharge your billable hours. I know for a fact that you trailed that Dalmatian for more hours than you claimed last week. That's not the action of a devious person." She sent Macayla a sideways glance. "I haven't billed the owners yet. You're low on cash. Could be you need to revise your hours upward by two."

Mac shook her head. "That's not my style."

"Sucker." Jefferina smiled triumphantly and shook her head. "So then, I trust you. End of debate. Okay?"

Macayla didn't have a smile left in her.

"We're going to have a serious talk, later, about who could be trying to set you up to take the fall for these crimes. But right now, you need food and then rest. Okay? So drink up."

Macayla gratefully sipped the coffee Jefferina had so thoughtfully brought her. Her car—Jefferina's cousin's car, that is—had been impounded for evidence collection. To be released later in the day.

Don't leave town. Those were Mullins's final words to her. As if she had more than bus money home.

She took a longer sip of coffee. The heat seemed to be opening up her windpipe.

They'd offered her something they called "dinner" in the cell last night, and "breakfast" before the morning's hearing, but she hadn't eaten anything. She was ravenous now but too queasy to think of eating. Every bone in her body ached from sitting for hours in the most uncomfortable chairs in America, and the unforgiving bunk of her cell. Maybe they were police-issue chairs, designed to numb the butt and eventually work that numbness up into the brain. But now her brain was coming back online, and one thought superseded everything else. It was one Jefferina had homed in on, too.

Someone is setting me up. Massey? And not just for misdemeanor petnapping. The Boxer, a show dog, would have been a felony. And who knows what others were too?

The hints had been there for a few days, she realized now. Sam's remarks. Then Massey's accusations. Then Gerald's rumor-spreading when he came to help out with her raccoon situation. She'd never taken any of it seriously.

But the police saw it differently. To hear Mullins talk,

she was the mastermind of a criminal gang. Why would she risk her freedom to steal dogs?

Oh yeah, for fame and glory. The very things she'd run from.

Her mind wandered through the myriad questions Mullins had phrased and rephrased over the hours of their interview. But there was nothing left but a jumble of fear, fatigue, and outrage. She knew she wouldn't be able to think of anything else until she found a thread of a clue she could hold on to.

The missing greyhounds seemed to be at the beginning of her problems.

Mullins hadn't even mentioned the shooting that occurred the night they were found! Did he not know about it? Had the St. Petersburg police not shared that little tidbit in their *serious intercity cooperation* notes?

Mac's pulse accelerated on that thought, but it was only to move from a slow *thump-thump* stroll to a *whoppidy-whop* lope. Adrenaline overload made for a bad morning after. Where was she? Oh yeah.

Was it a good thing her interrogator didn't know about the infrared video she'd shot? Or was the non-mention just more holding back by Mullins? Wouldn't it prove that she had nothing to do with the greyhounds or their death? All the proof the police had, other than the anonymous phone call, that shots had been fired had come from her. Who would invite the police to a dognapping gone wrong?

Of course, she'd hadn't called them. She'd been too busy trying not to die when they arrived. But someone had.

Point one in her favor. Find that someone.

She was too tired to look in her purse for a pen and a scrap of paper. She would have to remember that. What else about that night?

She hadn't known about the racing dogs being stolen

for ransom until two weeks after they were found. But the police knew. They had been called in at the beginning. Then, when they failed, Jefferina's private detective agency had gotten a call from the owners to try to locate them. And that's where her part in the discovery came into play.

She glanced at Jefferina, who was mouthing obscenities at the slowpoke driver in front of her. She'd said no talk until later. But one question couldn't wait.

"Why didn't you tell me the missing greyhounds belonged to Jarvis Henley?"

"How did you—?" Her boss's full mouth flattened out. "Detective Mullins."

"How well do you know Jarvis Henley?"

Jefferina shrugged. "He's a local wealthy businessman with fingers in a lot of pies. He's driven business my way since I opened. Before you ask, our interactions are something I cannot discuss with you. But I consider him a good client. He pays promptly. Or is that what you're asking me?"

Macayla debated her next question. Jefferina hadn't said Henley himself was a regular client. Yet private detectives kept confidential their clients and their sources. A cheated-upon spouse often didn't want that information to become public knowledge any more than the cheater. A businessman would have multiple uses for a PI. Not her business, perhaps. That's why she hadn't asked about the owner of the greyhounds at the time. Her job was to find the animals.

Would it have made a difference if she'd known wealthy, powerful people were involved? Maybe. She'd have been even more careful than usual, that's for certain.

Mac glanced sideways at her boss. She needed to know how much her boss knew. And that meant trusting Jefferina in return.

"You haven't asked me much about this."

"I was waiting for you to settle. You're still shaking. Finish that coffee while it's hot."

Macayla sipped her coffee before saying, "Detective Mullins says he's got a good case."

That brought Jefferina's head turning her way. "What, exactly, are the charges? What did they ask you?"

Macayla told her boss about how she had been picked up. It had been a sting meant to capture the real thieves. She told her about how strangely Ms. Siler had behaved when Mac brought the Boxer back. And how she'd insisted on handing her money, which turned out to be marked bills that the police had given her to pass on to the person who brought her dog back. They'd used Mac's possession of the money to arrest her. Who had set her up? That was the question uppermost in her mind.

A day ago Mac might have been less direct, but her reputation, to say nothing of her possible freedom, was now on the line. "You sent me to locate the Silers' Boxer. Did Ms. Siler call you?"

"No." Jefferina turned off the street and into the drive-in lane of a fast-food restaurant. "Marcia took the call." Marcia was the office secretary.

"Ms. Siler seemed to think she'd spoken to me."

Jefferina glanced at Mac, dark eyes flashing in the console's reflected light. "You sure she said that?"

"Absolutely. Ms. Siler told the police the person she spoke with when her dog was snatched had demanded half the money upfront. The bills she gave me were a 'second payment.'"

"That's how she phrased it? 'Second payment'?"

Mac frowned. "Yes. I'm certain of the wording because it struck me as odd. Does Marcia accept clients' payments?"

"Hell to the no. I handle all the money. Hold that thought."

Mac breathed in the greasy aroma of fried food as Jefferina leaned out her window to order two breakfast sandwiches, one with extra Tabasco sauce, and more coffee.

Macayla tried to look casual as she checked her purse for cash. The thought of breakfast was quickly gaining ground over her former queasiness. She found just enough to pay for a sandwich. She'd have to owe her boss for the coffee.

When she tried to offer the cash, Jefferina gave her a look that made her jerk her hand, and the cash, back. "Thanks."

Jefferina paid and handed Mac a bag of sandwiches. The smell emanating from it made Mac's stomach crimp and her mouth water. Maybe food would go down after all.

Jefferina's simple kindnesses were piling up fast, none because of anything Macayla had done to earn them. In fact, she'd deliberately kept herself apart.

It struck Mac that she'd been sailing through her life for the last year, only skimming the surface, never looking deeply into anything. It was the opposite of the life she'd lived before, where she'd become deeply invested in the lives of each of the children she advocated for. When she'd bottomed out, it was all the way to the deep end of the pool. Only in the past week had she begun to surface with a sense of clarity and sensation.

Since Oliver.

She'd felt a lot of different things in his company. Not all of them toe-curling orgasmic. Her reawakening to feeling was like a foot gone to sleep now stinging to life. He'd made her ache like crazy to touch him. And touch him and hold and kiss and—

Macayla jumped when she was elbowed by Jefferina. "Take a sandwich and pass the bag back to me. I'm starving."

Macayla dived into the bag, offering the first sandwich to her boss then unwrapping the second for herself. The first bite of scrambled eggs, bacon, and cheese made her sigh out loud. Coming alive even made food taste better. She had Oliver to thank for that, too.

That night on the beach after making love, they'd eaten two huge platters of stone crabs.

The remembrance of him sucking the butter off her fingertips made her face heat up. And other parts as well. He'd been so good for her. More than he would ever know.

Setting the sandwich aside, she checked her phone. Oliver hadn't called.

She sighed and tucked it away. She shouldn't count on him calling. She knew that. It was nice while it lasted. Better than nice. His interest in her had made her aware for the first time in a long time that maybe there were feelings worth taking a risk on. Her former trauma counselor would have been proud of her.

She took another healthy bite of her breakfast. OMG. When had she last tasted bacon? Definitely one of civilization's greater achievements. Ramen noodle budget diet be damned. She was going to have to get out more. Eat more. Make more money.

When she'd slept and showered and eaten again, she was going to have to do some investigating of her own. That didn't mean she didn't have to make a living first.

When Jefferina pulled up outside her bungalow, Macayla turned to her. "I will understand if you say no, seeing that you just bailed me out, but I could use something to do besides wash pups at the vet's until this is straightened out. Is there any kind of work I can do for you over the next few days? I can file, make phone calls, follow up with creditors."

"I'd have to fire Marcia. Those are her jobs. But what are friends for. Bye-bye, Marcia."

"Oh no, don't—" Mac saw her boss's slow smile a bit late. "Right. You wouldn't fire Marcia."

"But I do have some boring PI tasks you could do—using the computer to run down details on a few cases. I have a workers' compensation fraud case that needs a medical history check. Another where I need the time clock run on some employees' hours. And yet another case where we routinely check for criminal records and driving records for potential employees. These are things I fit in between more important cases."

"I can do that."

"Then I'll pick you up tomorrow morning and you can get right to work."

That surprised Macayla. "Honestly, I'd rather be working than trying to sleep during the day."

Jefferina gave her *the look*. "You're exhausted. Once you get in bed, you won't be arguing with me. Get your mind straight and your drama under control. I'll be by first thing in the morning. Six a.m. at the latest."

Macayla didn't argue. She was itching to shower off the flop sweat of having spent a night as a guest of the local police.

Jefferina was right about the drama part, too. Someone was out to get her. She doubted it would stop now. She needed to figure out who and why before it was too late.

She gulped. Too late would be after she was convicted.

Back in her home, Mac took a shower—then glanced at her phone, just to make certain she hadn't missed a call. And then, to prove to herself that she wasn't one of those pitiful people who sat by their phone praying for it to chime, she shut off the ringer so that she could sleep undisturbed. Twice before actually falling asleep, she checked to make sure she wasn't missing a call from Jefferina, or the police, she told herself.

Or maybe she was just feeling a tiny bit sorry for herself.

CHAPTER NINETEEN

Oliver prowled the lanai of his partner's home on Molo-
kai. Despite the vivid beauty of his surroundings, including flowering yellow and red hibiscus flanking the porch
and an uninterrupted view of Pukoo Beach, he looked
ready to erupt.

The two people watching him from the relative safety
of a sea-grass sofa stacked with colorful pillows pretended
to ignore him as they whispered quietly to each other
from the comfort of their loose embrace. Sprawled in sleep
at their feet were Kye's Toller, named Lily, and Yardley's Czech wolf dog, Oleg. At the moment they reflected
the mellow mood of their handlers.

It was well known that Oliver hated regulations, de-
lays, red tape—any and everything that interfered with his
god-given right to go to hell any way he damn well pleased.
Except that none of that was what was at the heart of his
fury today.

"I'm not even a fuckin' American citizen."

Kye looked up from fondling his fiancée's earlobe. "You could remedy that."

Oliver glared at his partner. "At least in Oz we've got sane laws."

"Did you get another court summons? I told you those speeding tickets add up. Next time, they may not allow you back in the country until you settle. And don't even think about asking BARKS to post bail if you're arrested."

Oliver ignored his partner, pausing to stare out at the vista of Pukoo Beach. He'd just flown in this morning from Concepción, Chile, and had been looking forward to a few days off and a long bake on a beach. They'd done good work. Saved many lives and helped get supplies flowing. Now it was up to the crew he'd left in place to continue the work.

But he wasn't looking at the water, or the huge black volcanic boulders that broke up the shallow waves and buttressed parts of the shore. Nor was he thinking this time about women in tiny bikinis. His whole focus was on the phone call he'd gotten hours earlier from a Detective Mullins of the Pinellas Park Police Department in Florida. Wherever the fuck that was.

Near Macayla. That much he knew. He'd called her, trying to find out what the hell was going on. But she must have turned off her ringer, or maybe her phone battery had run out because she hadn't returned any of his calls. The longer she remained out of touch, the tenser he got.

Jackeroo was as stressed as his handler, pacing next to him and watching his every move.

Guilt stabbed Oliver. He and his partner needed downtime. But he was very much afraid neither of them was going to get it. Not until he knew what was going on with Macayla. Too bad he couldn't explain that to a dog so faithful he matched his handler's every emotion without knowing why.

Finally he turned and made a rude comment about lovers before blurting out, "I met a woman."

Yardley yawned. "That's not news."

Oliver scowled at her unsympathetic reply. "I like her."

Kye yawned, too, so simpatico, these lovers. "You ever met a woman you didn't like?"

Oliver glowered. "The situation's impossible."

Yardley rolled a shoulder. "Isn't it your philosophy that the best way to get over a bad relationship is to replace it with a new one? Immediately?"

The fact that it was true only further soured Oliver's mood. "Don't you have somewhere to be? Shopping? Toe painting class?"

"No. She doesn't." Kye kissed his wife-to-be's bare shoulder. "She's right where she belongs."

Oliver stared at them as they made kissy faces. It was awful. Sad, really. Where was Kye's dignity? His cojones? His pride?

The diamond on the third finger of Yardley's left hand winked in answer. Their happiness was more than a grown man should have to endure.

Oliver wheeled away toward the exit. "I'm off then. Got to get away from the wedding cooties lousing up this place."

Yardley smiled. "Jealous, Kelly?"

That brought him up short. "Me? Do I look jealous?"

"You sound as pissy as a wet hen. Who ruffled your feathers? I'd like to meet her."

Oliver gave it a beat. He liked Yardley, most of the time. She and her dog could hold their own with any K-9 team in the world. In fact, she had trained a fair number of them.

But right now she was twisting a very pissed-off tiger's tail. None of the retorts running through his mind would be easily forgotten, or forgiven, if they got past his lips. And he really didn't want to have to patch up another problem.

Finally, all that came out was, "Huh."

"No need to run off. We'll leave you to steam up the afternoon alone." Kye stood and stretched. "I'm thinking a nap in a hammock is just what I need."

Yardley stood, too, and gave him a small intimate smile. "I'll come with you."

Despite his temper, Oliver took a second to admire his best friend's fiancée. Strictly in a brotherly, platonic way. Or as close to it as his nature would allow. Yardley was a stunner. What man would pass up a chance to glance her way? Dressed as usual in jeans and a tailored shirt, she'd learned this past year to go barefoot when not working, a concession to the sand that was a part of life on an island. Tall with a mane of unusual dark-red hair, Yardley had the black eyes and high cheekbones that were traits of her Native American heritage. She and Kye shared a history that went back further than his and Kye's. But only in the last year had they found each other again. Yeah. Maybe he was a bit jealous of that kind of emotional connection. But the awareness was so new he didn't know what to do with it. All he knew was that it was tied up with meeting Macayla. And that he had a problem he had no clue about solving.

Kye started to walk past him but Oliver shoulder-checked him.

"What?"

"We need to talk." He said it so low the words were no more than a growl.

Kye looked past Oliver to where Yardley was disappearing down the cool dark hallway toward their bedroom, hips swaying in an invitation he'd thought one short year ago he'd been denied forever. He glanced back at the tight face of his best friend. "This better be good. And you've only got five minutes."

"It'll keep"—Oliver pointed—"the happy in your pants."

"Yeah, it will."

He saw a small smile play around his friend's mouth as Kye glanced back down the hall. The boy had it bad. But then Kye had been looking for forever-after all along.

"Buy me a beer and I'm yours."

Kye and Oliver were opposites in many ways, but equally compelling men. Kye was native Hawaiian, handsome in a dark-eyed, thick-muscled way. He looked like a Pacific Island statue, broad face, bold blunt blade of a nose, full sensuous mouth. He gave off a solid, dependable air. As if he could stand between Doomsday and the world, and everyone would believe he'd have a fighting chance. In reality, he was something of a goof, when he wanted to be. He was also the cool head, the deliberate leader, which made Oliver appreciate him in the field. When things got ugly, Kye was always good for a smile. But he was also the linchpin on whom the rest of the crew depended. He kept the books, did the hiring, made the speeches, paid the bills.

Oliver was the scout, the point man, the lead, the risk taker, the audacious Aussie with a ready smile and a pirate's appreciation for rule breaking. He gave master classes in search and rescue, and he'd logged an impressive number of saves, some of them based on sheer grit more than calculation. When they'd met several years ago while working for other SAR companies, they discovered that their working styles fit like puzzle pieces, each one contributing to the greater good. That was because they understood and shared an appreciation for dogs, and what they could do.

They were dog men. Neither felt complete without their K-9 companions in sight. Kye's expertise had been honed in the U.S. military K-9 forces, as Oliver's had in the Australian armed forces. They knew discipline and the value of unshakable ethics, and what it cost to keep the world on its axis. Once they'd killed to defend the world. Now they dug in and tracked and trailed and searched to keep lost souls alive. It made them more than colleagues. It made them brothers. So they'd quit their employers and formed their own company, BARKS.

Oliver explained briefly about meeting Macayla. He even managed to hint at the fact that she'd been the one to get him to give the banquet speech. Not that he was going to own up to everything. Like the dyslexia. He and Kye were now friends for life, but they weren't girlfriends. The competitive edge remained strong between them. It kept their bond fresh.

Oliver passed along one of the two beers he'd found before he ended with a palms-up shrug. "She's different. Not really my type."

"Flat-chested, no ass?"

"None of your goddamn business." Oliver cracked a smile. "She's cute."

Kye nodded thoughtfully. "Cute works. Why not invite her over to the island for a few days?"

"She's not that type of woman. She has a job, responsibilities she can't leave."

"Totally out of your league then."

"Would you give it a rest? I'm trying to have an adult conversation."

Kye grinned. "Touchy."

Oliver pushed two hands through his hair, pulled a

black hair band off his wrist, and twisted his hair up into a bun. "She's got something about her. Total commitment to a piece-of-shit job that she's really good at but it doesn't pay well. Pet detective. You ever hear of anything like it?" Not waiting for Kye to reply, he went on. "She's got this touch with animals. People, too. She talked me into getting on that stage. And I'm not easy to deal with. But she handled me. And I didn't mind."

"I'd have given my left nut to see that," Kye inserted quietly, but his partner wasn't paying attention. He was back to pacing.

"All those lost dogs, they like her. And she's not just a softhearted dog lover. She's got grit." He bent down to love on Jackeroo, who had been growling low and nipping at his handler's heels as if Oliver were a straying sheep who wouldn't return to the fold.

"How did you meet?"

"On the beach. She was dumpster-diving to save a rat-faced overpampered pet. Thirty minutes later she tried to face down a couple of thugs destroying her car with baseball bats. Then she took on a bully over his treatment of neighbor dogs. That was all before lunch." He was grinning. "Think what she could do with some training. She'd be perfect in SAR."

Oliver stood up suddenly, looking as if he'd been struck by a eureka moment.

"So why doesn't she have a dog of her own? That's like a cardinal thing. No one who loves animals the way she does should be without one. You or me without a dog? We'd— Just wouldn't happen." He shook his head and began taking his hair down. "She needs a dog."

Kye watched his friend with a stunned expression on his face. This was Oliver Kelly, talking about a woman in terms other than her healthy appreciation for sex, or availability.

Here he was talking about the emotional needs of a woman that didn't end with the solution of him being in her bed. Kye had been waiting their entire relationship for his friend to realize that he might need a woman in his life who wasn't a buddy or a one-night stand.

But this was new and tender territory for Oliver. *I told you so* wasn't going to cut it. Might even scare him off. Look how he was fussing with his hair. *So* not a Kelly move. Half the time he looked like a street person with better hygiene opportunities. Now he was messing with his hair like a teenager at the mall. The man was in deep.

Kye set his beer aside, thinking of a shadowed bedroom with a hammock for two. "What are you going to do?"

"I need to catch a flight."

"Where?"

"Florida."

"I'm asking *why* again because you're scheduled to teach a sea search-and-rescue class over on the Big Island this weekend."

Oliver hesitated, but he'd been jonesing to see Macayla again before the call from the police came in. Maybe it was just a ready excuse. See. This was why he didn't do relationships. A man had to figure his emotional stuff out if he was in a relationship. And he didn't do emotions. Yet all he had to do was think of Macayla and this little ache pulsed deep inside him. Yeah, he wanted to see her. For any reason.

"Macayla's in trouble."

Kye's brows rose. "What kind of trouble?"

"She's a suspect in a crime. That's the vibe I got from the police when they called to ask me about her."

"The police called you in Chile about a woman you met in Florida over a long weekend? Just how involved were you two?"

Oliver scowled at Kye. "I'm not sure how closely they're looking at her, and I hope they've already ruled her out. I won't know that until I talk to her, and she's not answering her fuckin' phone. That's why I'm heading out."

Kye's surprise expanded. "What crime is she suspected of committing?"

"Theft. Dognapping."

"The Pet Detective steals dogs?" Kye laughed. "Now, that sounds like an Oliver Kelly kind of woman."

"Get stuffed, Kye."

And, because they were friends, Kye pulled him into a quick chest-bump embrace and let him go. "I hope you can help her. If she needs you."

Oliver nodded. "Thanks. I'm thinking I'll bring her back here. For a visit. For a while." He looked suddenly very nervous about voicing that protective thought. "She's had a hard time, before this happened, and could use a break."

"You do that." Kye turned aside before his expression gave him away.

A few minutes later, Kye located Yardley in a hammock he'd hung in their bedroom. She was wearing the thinnest bit of feminine attire he'd ever seen. Those who knew Yardley would never believe it of her. Only he knew the secrets of the woman who could swear like a drill sergeant and make grown men quake in their boots if they made a mistake with one of her K-9s. But right now, all that mattered was that she was his. He was here to do the possessing.

He slid down beside her after dropping his shorts.

She welcomed him with open arms. "What's with your friend this time?"

Kye told her quickly all that he could remember.

She pulled a face. "Serious then?"

"Sounds like."

"Will wonders never cease."

"Yep. Our boy's fallen in love."

"Does he know it?"

"Not yet. He thinks she needs a dog. At least he's got the partnership part sorted. Should be fun to see how long it takes him to connect all the dots."

"That was quick."

"It can happen that way. He's seen and done just about everything there is out there in the world. When the real thing comes along, there's no mistaking it."

Yardley reached up and kissed him. "Still, he's known her, what, a few days?"

Kye pulled her down over him. "Oliver's never been one to waste time, whatever he's doing. Neither am I. Let's do this."

CHAPTER TWENTY

Something was wrong.

Macayla stood in the doorway of her bungalow, eyes scanning left and right as the hair lifted on her arms. Yet everything was as she'd left it this morning when Jefferina picked her up for work.

Easy to see everything in a glance when her living room was furnished with only a used sofa covered in denim and two plastic rockers from Walmart. Two suitcases were stacked to hold her small TV. But she knew in her gut that something was wrong. A surge of adrenaline spiked through her, preparing her for fight or flight.

She slipped her phone out of her pocket and slid it open to emergency numbers. This was becoming a habit she didn't want to form. She took a few more steps across her living room floor. "Hello? Anyone there?"

No answer. But then, who would out themselves if they had broken in?

The police, maybe. Had they gotten a warrant to search her apartment?

She remembered entering the home of a child in protective custody after a police drug raid that snared both parents. The place had been tossed like a salad, nothing left undisturbed. If anything, her little six hundred square feet of space felt too neat.

Okay. She sucked in a careful breath. What was spooking her?

It was uncomfortably warm. Nothing new. She always turned the air-conditioning to eighty degrees or higher when she left, to save on electricity. But this humid warmth was like entering a greenhouse at a local nursery, an atmosphere that always made her head ache. It even had a faint sweet smell.

She tried to place the source as she shut the door behind her. She didn't keep scented candles, as many people did. The dish detergent? Her new shampoo? No, something sharper, more specific than those all-purpose floral fragrances used by cleaning agents. Even as she tried to breathe it in, it dissipated.

She dropped her purse by the door and went looking for other clues that someone had been here while she spent her day behind a computer running down the records of job applicants.

The one-bedroom bungalow didn't have many obvious places for a person to hide. But as she looked closely, things felt disturbed, touched, searched. Quite possibly she was the thing touched and disturbed. Her dreams last night had turned out to be as troubled as her waking life had become.

She began looking at her possessions as if she were searching for something to steal, like her jewelry. No, the small but nice diamond studs given her by her parents upon college graduation were still in place in her top drawer. They gave her a pang of yearning. Her parents were under strict orders not to contact her until she was ready. The fact that they had kept the promise wasn't as wonderful as it might have been.

Not robbery? What then?

It took her less than ten minutes to search everything else she owned. Nothing missing.

So finding five one-hundred-dollar bills tucked between two pairs of her panties gave her a start.

The money might have escaped her attention for days if she hadn't decided to lay out fresh clothing to put on in the morning. Even then, the money lay folded between a pair of red undies and a pair of jaguar-print ones, not her usual choice for a working day. She saved these pairs for a special occasion, like a date. But she was feeling the need for a show of bravery tomorrow. When she reached for them, out slipped the bills, crisp and clean, and possibly marked by the police as had been the ones Mrs. Siler thrust on her the night before.

Mac dropped the bills and the panties back in the drawer. But even as she did it, she knew it was too late. Her prints were now on the cash. That meant it had to go.

She considered burning the bills in the bathroom sink and then flushing the remaining ashes down the toilet. No one would ever know she'd found it.

Except the person who put them there.

How had they gotten in? She found the answer in her bathroom. The latch to the small window above the toilet had been jimmied open. It seemed a small space for an adult to climb through. But maybe a skinny string bean like Massey's grandson Woody could get in.

She looked down at the mat she was standing on. Were there footprints on it?

Someone had broken in to stash money in her house. It couldn't have been left for her to find. The cash was a plant. To catch her in a lie with the police.

Several emotions rose up to almost choke her: anger that someone had violated her home, rage that she had no clue about who it could be, and finally fear. That final emotion seared her throat, leaving it dry as sand. She was someone's dupe. And they thought they could get away with it.

It wasn't the first time she'd thought that in the past thirty-six hours. It was becoming a habit.

She wiped the sweat from her face, feeling a little light-headed from lack of sleep and the suffocating heat. She should turn the air down. But her thoughts, not her feet, were moving at light speed.

She recalled the Boxer's owner saying she had already paid money upfront. The marked bills she thrust into Macayla's hands were a second payment. Who else would know that but the person who'd asked for the ransom? That person must hope the police would find the money before she did.

Panic torpedoed through her as she pulled the cash out of the drawer. She needed to hide it before the police arrived. What if they were at this very second walking up her sidewalk with a warrant to search her home? She whirled around and headed for the front door to check.

The peephole showed no police or cruiser out front. But that didn't mean it would stay that way.

She glanced at the money now fisted in her hand. What to do with it? It couldn't stay here. In fact, why hadn't the police searched her apartment while they had her in custody?

Because she'd been arrested in Pinellas Park! The thought gave her a rush.

No matter how much Detective Mullins had bragged about the cooperation of the various local police departments, it would take paperwork to get the Gulfport police, the town in which she lived, to get a judge to issue a warrant to search her house for a crime committed in another town. But that was probably already under way. Whoever had planted the money would be counting on that. Who was that person?

The money crinkled in her hand as her fist tightened with nerves. She looked down. No. First things first. Destroy the evidence.

She marched into the kitchen and grabbed a box of matches from a drawer. But by the time she'd made the trip back to the bathroom sink, she was having second, third, and fourth thoughts. What if she destroyed the money and the police somehow found out—for instance, a bit of ash in the sink pipe that could be identified as paper money. She'd seen something like that on *CSI*. Then she would have just added a federal crime of defacing money to whatever else the police planned to charge her with.

Plus, it was destruction of evidence.

Plus, it was *five* hundred dollars. That was a lot of money.

Of course, it didn't belong to her. If it belonged to anyone, as a fee for a pet recovery, it belonged to Jefferina.

"Jefferina." Her boss's name hung in the air.

Jefferina had told her to call her first if anything else happened. But she wasn't even certain what had occurred. Who broke into a house to leave money? And why? And, if she couldn't explain those two things, how could she expect Jefferina to believe her?

She could easily imagine their conversation.

Someone broke into my house and left me money.

Could be the Tooth Fairy catching up on back payments. Jefferina's dry wit always carried a sarcastic barb.

Mac's mind switched sluggishly to other possible perpetrators. She recalled the Boxer's owner saying she had already paid money upfront. Who else would know about that but the person who'd asked for the ransom?

Marcia, Tampa/St. Pete Recon's secretary? Not a motive in the world came to mind.

She wandered back into her living room and spied the twenty-inch Mongoose girls' BMX bike she'd borrowed from a neighbor's daughter before Jefferina had hooked her up with a cousin's car. The scamp had wanted fifty dollars a day for rent. She'd settled for ten.

She walked over and twisted off the left handlebar grips. After rolling the bills into a tight tube, she stuck them in the hollow end of the metal bar before replacing the grip.

She returned the bike to her neighbor with the explanation that she might need it again, in a day or two. One problem temporarily solved. Money safe and *not* in her home. She would tell Jefferina about it, as soon as she was certain what she wanted to do about it.

After a shower made her feel less violated, Macayla sat down at her kitchen table in her robe and made a plan.

If she talked with everyone she'd done business with in the past three weeks, a pattern might emerge. It was better than sitting and waiting for her enemy to make the next move.

There was Cedric, who had first tipped her off about the possible location of the greyhounds. He might have forgotten to tell her something. But she'd have to be careful not to give the police a reason to talk to him. Surely Detective Mullins had better things to do than follow her around Pinellas County. But she'd wait until evening. Dougie liked to beg treats from outdoor diners on the bay. A casual meet could be arranged.

Mr. Massey, definitely. He'd already filed a false claim against her when he'd been the one to destroy her property. Not a large leap to think he'd plant the money. He would fit through her bathroom window. That would be gutsy. And sneaky. And very like him.

She'd love to question Sam and Gerald again, too. But Sam was a cop and right now she had more cops looking at her than was comfortable. Plus, he'd want her to turn the money in. And that, she was certain, would be probable cause to lock her up.

Gerald was a blabbermouth. Talking to him would just get the word out that the police liked her for a crime. That wouldn't be good for business if—when, *when* she was proved innocent.

And definitely a trip to the racetrack seemed in order. That was where it all began. The night she found those stolen greyhounds. She could look up Jarvis Henley. Ask about the details of the dognapping.

Macayla tapped her pen against her lower lip as she studied the list. After a moment, she added more names.

She needed to chat with all the owners whose animals she'd rescued during the past few weeks. None of them had told her their dogs had been stolen. But now that she knew about dognappers working the Tampa/St. Pete area, they might be more forthcoming. Maybe they'd been reluctant to get the police involved. With their pets safe at home, though, they might admit the truth to her. That way, she'd know how many times she'd inadvertently thwarted the thieves.

"Huh." Macayla sat back to ponder that thought. Was that the reason someone wanted her out of the Pet Detective business? Was she cutting into their profit margin by finding missing dogs? Or was it related to the shooting she'd witnessed? Did someone hope to discredit any testimony she could provide by painting her as a thief?

Something deeper than theft was going on. She could

feel it, though she had no idea what caused the hunch burning like acid through her belly. She was being set up to take the fall for something bigger, more important.

Exhausted and sick at heart, she walked into her bedroom and sat down on the bed. "Why me?"

She looked around but nothing answered her. Not for the first time this week she felt the burden of her solitude. Her plan when she left Tallahassee had worked out perfectly. She had wanted to disappear, escape from the notoriety of being labeled a heroine. The idea still made her feel ill. She wasn't a hero. In a way, she was a victim, too. But who would understand that?

So she'd done everything she could to become a shadow in her world, without her family or close friends, without a confidante. Now she wanted to be connected again, to belong.

She reached for her phone and dialed Oliver, something she'd promised herself she wouldn't do. He'd left her a series of messages in the past twenty-four hours. He even told her he'd been called by Detective Mullins, so he knew about her arrest. And still he called twice more. But after she'd woken and found the messages, she realized she didn't know what to say to him beyond *Help*. This morning that had seemed liked like a sad ploy for attention. So she hadn't called him back. He didn't deserve to be drawn into the crazy-quilt nightmare her life had become.

Now, after finding the planted cash, he seemed like a lifeline she very much needed. And she wasn't, she discovered, above asking for his help.

The phone rang and rang and rang. And then his voice message played.

"Kelly here. Start talking, you wanker."

"Hi. I, uh, call me. Macayla. There's stuff happening. Bye."

Macayla sighed, determined to resist fresh fear and doubts. He would call her. She wasn't alone. Meantime, she had a battle to fight. How did a perfectly nice person doing her job end up in so many messes?

"I was well adjusted. Once." Nothing stirred in answer. "Well, I was."

She sprawled back against the bedding and fell instantly asleep.

He watched her from a chair by the open window. The cool, salty night air slipped past him on the breeze of first light and moved on to caress the almost nude body of the woman asleep on the bed. She lay with her robe open, feeling safe from the world behind her closed lids. If only she knew how tenuous that safety really was, with him in her room.

Hers was a woman's body, full and curved. Asleep on her stomach, the slope of her shoulders swooped steeply down into the valley of her waist before rising again on the full swells of her buttocks. He knew those swells intimately. Those legs, slightly parted with one knee hitched up, invited him to skim a hand up toward the shadows that hid her sex.

Oliver felt himself stir. Instead of the instant erection of his teen years, he had learned to enjoy the slower but steady build of desire. He took a deep breath, allowing himself to expand and harden by increments in appreciation of this woman. She deserved that. And she was worthy of appreciation.

With her, lust was a luxury. No hurried fucks with one eye on the door. No calculations. No need to strategize on how to get out afterward without a shitstorm of recrimination following in his wake. With her, all he wanted to do was get closer, to get in so close *he* and *she* lost all meaning. And remain there hard, and throbbing, on the brink of everything.

He resisted leaning in to catch her breath as it feathered out between her parted lips. Instead he imagined feeling the tremble of her fuller lower lip as he sank his teeth gently into its ripe moist warmth.

His dick lifted, stretching out long and thick beneath his fly. He'd shed the rest of his clothing before taking up his position by the window. Now he was having second thoughts about climbing into bed beside her. No. He would control himself, for her.

He smiled and sank a little lower in the chair, pushing his legs out in a wide vee to relieve a little of the building pressure. And concentrated on her face.

The faint light coming in through the open window bleached the vivid blue swath in her dark hair to an indistinct shade. But he knew her hair was a glorious, thick chocolate, with that sassy streak of turquoise. So alive, it tangled around his fingers with a mind of its own, intent on holding on to him. Sexy as hell.

Funny how he'd thought at first that she was not his type. Twenty-four hours in her company was all it took to realize that he liked every damn thing about her. Down to and including her fingertips. Her short buffed nails reminded him of the inside shell of an oyster. Ah, yeah. He had it bad.

He'd fooled around and fell in love!

He'd finally figured out the emotion that had been pushing at him for more than a week on the twelve-plus hours of flight time to get here. Worse yet, he knew it wasn't going to be a revelation that he could walk away from. But first he needed to keep the novelty of the feeling to himself. Until he was comfortable with the idea.

He was still vibrating with the unexpected surprise of

it all. They'd only shared one night of sex. Great sex. But still.

A man had his pride. His priorities. And he had no idea how she felt. She'd been pleasant when he called, but he'd not detected a single vibe of longing in her voice. Nothing to suggest why he was sitting here like a phallic symbol from an ancient tribal totem.

She hadn't been impressed by his appearance. Most women were first drawn to him by his looks. It didn't make him arrogant to think so. But not Macayla. She'd looked at him as if he were a peacock on the loose from the zoo, too good to be real. No, she'd held his sex appeal against him, going so far as to imagine that it was his job to exude sex. A stripper!

He'd felt objectified in her eyes. A rump roast she didn't want a slice of. She resisted his offer of help, had even tried to get rid of him after he'd saved her cute butt from bat-wielding assailants. She was not like the other women who'd briefly populated his life. She'd made him think differently about sex and sexuality. About what mattered. About himself.

He didn't know how much he'd been stuffing down negative feelings about himself until she came along. He didn't know that until a week ago he still felt, deep down in the tender parts of his soul, inferior. An idiot who could barely read. That much of his bravado came from overcompensation. Because he felt broken.

Only when he'd revealed his weakness had she shown her first real interest in him.

No, that wasn't right. He wasn't simply another wounded animal in her eyes that she'd felt a protective instinct toward. She'd stopped and really started listening to him when he stopped projecting Oliver the Aussie male whore and showed her simply the man. A man with a fear of

208

D.D. AYRES

public speaking. But that was common enough, even among famous actors.

He smiled. She liked him. She'd offered him a soothing shoulder massage even before he'd blurted out the real source of his stage fright. And then she'd helped him work through the terror, without taking away his pride. She was bloody awesome.

That's what had kept him thinking of her in Chile. Not the sex, good and fun as it was with her. It was her intense interest in him and what he had to say. He'd felt stronger, more capable, and a better man basking in her view of him than he had in maybe forever.

He hadn't ever known before what it was like to be admired for more than his masculine exterior and his expertise with SAR K-9s. He didn't know who he was without those things. But he suspected Macayla did. And that was part of what had brought him back here without her asking. He didn't want to hear *no* before he saw her again.

The quiver in his belly was not all lust. It was a rush of protectiveness, a nearly overwhelming need to scoop her up and carry her off to some quiet place so that he could have her all to himself for a while.

Another emotion immediately spiked through all that tenderness. It was fear.

Crikey! He was beginning to psyche himself out of being here. What if she opened her eyes and looked at him not with longing but with disappointment, or even hostility?

He'd entered her bungalow only after she didn't answer his knock. The fact that the door swung open under his hand didn't make him feel like he could simply walk away. Who didn't lock their door? And so he'd come in. To find her asleep. Unguarded. Unprotected. Not even fully clothed.

It had given him a split-second heart attack as he'd practically jumped on the bed to check her pulse and breathing. At the last moment she'd sighed and moved, and he knew she wasn't a victim of any attack. She was bloody zonked out. And so he let her sleep. That was two hours ago.

He sighed and rubbed his chin. He was exhausted. Hungry. Eager to see her face when she realized he was here. But he was content to wait, and watch, and enjoy. Each thing with her was new. He had patience he didn't know he possessed. For her. Contentment in being her guardian angel. Protector. Yes, he liked the sound of that.

She frowned slightly, as if her dreams were not happy. But that wasn't true. He knew her well enough now to suspect she was concentrating on a subject deep in her mind's eye. Probably chasing a puppy from the street. Or a parking lot, more concerned about the animal's safety than her own.

He wished he could stay. But even as he'd taxied toward the terminal in Tampa his phone had blown up with messages. There was another job on deck. He passed it on to another BARKS team leader.

There would always be another job. But first, there must be a few precious days of just *them*.

For the first time, the job wasn't all there was for him. No matter where or what, he knew a part of him would ache to be with her. Even if she didn't feel as he did.

That scared the shit out of him.

Her eyes opened, popping wide in surprise before she recognized who sat there watching her. "Oliver?"

His dick stirred. Even her voice had the power to arouse.

Yes, definitely. He was going to have to do something about this first-time ache for permanence in his life. But, first things first.

"Hi, Macayla."

He thought she'd be pleased. The look on her face

altered to anything but. She was suddenly wide-eyed furious.

She sat up making shooing motions with her hand.

"Get away from here! Get out! Now!"

CHAPTER TWENTY-ONE

"Did you hear me?" Macayla had started to rise, pushing up on an elbow. "You can't be here. How did you get in? Did the police send for you?"

His worst nightmare. She didn't want him here.

But that thought was quickly overridden by the obvious. She was in a panic. He wondered what that was all about but didn't ask. She'd been dreaming deeply. Probably a dream.

"*Shh.*" He came and sat on the edge of the bed, watching her breasts rise and fall slightly with each breath she took. He ran a palm up one of her thighs, smiling at the ripple of her body at his caress. The pleasure was returned by the twitch deep in his groin. Her skin was warmer and smoother than his memory of her.

"Aren't you glad to see me?"

"Yes. Of course. But how did you—?"

He put a finger against her lips, leaned in, and kissed her shoulder. "Can it wait until morning? I promise I'll answer all your questions then."

"No. It can't. What time is it?"

"Something after one a.m."

"How did you get in?"

"The front door was unlocked."

"That's not possible!" She scrambled out of the bed, heading for the door, but he reached for her arm.

"I locked the door after I came in. You're safe."

She swung around on him. "I'm many things at the moment, but safe isn't one of them."

"That's what I was worried about. And that's why I'm here."

"What do you mean? Did the police call you?"

He couldn't see her expression well in the dark, but he felt the tension running through her arm. "I promise it's safe for now. I'll explain everything in the morning, and we'll secure the place together."

She hesitated. "I left my door unlocked?" Her voice sounded small, like a bewildered child. But he knew better. She was all woman.

"And here I thought you were expecting me. You dressed for me."

She looked down at her open robe and quickly pulled it closed. "Not a good time for humor, Kelly."

There it was. The spark. She warmed him in all the right places though he could tell she wasn't there with him. Unfair to jump her bones when she was clearly half asleep and worried about other things. Better tone it down.

"Honestly, I'm dragging knuckles after my flight. I just want to share your bed." He patted the place beside him. "I promise not to jump you."

She sat down, her hand accidently brushing his lap, and chuckled. "You sure you can keep that promise?"

"Yes." He took her hand and lifted it away. But if she

made that sound again, that purely female response to his touch, he'd be on her like a stallion in rut.

"That's just my dick. Thinks he's a bloody porn star. But the rest of me is brain-dead knackered."

She nodded and crawled back onto her side of the bed. "Just stay on your side. All parts of you." But even as she said it, her hand found his and grasped tightly.

He squeezed back, wondering if he could keep his promise not to touch her as he lay down beside her. He really did need to sleep. He . . .

Macayla woke with a start at dawn. The mattress was weighted on her left side. She was not alone.

She bolted up into a sitting position even as her gaze fell on the outline of a kangaroo on the large biceps she had been leaning against. She blinked as a slow smile caught fire on her face. Oliver Kelly was back. In her life. In her bed.

She gave him a little shove. "Hey, Aussie. Wakey, wakey."

"Thirty minutes. Macayla. I swear, I need just thirty more minutes." His voice was all slurry and his eyes didn't open. But he found her hand on the bed between them and pulled it to his groin. "See that? You do that to me. And, damn you, I love you for it."

Love? Macayla knew better than to put any stock in bed talk. Especially from a half-asleep man. A loud snore issued from him on the back of that thought. Make that an all-asleep man.

She snuggled down next to him. The scent of clean male sexiness was a shock to her system. The bed was virginal. No man had slept here before. There'd not been much sex in her life during the last year. She'd never brought anyone here. Which begged the question: How had he found her, and why? Why didn't he call ahead and let her know he was coming? Was he really that interested in her? Okay, that heavy hairy thigh pressing in against hers was saying a big *hell yeah* to that last question.

The heat of his bare skin seeping into hers was like a drug, a sex drug that simultaneously soothed and aroused her. She slid an arm around his waist and then across his belly and into the gap of his shorts when he exhaled. His body twitched. His breathing hitched.

He turned toward her and ran his hand up her thigh, making her butt cheeks tighten and a little laugh escape her. "Twenty-nine minutes," he murmured.

It was only ten. At thirty minutes, he was snoring again and she was in the shower luxuriating in the mood-brightening benefits of sex before breakfast.

"I can't believe Jefferina told you how to find me." Mac had poured coffee for both of them, offering the container of milk and several packets of sugar, both of which he ignored.

He slurped his coffee loudly and then gave her a wink. "She's a hard nut to crack."

"She was a cop."

"That explains it. Looked at me like I was a slab of meat she needed to roast and carve. Gave me the willies."

"Have you been in trouble with the police before?"

"As a kid. Yeah."

She wanted to ask how he had handled himself. Was he as rattled as she had been when arrested? But that question would require a whole lot of explanation that she wasn't sure she should burden him with. "How did you get her give up my address?"

"Told her we'd met on the beach last weekend when I was in town with the Thunder from Down Under review.

Sex with you was amazing. Since I have a few days off the road I wanted to hook up with you again."

She gaped. "She believed you?"

"Every blessed word."

"A hot hookup is not reason enough to persuade Jefferina to give my address to a stranger."

"I wasn't exactly a stranger by the time I had your address." He grinned at her shocked expression, laced with threads of outrage. Jealous, maybe? "She'd run me through her system and taken video and photos of me, with and without my shirt. I told her she'd missed the best part." He pointed to his pants. "She also fingerprinted me and took photocopies of my passport and driver's license. She's even got photos of Jackeroo."

"Sounds like Jefferina." They both glanced at Jackeroo, who was asleep on her sofa. Long plane rides seemed to wear out this SAR team.

"So why are you back?"

He took another long swig of his coffee. If she didn't know better Mac would think he was trying to get a rise out of her with all that excess noise. But she wasn't going to be baited by irritating behavior. "Maybe for the same reason you didn't tell me you were attacked before we ever met."

Macayla thudded to earth. "What exactly did Jefferina tell you?"

"Enough." He quickly related the events the night Mac had found the greyhounds.

"Is that all?" Jefferina knew about Tallahassee, too.

He jerked in mock surprise. "Is there more?

Macayla stared at him.

"She said that your being arrested and out on bail was no reason for me to worry. She said you were a good person, when your drama is limited."

"I'm not dramatic. I'm just—unlucky. And I wasn't attacked. Not me personally. I saw something the night I found the missing greyhounds."

"Something?" He put his cup down, finally giving her his full attention.

"A shooting."

He sucked in a breath. "You're a witness to a murder?"

"Sort of. Maybe." She shook her head. "I thought I'd captured the shots being fired on my cell phone. But it isn't on the video. The police haven't found a body. No one else has corroborated my statement. And now the police think I'm the brains behind a ring of dog thieves."

He looked at her for several long moments. "This is going to be more complicated than a cup of coffee can handle. If you have eggs and cheese, I'll make omelets while you start at the beginning."

Luckily, she had eggs and cheese, and a few cherry tomatoes and lots of coffee. While she began her story with her search for the stolen greyhounds, Oliver went into her small kitchen and whipped up the best breakfast she'd ever eaten under this roof. He unearthed a couple of potatoes and half an onion to make skillet potatoes to go with the cheese omelets. He was quick, efficient, not wasting a single stroke of the knife as she made her way through the events of the past three weeks. By the time she got to her arrest, they had cleaned their plates.

He hadn't said much while she talked. Only stopped eating a few times to ask her to repeat something. That was how he remembered.

"So you see, the last two days have been a nightmare."

He nodded. "You've been framed. It's dirty. It's brilliant."

"What is?"

"Your enemy's tactics." He tapped his napkin. "He's using your job skills and your boss's connections against you. That takes a clever fella."

"You could try not to look so happy about that. I could go to jail."

Oliver shook his head. "There's no motive. Absolutely none for you to commit these crimes."

She drew her gaze from his. Time to tell the final part, the hardest part. The part she'd been trying to leave behind for a year. The distance made her voice hollow and her insides feel weak. But it was the final truth that made the lies close to real.

"I'm not just a Pet Detective. I'm a trained social worker. Until a year ago, I was a Trauma Services Child Specialist with Children's Advocacy Services in Tallahassee."

He looked at her a long time. "What changed?"

"Everything."

"I'm listening."

As she told that story he got up and began cleaning the kitchen, as if he realized she might not be able tell it if she had to bear the weight of his gaze on her. But the story came, shaping the horror of that day in the courtroom into words that seemed not quite enough for all they needed to tell. By the end, she was wondering, as she often had on that job, why anyone had to live lives like the ones she'd seen in the field. The abuse done to innocent children was obscene. It was inhumane. It had broken her innocence. And she'd wanted it back so badly, to piece together her popped soap bubble of ignorance. That was why she'd sealed up and put her former life on the shelf while she tried to find a new one that better fit her idea of how life should be.

She wasn't certain how much of her thoughts she'd put into words. Probably more than was wise when a new man friend was listening.

When she paused finally, she realized that the dishes

were done and that Oliver was sitting in front of her again. There was no real expression on his face beyond thoughtful interest. She couldn't tell if he was appalled, or confused, or, "What?"

"I saw the scar the first night we made love." He pointed to her middle. "I was a soldier. I know bullet wounds. But you didn't say anything, and I didn't want to embarrass you by asking about it."

"Oh." Macayla wrapped a protective hand over her middle. "I didn't know what to say."

He gave her a funny look. "You deliberately took a bullet for a child. That's as courageous as it gets in this life."

"No." She stood up. "I'm not that."

"Not what?"

"A hero." She said the final word so softly Oliver wasn't certain what she'd said until he played it back in his thoughts. And then he thought he understood her a little better.

He stood up, too, blocking her path. And then he gently reached out to frame her shoulders with his hands. "If I Google Macayla Burkett, what will I find?"

She shrugged under his hands, refusing to look at him.

"It will say Macayla Burkett is a hero, or heroine. Won't it?"

She moved her head back and forth. "I never wanted that. I had already burned out long before the shooting happened. But that was my breaking point. Being celebrated as a hero seemed like a horrible joke."

"I'm sure it was extremely hard for you."

She looked up, her damn eyes feeling damp. "Detective Mullins says I crave being the center of attention. And that's why he thinks I steal dogs, so that when I return them and the owners shower praise on me, it reinforces the praise I crave from once being called a hero."

"Detective Mullins is talking out his ass."

His blunt response startled a short laugh from her. "You're right. If I'd wanted attention, I'd have stayed in my job. I was being asked to talk to every group in the area who needed a speaker. They wanted to know how to be brave in the face of danger, how to be like me. But I couldn't do it, I just couldn't." She bit her lip, the impression of her teeth draining the color from her lower lip. "I wanted to say, I'm not brave. I was just there. Just there."

Oliver pulled her in. She hesitated only a moment before going willingly in against his warmth. She shivered against him, shoulders heaving though she made no sounds. He held on tighter, as if he could absorb her pain and anguish into his own bigger, sturdier frame. She was small, but not delicate. There was a lion in this woman. When it had come roaring to life, she had scared herself. That's what people forgot about bravery. It wasn't about not feeling fear, as everyone else did. It was feeling the fear, and acting anyway. The brave man or woman dealt with that fear afterward, when the danger had passed. That became harder to do when no one wanted to hear anything but the tale of bravery.

After a minute Macayla's shoulders stopped gently heaving and her breath evened out, but he didn't let go even a fraction. Holding her body to his felt right, normal. Something to be repeated as often as possible. They fit in ways he couldn't explain, or cared to try. It was enough.

Finally she unballed her fists and spread her fingers across his chest in the fractional space between them. He knew that she was about to push him away so he raised a hand to turn her face up to his. Looking down into her tear-streaked face made his gut quiver. Had he once said she was just cute? She was simply beautiful.

"I didn't mean to break down like that." She looked a bit ashamed.

"It's okay not to want to be brave all the time. You don't have to pretend with me. You can be needy. I'll just hold you until you feel stronger."

Pressing her cheek to his chest, Macayla allowed herself a little sigh of relief. Great sex notwithstanding, this was the best moment of the day so far. Feeling not alone.

"You're not responsible for a man with a gun and a sick mind," he said from someplace above her head. "You saved that child's life."

"It didn't feel like that. I lost Katie." She swallowed before going on. "Katie was my service dog. She was shot, too." She shivered. "I couldn't protect them both."

"It was a horrible choice."

"No, it was no choice at all. The child needed to live. I'd had twenty-six years."

He clutched her a little tighter, his chin resting on the top of her head. "That's not much."

"It's four times what Jily had lived."

"The girl?"

"She's fine. If witnessing all those terrible things could end with anyone being fine."

"She has more years now because of your sacrifice, and Katie's. More time to heal and build a better future."

She looked up at him, surprised that she hadn't thought of it that way before. "Katie was a hero, too."

He nodded solemnly. "Why did you walk away from your life? It was more than the label *hero*."

She looked away, not wanting him to see her cowardice. "I didn't want to be responsible for any other child's life. Ever again."

He said nothing for a long moment. "So now you save dogs?"

"Dogs don't have parents who think that killing them and then themselves is a good way to solve their problems."

"The father shot himself?" She heard him expel a harsh breath that ruffled her hair.

He loosened his hold on her and she reluctantly lifted her head, ready to free him, but he held on to her. "Do you want to hear what I think? Because I haven't been in your life long enough to have a right to an opinion."

"It hasn't stopped anyone else. Another reason I left." She sounded a little defeated.

"It's this. Stop trying *not* to be a hero. Because you already are one. You just have to learn to live with who you are."

"Don't say that."

"There is another way. Stop reaching for the prize."

"What are you talking about?"

"I've watched you. You're a natural protector. It makes your heart beat. You step up every time, in every situation. The damn Pomeranian wouldn't have made it another day if you'd given up chasing it. You face down the guys with bats then take on the local nutter Massey. If you really don't want the title, stop stepping up."

Macayla felt offended, right down to her shoe soles. "You just said it's part of my nature."

"Yeah. I did." He was watching her with kind eyes, no laughter or teasing glint. "So what does that tell you?"

"I'm screwed."

"That's my girl." Oliver hauled her in close and kissed her hard, feeling all the anger and frustration that had been building up on her behalf while he kept silent under the litany of her ordeal. It burst from his chest, powering the emotion of fierce protectiveness that was double-helixed into his own bones and blood. It was pleasure and pain to hold her and absorb her hurt. He wasn't sure which he felt

more until she groaned in his arms and he realized he must
be hurting her.

He released her. "I'm sorry. That wasn't what I meant
to do."

"It's okay." She pushed back shakily out of his embrace.
"We got carried away. Mixed up the emotions."

"Yeah. That's it." But the words surprised him. Mixed
up their emotions? He'd thought until this second that they
were absolutely together on the same page. "Maybe I
should get out of here for a bit. Find a place to stay."

She looked at him with large eyes brimming with possibilities but she only said, "That would be best."

For whom? He had to wonder. Irritation burned in his
chest that, just like that, she was shutting him out.

She didn't seem to notice how hurt he was about it. Not
that his face gave anything away. Yet she knew him, didn't
she? He'd decided on the flight to the States that she knew
him better than anyone else in his life at the moment. And
that made him vulnerable. It wasn't a feeling he enjoyed.

He looked away, settling his gaze on the sink to keep
from saying the words locked behind his teeth. She lifted
him out of himself, made him want things he'd never wanted
before. That scared him. Maybe instead of surging ahead,
as he'd come here to do, he should take a step back. Reassess
the situation. He was emotionally involved, always a dangerous position for someone making a huge decision. He
wasn't dispassionate enough to know his own mind.

His gaze dropped to Jackeroo, who had come to stand
before him, head kicked over in canine inquiry. He ruffled his K-9 partner's fur, a sign that he was okay. Jackeroo might be able to read his chemical pheromone
cocktail like a road map of his handler's emotions, but
he couldn't always know what was motivating his handler. Oliver felt old habits like muscle memory click into

place. A giant step back. Yeah. That's what he should do. Reassess.

He got as far as the door before turning around. "Fuck it. I can't leave. Someone has made you a target for the police. We can't wait to see what his next move will be. We need to counterpunch, and quickly."

She stared at him in surprise, as if she'd thought he'd already gone. "But I don't know who he is, so it's like punching in the dark."

"We could start with suspects. What about Massey?"

"I made a list yesterday of people I'd like to talk with." She looked around for it.

He came toward her, feeling energized. Action was what he needed. He'd like to bust a few heads and smash a few things on her behalf. Action, he could handle. "Who's on the list?"

She stared at him. "You really don't mind getting involved?"

"I was coming back to see you, Macayla. I thought you understood."

She smiled suddenly, and it broke his heart a tiny bit. "I was afraid to."

He shook his head and rolled his eyes, not daring to be as happy as her words made him. "Women. A man's lot always to need to draw a bloody map. Get over here, woman, and show me what you've got."

She found it and they sat down together while she explained who each person was. When she was done, he was grinning.

Macayla watched him cautiously. "You see something I'm missing?"

"Not yet. But we can find some answers by asking questions. Someone on your list is bound to know something. Let's go see a woman about a dog."

Oliver whistled and Jackeroo jumped up, fully awake. "Let's take a ride."

Jackeroo barked in reply. There were few things he liked better than a ride in a car with an open window.

CHAPTER TWENTY-TWO

Lisa Peterson smiled a little too broadly as she held the Pomeranian named Wookie in her lap. "You can see he's as good as new. And so much better behaved. We've been going to obedience classes." Her gaze darted from Macayla to Oliver and back. "Is everything all right?"

"I'm not sure, Lisa." Macayla tried to sound at ease because the woman had insisted on the informality when she'd let them into her home. "I've heard some disturbing rumors on the street and from the local police about dog-nappings taking place across the Tampa/St. Petersburg area. I wondered if you knew anything about that."

"I don't. Why would I?" She paused in stroking Wookie to dab at a bead of perspiration rolling down her forehead. They were seated on her patio though the day was swollen with humidity, and glassy bright, and the air-conditioned air that surrounded them when they walked through the house would have been more appreciated than the muggy garden view. The glasses of iced tea she served sat in puddles on the glass-topped wrought-iron table around which they sat.

Thinking ahead, they'd dropped Jackeroo off at Tampa/St. Pete Recon. Jefferina wasn't in but Marcia offered to look after him. No leaving a dog for even a minute in a car in this heat.

"You told my employer that Wookie has disappeared several times in the past month."

"That's true. He has a habit of darting away when I take him to the dog park. Sometimes he gets out of the gate."

"You don't keep him on a leash?" This surprised Mac.

"I did, after the first time. Now we just don't go there anymore." She stroked Wookie lovingly. "I should have known better. But it won't ever happen again, will it, sweetums?"

Macayla saw Oliver's eye roll at the endearment. She was more interested in the "after the first time" part. "The police tell owners who refuse to pay the ransom to check with shelters and put up signs in their neighborhood and on lost-pet Internet sites because most often the dogs are simply released on the streets."

"How awful." Lisa took a sip of her tea, ignoring the drips from the glass falling on Wookie. "I can't imagine not paying if Wookie were taken. I'd be frantic about him being hit by a car, or killed by wild animals."

"I'd pay. The first time," Oliver volunteered. "But if the little fella got snatched a second time, I'd think that paying the first time made me a target. And that it would happen a third time if I paid again."

Lisa glanced at him and smiled the smile of a woman confronted with a gorgeous man. "I'm afraid I would pay a second time, too. It's Wookie we're talking about."

"You wouldn't call the police?" Macayla tried to make her voice as nonjudgmental as possible.

"Well, yes, I suppose I would do that, too. The second time."

"Crikey, Lisa. If I'd paid the ransom the first time, I'd feel like the police might accuse me of having abetted a crime by not reporting it the first time."

Lisa's gaze fell before his. "Yes, there is that."

"So you called Tampa/St. Pete Recon, instead." Macayla smiled. "You aren't the only one. I've talked to two other pet owners whose pets I recovered." Neither of their dogs had been snatched, but that wouldn't be helpful to say at the moment.

The woman didn't reply.

"The problem is, Lisa, I'm now being accused of stealing the pets I'm paid to find and return. You know that isn't true because you've dealt with the real culprits. I'm not asking you to go to the police." Not yet anyway. "I just need to know all you can tell me about the real thieves so I can find them."

"We can find them." Oliver's voice held the threat of bodily harm.

Lisa bent and kissed one of Wookie's ears. "Two men. Young. Wearing hoodies. White, I think. They were hanging around the dog park. I noticed because neither of them had a dog. But they stayed on the outside of the fence. It was only when I realized Wookie was missing from the crowd of dogs he plays with that I noticed one of them had left. Of course, I was frantic. Wookie's never left outside, not even in the yard, without supervision. I asked everyone if they'd seen him. Even the guy outside the fence."

Her face tightened. "He pointed across the street to where his friend was holding Wookie. He demanded one hundred and fifty dollars. He said if I gave him the money right then, he'd have his friend bring Wookie back. All I had on me was the hundred-dollar bill I keep tucked away for emergencies. So I gave it to him. But he took off and the other one only dropped Wookie in the grass and ran. I ran to scoop Wookie up but he seemed to think the boys were playing a game and he ran after them and disappeared."

"Feeling a little better?" Oliver smiled at Macayla as they walked back to his rental car a few minutes later. "That's the first confirmation of the day."

Macayla shook her head. "Second. The Boxer's owner said a young man snatched her dog's leash out of her hand as they walked in the park."

"Remind you of anyone?"

"Massey's grandson Woody's buddies." She slid into the passenger seat as he slid behind the wheel.

"Sounds like I need to do a follow-up."

"Oh no you don't. You can't harass a witness. That's all the police will need to scoop me up and sit my butt in jail until trial."

He slanted a frown her way. "Since you didn't commit a crime, he's not a legitimate witness, so we're doing nothing wrong. It's definitely worth a trip to see what he knows. Someone put him up to this. Don't think it was the old man."

Macayla shook her head. "Later. This isn't just about them. The thieves sound like opportunists. The kind Sam told me about. I'm involved in something bigger. Whoever planted that money in my house had the extra cash to spend setting me up. Let's face it, if I had five hundred dollars, stolen or otherwise, I wouldn't waste it trying to frame someone with it."

"Fair point." But she saw something in Oliver's gaze change, as if he hadn't thought about her dismal financial situation. How was that possible when he'd seen her former car, and now her home? But he didn't say another word

PHYSICAL FORCES   229

about that. "What kind of thief would be wealthy enough not to worry about losing that kind of money?"

Her eyes got big at the thought. "The dognappers of the greyhounds."

"I was thinking the same thing. Dognapping in the park is a long way from breaking into a racetrack and stealing professional dogs. Have you ever been to the dog track?"

"No. I hate the whole idea of making dogs race. I've signed several petitions against it."

He grinned at her. "The Boxer, Wookie, and the greyhounds. One of these things is not like the other. Let's find out why."

Derby Lane Greyhound Track was a racino, a combination racetrack and casino. The main building was white stucco with pinky-beige trim and a shutter-green crown. At the moment it baked like a birthday cake in the heat, a plume of white clouds rising like steam behind it. Nothing moved in the heat. It was as if all the oxygen had been sucked out of the air. At least that's how it seemed to Macayla as she and Oliver walked toward it from the parking lot.

Oliver gave her a reassuring smile when they reached the entrance. "You go talk to the manager. See what he's willing to tell you about what happened that night. I'm going to nose around the kennels and talk to the guys who really run the place. If there's smut in the wind, they'll have a sniff of it."

The moment she entered the casino, the skin on Macayla's arms puckered. It wasn't just a reaction to the iceberg temperature freezing the sweat on her body, or the sudden switch from too-bright sun to the dim interior, or the weary worldliness of Frank Sinatra's voice pervading the space, or the incessant mechanical sounds of slot machines churning above the murmuring voices of gamblers.

By nighttime and weekend standards the place was nearly deserted now, at midday. It was the sense she was out of her depth.

Desperation was taking her down some very iffy roads to some very shaky destinations. What was she going to say to the manager? *Hi. Do you know who stole those greyhounds because the police don't have a clue? And, oh, by the way, did anybody from here leave five hundred dollars in my underwear drawer?*

"May I help you?" A young woman in a formfitting navy business suit had paused before her. From her sassy ponytail to her red lips and spike heels, she looked both business-like and sexy. How did she do that? The length of her skirt, of course. It stopped halfway up her toned thighs.

Macayla licked her too-dry lips. "I'm Mac Burkett of Tampa/St. Pete Recon. I'd like to speak with the manager."

The young woman gave her a cursory smile. "Follow me."

Mac stepped onto the elevator feeling as if it were a rocket to the moon. If the casino itself was Vegas retread, the upper offices were Seattle modern: spare lines, grays and chrome.

The moment the doors opened on the mezzanine floor she spied the silver hair of Jarvis Henley. She thrust her arm into the gap, saying to her hostess. "Never mind. I see Jarvis. He'll tell me what I need to know. Thanks."

She stepped out and moved quickly toward her quarry, who was in a discussion with a man who wore chinos and a white golf shirt with the words HENLEY KENNELS embossed across the shoulders. No doubt who he worked for.

"Put the last three back in their crates. They're not running well in this heat. Must be reacting to the pressure changes of the storm."

"Mr. Henley?"

The man turned as Macayla approached. He squinted at her, eyes rising to the blue in her hair. "That's right. But I don't believe—" His bland expression switched to razor-sharp. "Wait. I do know you. Ms. Burkett, right?"

"That's right. We met at that SAR banquet." She shook his extended hand and felt her knuckles crunch under the pressure. At least she didn't feel the terror of their last encounter. Yet he was a power player all the way. "Lucky thing, running into you. Do you have a moment?"

"Always for a good-looking woman." He waved her toward the dining room. "I was just about to have a little lunch. Do you come here often? If so, then you'll know how great the menu is."

"No. I've never been here before. And sorry, but I can't join you."

He paused and assessed her again. Did he have a thing for biker shorts and oversized tees? "The way you say that I sense disapproval."

"No disrespect but, yes, I think dog racing is unnecessarily cruel to the dogs."

"I see." He looked as if she'd punched him in the nose. "In that case, what brings you here?"

"Doing a little customer service review." She wasn't surprised to see his brows rise in skepticism. She was about to screw things up before she got to ask her first question. "And I seem to have forgotten myself. Never insult the customer. I gave you my personal opinion. Not that of my employer. I'd appreciate if you didn't report how badly I messed up my first outing as a Tampa/St. Pete Recon representative."

He didn't smile. "Have you been with them long?"

"Less than a year. I actually came to say how sorry I am that we weren't able to return your dogs to you in good health."

"I suppose you did your best. Though it took a while to find them."

"Actually, I ran them down less than twelve hours after being given the assignment. The police were in charge before that."

He seemed surprised that she defended herself. "How did you find them so quickly when law enforcement couldn't?"

She smiled. "Now I'll have to plead PI–client privilege."

"I'm the client."

"PI–informant privilege then." It felt as if she were dancing with a bear. "One hears things on the street."

"And, being a pet detective, you have lots of ears on the street?"

"People who would never agree on religion or politics agree about animals, Mr. Henley. Everybody loves them, and wants to help protect them."

"Except racing dog breeders." He was daring her to cross him again. Money made some people bullies.

"Good one. I know you were honored for good works for local K-9 search-and-rescue teams. Perhaps you aren't like other racing dog breeders."

"Is there a point to this, Ms. Burkett?"

"Only that I hope you were satisfied with my diligence in your case. It came at great personal sacrifice."

"What sacrifice would that be?"

It struck her then that maybe she'd said too much. The point was not to throw further suspicion on herself, but to fish for what he knew.

"A few cuts and bruises. But something about this case still bothers me. I wonder if you've had any more thoughts about on who might have stolen your dogs? As I came in, I noticed how professional the facilities are. It's clear the track has good security. I'm told the dogs live on the premises."

"Yes, at any given time there are between three and five hundred dogs on the grounds."

"Whoa. I'm amazed you noticed two were missing."

"They were a special pair, my wife's dogs, favored to win a big race the next day."

"How big?"

"The biggest purse since the famous Derby Lane Million."

"Wow." No one had mentioned that before. Her mind kicked into high gear. "That had to be a blow to you, financially."

He smirked as if she'd made a joke. "One doesn't own racers without the wherewithal to absorb the occasional disappointment at the track."

Message received: Henley was stinkin' rich. "But it might be enough so that someone might have wanted to fix the race."

"The police have always looked at the case as an inside job." He said this as though she was slow and needed to be told she was out of her league. "I really can't discuss details with you because it is an ongoing matter with the police."

"Because?" She had to try.

He just stared at her.

"That must be because they have a suspect, or suspects. Someone who works or worked here, I'd guess."

No reply. He glanced at his watch. "I have an engagement coming up. If you'll excuse me." He was done being polite and walked away.

"Mr. Henley? Did you know that here's a dognapping ring working in this area?"

He paused. "No. Why?"

"I was just thinking that the theft of your dogs couldn't be connected. The guys in the local ring are amateurs. Anyone getting in here would have to know what they were doing and how things operate. That makes it a bigger job, one that would require more sophistication."

She didn't know why she was being deliberately provocative. Probably because he'd rubbed her face in his wealth while she knew too much about how miserably maintained racing dogs were. Hundreds of dogs in metal cages stacked several levels high for up to twenty hours a day. Without the benefit of heat or air-conditioning, rain or shine. He had the "wherewithal" to make their conditions better, but chose not to. That made him an asswipe in her book.

What the hell—she'd already been arrested. Once that became public knowledge, no one would talk to her. Maybe if she told Henley what had happened that night, he would talk about it among his friends, and that might flush out whoever was behind the attempt to frame her.

"It was a busy night in the neighborhood the night I found your dogs. The police were called to that block before I'd had a chance to call them myself."

He looked surprised. "Why were they called?"

"Shots fired."

"You were there when shots were fired?" He didn't even blink. "That must have been frightening."

"Terrifying." She hesitated. Up until this moment, she'd been grateful no one knew she'd been there. Now it seemed a liability. Someone had committed a crime greater than the murder of those poor dogs. Someone had shot another human being.

"The police are holding back but you are the client, as

you just reminded me. So I'll tell you, I was able to video the shooting."

This time he did blink. "What?"

"I was using an infrared camera at a location I'd been given to try to detect live activity—in this case, your dogs—without needing to enter the premises. That's how I came to accidentally witness an altercation in which one man shot another."

"If what you say is true, why haven't the police arrested anyone?"

She shrugged. "I can't say." She wasn't quite sure why she felt the need to hold back the detail about the recording being unclear. Maybe to see if it made him nervous, to help suss out what he did or didn't know.

"That's a very interesting story. But what does it have to do with my dogs being taken?" His expression remained cool, almost too cool.

"Nothing. Just wanted you to know how dedicated Tampa/St. Pete Recon is to doing a good job for you. Thanks for your time. Have a good day."

She turned and hurried toward the elevator. Thankfully the wait wasn't long and she sank back against the wall in relief. *Holy crap!*

Her brain was buzzing. She had never been more sure that the greyhound dognapping and the shooting were related. It once seemed so random. Not anymore.

The events of the night flashed through her mind like a PowerPoint presentation on fast forward. The details were surreal, seen through the lens of the infrared camera in splashes of neon colors. The shooting she'd witnessed had taken place next door to the house where the dogs were. Maybe they had talked there to throw off suspicion in case they were seen.

Maybe she *had* been seen. *Professional hit*. That was Sam's opinion, when he'd believed her. Maybe she'd been tracked down.

No going back now. She'd told Mr. Henley enough to set in motion a series of events she wasn't certain she could handle. But she had to try. To do that, she needed more information.

The police hadn't shared information with her about who owned the house where the dogs were found, or where the shooting had taken place. Not her business. And it didn't seem important. But she knew someone who could find out the answers to both those questions.

Fresh sweat squeezed out of her pores as she stepped outside. The day was a bright oven after the chill, dim enclosure of the racino building. She gnawed her lip, wondering whether she should go in search of Oliver when he appeared around a wall and waved at her. They needed to talk. But not out in the open where they might be overheard.

When they met, he slung a familiar arm about her shoulders as he steered her toward the parking lot. "How did it go?"

"I ran into Jarvis Henley. I don't like him. You?"

"I had a conversation with several of the kennel hands."

"Don't say any more until we get to the car."

He nodded. "You're going to like what I have to say."

You won't, she thought as she slid into the passenger side.

Oliver got behind the wheel and turned on the engine, cranking up the air to full blast. "The trainers wouldn't talk to me. But my bastard Spanish came in handy while the kennel hands argued among themselves about what they weren't going to tell me, and why. One of them said that a guy named Nico, one of Jarvis Henley's trainers, hasn't been seen since the dogs disappeared. Mr. Henley says he fired him but they aren't sure."

Mac leaned into the air vent, grateful for the gust of re-frigerated air hitting her face. "You think this Nico took the dogs?"

"Possibly. If it was an inside job, one of the trainers would be the likeliest suspect. He'd know the security, how to handle the dogs. For the right bribe, many people aren't rigid about their loyalty."

Mac thought about that a beat. "There's something you should know. I kinda outed myself." She went on to explain her conversation with Henley in detail.

Oliver was shaking his head by the end. "That was pretty stupid, Macayla."

"Oh, thanks for the vote of confidence."

He sent her a dark look. "I don't like the idea of you making yourself a target."

"I'm already a target. I'm just trying to figure out *whose* target. I needed to push Henley to see how he responded. Now I'm certain he knows more than he's letting on."

"What happened to not being brave and shit?"

She shrugged. "There's something else. Henley lost a large purse on a major race the day after his dogs went missing."

Oliver glanced at her sharply. "Who won?"

"Let's see." Macayla pulled out her phone and found the answer after a minute. "A long shot won, nearly four hundred thousand dollars. The rest was split seven ways from Sunday because of a multiple tie. No big day for anyone."

"Except the persons who put a bet on the long shot. There was probably major off-track betting going on, too."

Macayla eyed Oliver. "You know a lot about betting?"

"Not really. Me granddad liked to bet on the horses. He always went for the long shot. He didn't win often. But when he did, he won big. Are you thinking someone took the dogs to throw the race?"

"I'm thinking Henley must have lost a bundle because his dogs were the favorite to win. Which is interesting, but it doesn't help me with the dognapping charges." She tapped her fingers. "Turn left here and head south. Maybe Jefferina will be able to make something out of what we've discovered."

CHAPTER TWENTY-THREE

A few clicks of her mouse and Jefferina nodded to herself. "I have the names of the owners of the greyhound winners but I don't know what good it's going to do us. They're scattered over the country." She looked up at Macayla and Oliver. "Any other ideas?"

Mac leaned in. "Aren't any of them local?" She'd been hoping the winner would be connected with Henley somehow, helping them zero in on the mastermind.

"Henley didn't win the big purse. The long shot came in from Texas." Jefferina rolled her head on her neck. "I've got to tell you, what you did by approaching Henley was beyond stupid. I don't need you antagonizing my best customer."

"Yes, well, it was an accident. I just couldn't see passing up an opportunity to ask him directly about the greyhound abduction. I still think there's something hinky about it. He seemed like he was freezing me out. And when I told him I was doing a follow-up customer service call, he didn't even respond. Not a *good job* or a *you stink*. Nothing. It was like my finding the dogs was no big deal."

"Customer service?" Her boss was eyeing her with a squint. "When did we start doing that?"

Mac blushed. "I needed a reason to talk to him. It just popped into my head."

Jefferina smirked. "Keep up that kind of thinking on your feet and we'll make a PI out of you yet. But meantime, you're supposed to be holding down a desk here."

"I know. And I'm sorry I'm late. I just thought if I could talk to—"

"Witnesses. Tampering with witnesses. You're just racking up charges, Mac. What kind of crazy do you plan to pretend to be in jail? Because you are going for the gold with lockup time, the way you're going about it."

"Lecture me," said Oliver. "I'm the one to put her up to it."

Macayla glanced at Oliver, who was riding the edge of Marcia's receptionist desk with one leg cocked at a provocative angle and arms crossed, showing off tats and attitude. "But be warned, I'm not a good listener."

Jefferina eyed him up and down like he was something she might be thinking about purchasing. "You told me you could protect her. This morning was your idea of protection?"

"It was that or lock her up in her bedroom. But she seemed to think my style of lovemaking should be indulged in sparingly."

Jefferina chuckled. "She's young."

"I'm right here. And I'm listening. And neither of you is the boss of me. Especially in matters sexual." Mac shot Oliver a hostile glance. "Three times is enough for one day."

"Your opinion," he and Jefferina answered simultaneously.

Mac just remembered something she was supposed to be angry about. "You gave him my address."

"I wondered when you'd remember that."

"He's a perfect stranger."

"Perfect, maybe, but not a stranger. He knew things about you that said you two had been up close and personal. Don't look at me like that. I didn't know you had a birthmark shaped like a duck on your ass."

"I don't."

Laughter burst from her boss. "I like him, which is more than I can say about the other men I've seen you with."

"You haven't seen me with anyone."

"I rest my case." She glanced at Oliver, who was putting the charm moves on Marcia. "He's a handsome beast. I am hella impressed with you. He came a long way just to get you to drop the panties. That speaks of devotion. Question is, how interested are you in him?"

Mac narrowed her eyes as she looked at Oliver, all taut muscle and masculine cool. Devotion? For her? How did she feel about him? "He makes me want to set fire to my hair. Worse, I can't tell if this is a good or bad thing."

"I'm here and I'm listening," Oliver added. "Careful you don't hurt my feelings, they bruise easily."

Mac rolled her eyes but she couldn't help grinning. "I think we're both highly interested, so get me some work to do before I fall in so deep I won't come up for air for months."

"Funny you should mention work," Jefferina said. "I wasn't going to ask. But since you're offering."

That caught Macayla's attention. Jefferina didn't do coy. Ever. "What?"

"I had a job come in, starting today. I usually take

something like this myself. But there are animals involved, and there's no way with my allergies. It's a house-sitting job. Three–four days at most. Until the storm blows through."

"What storm?"

"Mac, where is your mind? Oh, right. Over there in that man's jeans. That Gulf low that's been piddling around all week has decided to make landfall in the area tonight. People have been talking about nothing else for the past twenty-four hours. The mayor's office is advising people to move away from the usual low-lying areas."

"But you want me to go out to a low-lying area."

"The house is on the water but it's on the bay side. Second home for the summer for a family with two small kids. You know how it is with folks who don't live near water. Every tropical storm is, for them, a Category Five on the hurricane scale. They're taking the kids inland until the storm blows over."

"I don't know. I'd like to keep talking to people."

"No. Someone's out to get you. We don't know who that is. I'm trying to protect you. If you aren't at home they–whoever they are—will have a much harder time getting to you."

Macayla thought about that for a few seconds. "There's probably something else I need to tell you."

Jefferina was chewing her lip by the time Mac finished her story about finding the cash in her underwear drawer. Her black eyes were dead serious as she made eye contact. "I don't know how or why, but this is a lot bigger than petty dog theft."

"It has to do with Macayla witnessing a shooting."

Both women looked up at the sound of Oliver's voice. He hadn't moved from the desk but his attention was riveted on them.

"You told him everything?"

"I did, after he came back."

Jefferina nodded. "I don't like what's going on. We need to tuck you safely away while I do some serious investigating of your situation. Go home and pack."

She looked up at Oliver. "Don't let her stay in her place more than fifteen minutes. If you see the police, don't even go in. Then deliver her to this address."

Oliver nodded, expression as serious any Macayla had ever seen as he took the paper Jefferina offered him.

Mac felt a sudden hit of emotion she didn't want to examine. Oliver had come, and gone. And come back. A beginning. Of what she wasn't sure.

She turned to her boss. "What do they want me to do?"

"Mostly feed the dogs and cat, and walk them."

"People don't usually walk cats."

"Do I look like an animal lover? Work it out. The management company sent over all the instructions in an email I'm printing for you." She grabbed the first sheet of paper off the printer.

"Sounds easy."

"Yes. Basically they're paying for you to watch videos twenty-four seven. Make the most of it." She cut her eyes to Oliver. "But not you. Sorry, but you don't work for me and I can't take responsibility for you being on the property."

"Then I'll be off the property. Two inches, maybe."

Macayla shook her head. "You don't—"

He scowled at her, daring her to continue. "I'm not leaving you alone anywhere until you're cleared of suspicion and the culprit's caught."

"You heard the man," Jefferina added with a smile. She glanced down at the papers she'd snagged. "Oh yeah. There're saltwater fish tanks in the house. A guy will come by daily to take care of that."

Macayla took the paperwork and read it for herself. "Any teenager could do this job. Why did they call a private investigation company?"

"You do remember that reconnaissance is part of our name? We do low-tech security for vacation rental companies. House-sitting expensive properties comes under that umbrella. You do want the job?"

"Hell to the yes." Macayla repeated one of Jefferina's favorite phrases.

Jefferina snatched the final sheet as it finished printing. "You can order in from the list of restaurants left on the kitchen island. The bill's already taken care of. As long as you don't order food for more than one person. And you can't buy booze."

When Jefferina showed her where the house was located on the local map, Macayla frowned. "I'll need wheels."

Jefferina pointed to a line on her computer screen. "There's a jeep available for use on the property. You're free to use it as long as you don't leave the greater Tampa/St. Pete area. It's got a car locator."

"You can't be serious? Free food and a car loan?"

Jefferina smiled. "This might not be Palm Beach but we've got our share of heavy hitters. From time to time they need a house-sitter. I've been trying to break in with this level of client for some time, so bring your A-game, okay, Mac?"

"What if the family learns that the person fish-sitting their tanks is out on bail after being arrested on suspicion of dognapping?"

"I don't see how that can come up."

"Jefferina, thanks."

She waved it off. "Now about your Aussie. Take him

home. Make him happy. And then lose him. You don't need the distraction, and he can continue to make inquiries on his own."

"All that, and pack, in fifteen minutes?"

"You'll think of something."

CHAPTER TWENTY-FOUR

Macayla frowned as Oliver pulled up before her new temporary home. The totally modern house was built at the dead end of a point of land that jutted into Tampa Bay. It didn't look at all like the description Jefferina had given her. *Mansion built on 180 feet of prime waterfront property.* It was certainly nice. What electronic-gated, four-car-garage mansion wouldn't be? Still, she was disappointed because from where she sat in Oliver's front seat, there wasn't a bit of water view to be seen. In fact, the house looked like any nice house on any block anywhere in the area. It was a split-level, two-story stucco surrounded by tall matching stucco walls and lush tropical plants on either side of the drive so that one could not see the neighbors.

"Well, it's not the estate I was expecting, but it'll do."

Oliver shook his head, his expression grim as he turned up the radio. "The storm is intensifying. I should be in there with you tonight."

"Sure you should." Mac grinned. "But I'd get nothing done. I have responsibilities, animals to take care of."

The old twinkle in his blue eyes flashed to life. "I'm an animal. You could feed and pet me."

"You heard what Jefferina said. Not gonna happen." She leaned in to land a quick kiss good-bye.

His hand shot out and snagged her behind her head and held her month to his. The peck turned into a full-mouth drown in his scent and heat and taste. When they finally drew apart, she was in his lap and her bra was unclasped, his shirt pulled up, and skin-to-skin contact felt so good her nipples were gumdrops glued by humidity to his chest.

"I could come in and we could christen each of the beds in the seven bedrooms."

She grinned at him. "We wouldn't make it past the entrance floor."

"Fair dinkum." He grinned back.

"But you need to hold that thought. For three days."

He pushed her hand down between them so there was no doubt about how ready he was for action. "Why don't you hold this instead?"

She hadn't meant to leave her hand there, but his dick was so hard beneath the denim of his jeans. And it just seemed like the thing to do, to squeeze and lightly knead and— She jerked her hand away. "You don't play fair."

"Am I winning?"

He stroked a thumb across the seat of her shorts and grinned. Busted. It was damp. "I won't stay long. Promise. Just a quick screw and I'm gone."

Macayla moved her head slowly in a negative but her hand had moved back to his erection. After a hard squeeze that drew a gasp of need from him, she fumbled for his zipper. "That quickie needs to be here. I promised Jefferina I wouldn't let you in. However, if we get arrested for lewd public conduct . . ."

"We won't. Just let me make room." His hands had found her waist and he lifted her back onto her side of the console.

Macayla was trying to wriggle out of her shorts when he suddenly let his seat back in a reclining position. A second later he had skinned out of his jeans, revealing a fully equipped erection of impressive size. He pulled out a condom and rolled it expertly over himself before turning to her with a grin. He rolled his hips provocatively. "Ready for a ride?"

She shucked her shorts and then climbed back on top of him. That's all the invitation he needed to scoop his hands behind her and palm her butt cheeks.

She leaned over and kissed him as he maneuvered their bodies into the right position. She felt his fingers delicately part her, and then the tip of his penis slipped in. With a sigh of satisfaction she sank down farther on him, until inch by inch he filled her completely.

It was a wild ride, fast and hard, no time for subtleties or luxuriating touches or prolonged tension. This was sex pure and raw and intense. They were both sweating within seconds. He grunted with every thrust, as if he thought he could bury himself so deeply inside her they would never be able to separate again. It didn't seem to matter that there was very little room in which to maneuver, or that her butt kept bouncing against the steering wheel. They were lost in the moment of urgent heat between them, a tangle of surging lust, damp skin, and warm mouths.

The climax came quickly, as if it had been months instead of hours since they'd been together. It was hard and sudden, almost painful. Macayla heard Oliver's groan of surrender on the back end of her tsunami of release.

For a moment the world stopped. And then she was nose-to-nose with Jackeroo, who'd been watching them with intense interest from the backseat.

A flash out of the blue suddenly lit up the late afternoon, landing so close by it made a cracking sound before thunder blasted the surrounding air. As if the razor of electrons had slashed open the clouds, rain splashed down around them in ragged sheets.

Jackeroo barked loudly in protest of the sudden pyrotechnics. Macayla scooted off Oliver's lap and grabbed her undies and shorts from the floorboard. "I've got to go. The dogs need to be walked before the serious weather sets in."

They both dressed quickly in silence as the moisture from the rain fogged up the windows.

Finally clothed, she darted a glance at him. He was leaning against the driver's door watching her with half-closed lids, as if he was thinking about jumping her again. She'd thought he would look sated. Instead he looked like a man who couldn't get enough.

She smiled to herself. She'd never thought she was the kind of woman a man couldn't get enough of. But what did she know?

She leaned across the console and kissed him quickly, a mash-up of lips and tongue that didn't contain a lot of finesse but put her shaky world on notice as her sex fluttered in tiny aftershocks of delicious desire.

"See you tomorrow." She grabbed her backpack of belongings, pushed open the door, and scooted out into the rain, gasping in surprise to find the thick splash of water surprisingly cold as it pelted her head and shoulders. She swung open the back door to grab her backpack and leaned in to give Jackeroo a pet. "Take care of the big guy. He's going to be a little cranky." She offered Oliver a sympathetic glance over the seats. "See you soon."

His grin dissolved. "Call me after you've checked out the place. I'm not leaving here until you do."

"Okay." She slammed the car door and ran for the front gate, where she punched in the security code she'd been given. Happy to hear the dead bolt grind and release, she pushed through to use the code on the keypad to the right side of a pair of leaded-glass entrance doors.

The view on the other side halted her just inside.

"Holy shit."

This was a house in which the view ruled. Across a great room decorated in expensive but casual furnishings, floor-to-ceiling windows offered an uninterrupted view of Tampa Bay. Everywhere she looked, the panoramic water view just didn't stop. It was magnificent. Or scary, depending on how much a person liked water.

She pulled out her phone as another brilliant flash lit up the interior. "I'm in. I'm fine." No point in torturing him with a description of a place he couldn't share with her. Damn shame.

"Use security even during the day. I don't like you being here alone. Are you sure you don't want me to come in?" Oliver sounded concerned, not sexy. Well, not deliberately sexy.

"I'm fine. Like Jefferina said, this job gets me off the street and away from the places I can usually be found. No one will be looking for me here. Now go find shelter before it gets ugly."

"Don't do anything heroic, Macayla."

"You mean like walk the dog?"

"Shit. I can do that for you."

Macayla turned back to face the front doors and could

see his car idling on the street. "If you so much as place one booted foot on the drive, Kelly, I'm cutting you off. Forever."

He chuckled. It was a low dirty chuckle and made all her lady parts tingle. "You've got until tomorrow. Did I tell you the clock's running on my visit?"

"No." Her heart gave a funny quiver.

"I just turned down the second job I've been offered since I flew in."

"Where do they need you?"

"Actually, it's local tonight. I'm on an Internet loop that allows professional search-and-rescue groups to know my location at any given time. That's how they found me. The local SAR groups are checking with one another just in case they're needed during or after the storm. I told them I'm busy."

"Why did you do that?"

He paused so long she thought the line had gone dead. "You're in trouble, Macayla. You might need help. I can help."

Not exactly a declaration of anything. But what could she expect? They may have smashed private parts together with lusty enthusiasm several times, but that didn't make a relationship. Yet he was turning down work to stay here. Did she seem that needy, or out of her depth? Or worse, was he feeling sorry for her? Pity was the worst.

"I'm not in trouble tonight. You saw the spec sheet on the alarm system in this place. Monitors and cameras. I'm afraid to scratch for fear it's being recorded. Please call back and see if they could use your help—and Jackeroo's."

"You wouldn't feel deserted or anything?"

"I'd be relieved that you're doing something important instead of knocking around in a boring hotel room." Or sitting in a bar attracting every woman with your eyes. "Go. Be useful."

"You're the best, Macayla."

With that thought keeping her company, Mac went to look out the windows at the bay.

The water was choppy with whitecaps, reflecting a lead-gray sky. The wind had yet to gain strength but intermittent rain spattered the patio and decks, dimpling the surface of the pool that took up a huge chunk of the backyard. It was a saltwater pool, she remembered from her paperwork. Beyond the bay itself, lightning flickered like a shorted bulb in the western sky.

A private dock with both a boat lift and a Jet Ski lift completed the backyard amenities. *Just what every house needs*, she thought with a chuckle. Of course, there was nothing to lift today, with a storm making headway toward land. Usually the bay was dotted with sailboats and tracked with water-skiers. At the moment, nothing rode the waves but a few brave terns and pelicans.

The rest of the huge outdoor living space was furnished with teak lounge chairs, an outdoor dining table for six, and wicker couches under a gazebo the size of her entire house. She hoped the furnishings were anchored because when the wind picked up, she wouldn't be chasing lawn furniture in sixty-mile-an-hour gusts.

In fact, it dawned on her as she picked up her damp things to go in search of a towel with which to dry off that the lightning and power of the bad weather to come would be impossible to get away from. The entire back of the house was made of the same floor-to-ceiling windows. Even the doors were mostly glass.

Not a single blind covered a window. The sheer drapes hung between wide expanses of glass wouldn't keep out sights or sounds when closed. No wonder a family with small children had left for a more ordinary hotel's solid walls and blackout curtains.

Once dried off with a towel from the master bath, she moved to the windows of the bedroom, drawn by the telescope that, once peeked through, allowed an up-close-and-personal view of the water and the neighbors on the far side of the bay. It occurred to her that while she could see the bay in practically every direction, there wasn't going to be a lot of protection from the effects of the storm. She would have a front row seat to the lightning, rain, and bay surge.

As a kid she'd hidden in her closet with a flashlight when thunderstorms rolled through. Now she loved them, but maybe not quite this much. She felt exposed.

She backed away from the telescope, wondering how many of them across the bay were focused in her direction. The sense of being in a fishbowl increased. She was isolated, now that she thought of it. If someone wanted to get to her—

"Get to me?" She thumped her forehead with her palm. No one would even guess to look for her here. She hadn't known she'd be here three hours ago.

Just because her place had been broken into and—what was the opposite of robbed? Cash-infused? There was no reason to think her every move was being stalked. She was safe. The only way for anyone to get into this place was through a security gate or the choppy bay that would be churning up into scary very soon. Besides, the system was monitored. Any sign of a break in the grid and the police would be called in.

Just to satisfy herself that that this was true, she checked the security system again. It was the cautious thing to do. It had nothing to do with the paranoia that was her constant companion now.

She really did need to settle down and do her job. That meant finding and caring for the animals. Where were they? She'd never entered a place with dogs and not heard them barking from the first crack of the door.

She dropped the towel and bolted through the door toward the main house, ashamed that she'd gotten caught up in worrying about herself when there were animals that needed her help and protection.

She found the two dogs, Mal and Zoe, huddled in their crates in the kitchen.

She grabbed their leashes from the top of their crates, then bent down and opened the doors. "Sorry, guys. Really sorry."

A pair of mixed-breed dogs, some Lab, some something else, they were very *very* happy to see her. In fact, they did a little pee dance around her before she could leash and usher them out onto the rain-soaked deck. Served her right for making them wait. For the moment, the rain had stopped. But the bank of clouds swirling up from the south promised much more, and soon.

Mac looked around. The outdoor area was tiled from the house to the seawall. No grass in sight. "No. No. Come on. Mal. Zoe." She tugged on the leashes as the dogs were doing the circle-to-squat dance. She wasn't sure poop would stain the outdoor tile but she didn't want to be the one to explain it if it did.

She finally found a patch of grass, thanks to the dogs leading her over behind the gazebo near the seawall. This must be their regular spot. The splash of bay got her twice before they'd done their business. Tomorrow she would have to walk them outside the property, pooper scooper in hand.

Lightning flashed close enough to make her blink. Terrified by the flash, Mal and Zoe froze like deer. The accompanying rumble of thunder made them bolt for the house, tugging her in their wake. Poor babies. No wonder they were shivering when she found them.

An hour later, her charges had been fed, played with, and walked again, this time under storm-darkened skies that leaked rain. But they had no interest in relieving themselves. She moved their crates into the laundry room, the only room in the house she'd found that didn't have a wall of windows. She couldn't keep out the thunder but they didn't cringe with every flash.

Satisfied that they were good for the night, she checked her instruction sheet. There was a cat named Ninja. Look for in upstairs bedroom, the instructions said.

She was at the top of the stairs when something moved at the corner of her vision. Heart jumping from first to fifth gear, she turned toward the movement.

A cat emerged from the nearby doorway. The fluffy black Persian feline was not in a good mood. Back arched, tail down, it came skipping across the travertine floor toward her at an angle, hissing and yowling, spoiling for a fight.

"Hi, Ninja." Macayla held still, knowing she'd get clawed if she bent to try to pet it.

Three times the cat came at her then skittered away, as if Mac were pursuing it. But she remained where she was. When Ninja tired of that game, Mac reached in her pocket and pulled out a small toy mouse made of yarn with a jingle bell in its middle. She lobbed it gently to land halfway between them.

The kitty paused to watch the toy jingle its way across the floor. After it lay still for several seconds, Ninja pounced. The mouse jingled. Ninja sprang back. Pounce. Jingle. Jump. Pounce. Grab. Shake. Jingle. Keep.

Ninja tossed it in the air a couple of times, shook it

twice, and turned to walk away, tail loose and squishing as he wandered off.

"Yes! Final point goes to the Pet Detective." Macayla gave herself a fist pump as the Ninja carried her prize off. The phone rang somewhere deep in the house as she finished up cleaning the cat box. It was still ringing when she located the landline in the kitchen.

"Hello. Um, this is the fish guy, Roland." He sounded like a teenager whose voice was still changing.

"Yes. You were supposed to be here—" Macayla checked her paperwork. "—three hours ago."

"So, like, I can't be there today."

"Not an option. I know nothing about saltwater tanks except that they have to be serviced daily. That means today."

"Like I so know that? But the po-po picked me up on a totally bogus charge, and I'm, like, waiting on some righteous bail money to come in."

Macayla opened her mouth to blast him for the bullshit routine, but he kept talking.

"I'll walk you through it. There's a sheet of instructions under the table that holds the biggest tank. We keep it there for emergencies."

Emergencies that included arrests, Macayla supposed. She found the sheet. Under DAILY it read: *Check fish for signs of stress, disease, or death.*

"Death." Macayla rolled her eyes as she held the phone in one hand and lifted the lid. Death would be obvious. She bent down and checked the waterline for floaters. Then the bottom. Nothing lying unnaturally still. "No deaths."

"Now look for disease."

She leaned in over the top wondering what a diseased fish looked like. "Anybody in there got a cough? Feeling achy? Runny nose?"

She heard Roland try to laugh and choke on it. She peered in deeper, looking for broken fins or great abnormal growths distorting the menagerie swimming past her view. "Nope."

"Awesome. Now stress. That's a real bitch for marine life in the home environment."

Mac sighed. Stress was a silent killer, everyone knew that. No fish dead equaled no fish truly stressed. Unless it was that little yellow one hiding under the coral boulder. He looked pretty stressed. Eyes bulgy. Fins flicking nervously. Oh yeah. Fish.

Following Roland's next instructions, she checked the temperature and tested the water, marking down her findings.

Finally it was time to feed them. It was not a pretty job. Frozen bloodworms. Briny shrimp. Freeze-dried jumbo krill. Algal wafers and sinking pellets.

By the time she was done, Mac was pretty certain sushi was off the menu for at least a month. Just as well, because she couldn't afford it.

The full brunt of the storm moved in after nightfall, buffeting the house with keening winds and the sounds of surf stirred like food in the blender.

Macayla managed to tune out most of it. Dinner consisted of a cold chicken sandwich she'd made from leftover barbecue in the fridge. After eating three bites, she realized she wasn't really hungry. Nor was she interested in anything on the TV. The main channels were full of Doppler radar images of the storm, while nothing on the cable channels looked even remotely interesting. She checked the doors and walked the dogs again, though neither of them was interested in performing their duties in gale force conditions. She put them in their crates and hoped for the best.

Finally, after prowling around like a cat, she found a CD of *Up* in the DVD player and settled in to watch the adventures of a widower, a fatherless boy, and a dog named Dug. But it was not easy to keep her gaze on the screen when the storm surrounding the house was louder and brighter.

She was propped up in bed in the upstairs second master suite when she finally gave in and texted Oliver. *When I get rich enough, this is the 1st thing I'm buying. Memory foam mattress should be an inalienable right.*

Then she held her breath, wondering if he would be able to read her message. He'd said he had some help over the years. Two miserable non-self-empowering minutes passed before she got a reply. *Don't u need a car 1st?*

She smiled so hard she was glad no one was there to witness it. *I need this mattress. I'd do wicked things 4 this mattress.*

I have that mattress.

No u don't.

Will have as soon as doors open to Mattress World tomorrow.

U don't have a place to put it.

It can live at ur house. Plan to get wicked by sundown.

This is a three day job, at least, remember?

Ur place or that place. I got dibs on the mattress.

She laughed, really genuinely happy for the first time in a long time. *Be careful out there. I'm all tucked in.*

I will.

Oliver hung up and leaned his car seat back as far as it would go. Then he twisted until he'd settled his shoulders against the back. Jackeroo had climbed into the front seat and lay his head on his handler's stomach. As lightning flashed, lighting up the car like a lantern, Jackeroo whimpered.

"Easy, boy. We've ridden out worse." Of course, he might have thought about getting a heavier vehicle if he'd known he'd be keeping vigil in it while out in a storm. Right now they were rocking and rolling as the wind boxed with the chassis.

He leaned forward and checked the security gate of the house in which Macayla slept. He was certain she was safe. But he didn't trust himself to be far away if she wasn't. That's why he was parked across the street.

Macayla would be mad as hell if she knew what he was doing. That's why he didn't tell her. His gut was queasy, a sign that something wasn't right. He didn't know what or why. That's why he and Jackeroo were here. Just in case.

The wind had died down. That's why she heard the hum of the engine. A boat on the water.

"What an idiot," Macayla murmured, finding herself moored in the memory foam mattress beneath her. She didn't bother to open her eyes. The Coast Guard must be checking to see if residents along the bay were safe.

Please keep the first responders safe was her last thought before drifting back into unconsciousness.

CHAPTER TWENTY-FIVE

It was the clicking sounds across the travertine floor that woke Macayla. They reminded her of little taps on a door with a key. Only she was alone.

Supposed to be alone.

Heart thumping loudly in her chest, she sat up, reaching for her phone with one hand and her pepper spray with the other. She debated whether or not to turn on a light. To do so would give away her position to an intruder.

Intruder. Her heart accelerated.

Be logical, her mind told her scaredy-cat heart. She hadn't heard the alarm go off. And she was certain she'd set it because she'd checked three times.

Maybe one of the dogs had gotten out of its crate. Yes, that must be it. Mal or Zoe was wandering around, doggy nails clicking across the floor below. Might even be Ninja kitty. No, cats retracted their claws to walk. Dog. It was a dog.

Just as she was about to reach for the light, the clicking stopped.

She held her breath, straining for sound. She could hear the surf on the bay lashing the seawall. The rumble of thunder had abated. The storm was taking a time-out. The glow of the reflected city was too weak to penetrate far into the room, because the windows had become cloudy from condensation and streaked rain. But gradually things came into focus as her eyes adjusted.

If a loose dog chewed the furniture, or peed on a pillow, she could see her salary for this gig going back into cleaning fees. She should check on the dogs.

Click. Click. Click.

Her breath hitched in her throat. This time the sound was coming up the main stairs. And they weren't doggy steps. This was the two-legged variety.

The hair on her body lifted as she slipped off the memory foam, no small accomplishment on a mattress that clung like a lover. As her feet hit the chill tile she actually thought about hiding. There were six bedrooms on the second floor. Five chances for an intruder to miss finding her before she could summon help.

She punched 911 and put her finger over the sound. Maybe it would be enough for an intrepid emergency person to check the location of a cell that couldn't be answered.

A sudden gust of wind hit the house. And she ducked as if it were after her.

Click. Click. Click.

She could hear thunder again, a low rumbling like a distant train. They must be in the eye of the low. If lows had eyes, like hurricanes.

Click. Click. Click. An abrupt pause.

Mac held her breath, flipped the safety on her pepper spray, and stared at the open door to the bedroom she occupied.

"Ms. Burkett?"

The inquiry came through the dark in an impatient tone of voice. A man's light tenor voice looking for someone he considered slightly inferior. Boss to underling. Homeowner to maid.

Macayla bit her lip until she tasted blood. Someone was inside this house. Who? Was the renter back despite the storm? No one else knew she was here. That absolutely wasn't Oliver's voice issuing from the hallway.

"Ms. Macayla Burkett!"

A tall figure stepped into the dimly lit doorway of the bedroom. And for the first time in her life, Macayla understood why a person might want to have a gun in her bedside table drawer. Not that she had the guts to use one. But the idea was oddly comforting in a dreadful sort of way. "Macayla Burkett?"

Macayla realized that just as her eyes had adjusted to the gloom, her intruder's probably had as well. And in the glow from the night sky she could be seen standing by the bed. "Stop. I have pepper spray."

"Cute." Lightning flashed, outlining the figure. The silhouette was familiar. Too familiar. Even without the infrared enhancement, the tall figure with short hair and jacket clicked into place in her mind. Then a second bolt of brilliance slid briefly along an object clutched in the figure's hand. *Gun.*

The lights came on.

Blinking against the sudden brightness, Macayla tried to pull the world together. A woman stood before her dressed in a buttoned-up anorak rain jacket shedding water on the floor. She glanced again at the gun the woman held, not expecting it to be there. This was a mistake. Her brain was overreacting to memory stimuli that had nothing to do with the moment. "Mrs. Henley?"

The woman nodded. "So you do remember me." Not a man's voice after all.

"What are you doing here?"

"This is one of the homes owned by Stinton Vacation Properties, my family's business. We've been in real estate in Tampa for fifty years. I specialize in vacation rentals. The interior design is mine. Do you like the house?" She sounded honestly curious. As if she were holding a good bottle of wine for an invited guest—instead of a gun.

Macayla couldn't take her eyes off it. The only sane thought that came to mind was, "Nice. Very nice." Except that her adrenaline level was so over the top from the woman's sudden appearance that she was close to wetting the floor.

Obviously, Mrs. Henley had access to all her properties. Maybe she was checking them for problems. In the middle of a stormy night? Okay, crazy person move, but not her problem to solve.

She made an effort to smile. "Why are you here?" Had she screwed up the alarm and sent a silent message to the property owners? "Is there a problem?"

"Yes. There's a problem." The woman wiped at her wet face with her free hand. "Why couldn't you have found my dogs in time? That would have saved everyone so much trouble."

"I don't understand. And would you mind lowering that gun? It's making me very nervous."

Mrs. Henley didn't bother to smile. "Put down your canister first."

Mac sucked in a slow breath. *Disarm.* That's what she meant. The reasons why that wasn't a good idea didn't even have to be thought through for Mac to come to the conclusion that giving up her only defense was a nonstarter. At least until she understood more.

Her hand tightened around her pepper spray can. "Is there a problem with the house that brought you out to-night?"

"I hired your agency to bring home my greyhounds. But you didn't."

Mac swallowed the inclination to scream, *What the fuck's wrong with you, lady? It's two a.m. Call during business hours if you have a complaint!*

But the gun kept drawing her eye. A gun has a way of shaping the conversation. The need to remain polite seemed suddenly to be very, *very* important.

Mac couldn't find a smile, however. "I'm sorry, Mrs. Henley, but they were already dead when I found them."

"I know." She sniffed, but her expression remained calm. "Still, why don't you tell me about that night?"

Macayla wondered how much the woman already knew. "Where is Mr. Henley?" Downstairs?

"Screw him. I'm divorcing that bastard. He told me he'd bring my babies back home but I was right not to trust him. Turns out *he* took them. That soul-sucking prick!"

Macayla froze. Nothing was making sense. Her mouth had gone dry, leaving her tongue feeling thick and useless.

Mrs. Henley seemed to need to fill in the silence. "I'd put a lot of money into growing my own bloodlines. Those dogs were the proof of my success. After winning a big race I was going use them as breeding stock. Start my own business and go up against Henley Kennels after I left him. That's why Jarvis stole my beauties. He wanted to make sure I didn't win the biggest race of the season and show him up. Because of him my perfect animals were destroyed."

Stall for time. That's all she could think of. And hope that the 911 call had gone through. She'd pushed the END

CALL button in case the woman noticed her holding the phone. "That was pretty vindictive."

"Oh, Jarvis is an accomplished liar. He brought me the note and tried to pretend he was willing to pay the ransom but said it would take time. By then it would be too late for me to get them back for the race. But I called in the police and his hands were tied."

"I don't understand what this has to do with me."

Mac's question refocused Mrs. Henley's thoughts. "You were there the night they were found. You witnessed something. Tell me about that."

How did she know about— "Nothing important. I mean nothing worth—"

The woman lifted the gun muzzle a fraction. "You told my husband there's video proof of a shooting."

The world stopped spinning.

Fuck.

Macayla's mind hopscotched across her memories of that night. She'd been certain the infrared images had been of two men. One stocky in a hoodie. The other in a suit. Tall. Short hair. Suit. Click-clicking sounds of boot heels!

Clicks! They were part of the few sounds on the video. The police thought they were taps that some men wore to keep their heels from wearing down. But what if they weren't made by men's shoes?

Her gaze slipped down to Mrs. Henley's feet. She wore Top-Siders, a unisex shoe. Her eyes flew up to the short wet hair plastered to the woman's head. The footsteps coming toward her that night might have been made by a woman.

Macayla's vision blurred. A sudden chill threatened to buckle her knees. She took an instinctive step back from the bed. No point in being coy about her fear.

"Stop." Mrs. Henley leveled the barrel at Macayla's midsection. "Don't move again. I don't want to hurt you."

Macayla stopped in her tracks. "Maybe we should include your husband in this conversation."

"No!" It was the wail of a woman in pain. One whose gun wobbled as she cut off a sob. "I didn't go there to hurt him. I just wanted my dogs back."

She really cared about her dogs. Macayla grabbed onto that slender lifeline. "I understand how you feel, Mrs. Henley. No, really. I lost my dog a year ago."

She blinked. "How?"

Macayla shoved down sentiment. No time to indulge her emotions when her life was on the line. "A madman shot her. He shot my Katie." *And me.* But now was not the time to give this person any ideas.

"Did you want to kill him?"

"No. Maybe. I only know I had to get Katie to the vet. The police took care of the shooter."

Memory flashed clear as she spoke. *Katie had leaped over her as she'd covered the girl with her own body.* This was her first memory of that snippet of the event. Had Katie done it out of a sense of play, or for protection? She'd never know. But it helped to remember.

Mrs. Henley shut her eyes briefly, visibly pulling herself together. "It was an accident. After three days of searching the police gave up. That's why I called you people in. I couldn't just leave my dogs to waste away in the hands of the thieves. When I told Jarvis what I'd done, he went ballistic. He confessed that he'd arranged for my dogs to be taken. He promised me that they were in the best of care. Our head groomer, Nico, was looking after them. But I didn't trust him. I demanded that he tell me where they were."

Macayla thought she was just about out of rungs on the fear ladder. But with that statement, Sara Henley had added a few more. Confessing to murder, that's what she was doing. And that was a very bad sign.

Macayla backed up another step. "I'm sorry I didn't find them in time."

Sara Henley sucked in a breath. "By the time I found Nico it was too late. He didn't even apologize for what he'd done. He was angry, demanded more money. He said the dogs were making too much noise and the neighbors were getting nosy. With the publicity in the papers, he was afraid to move them. Jarvis wasn't answering his texts, so after three days he put them down. Can you imagine? Champion dogs put down like mangy curs?"

Macayla was imagining how once a person killed it might be easier to do it a second time. "I swear I didn't know it was you who—" Maybe it was better not to finish that sentence.

"Don't be cute. I knew you were there that night. At least I was suspicious. It was all over the papers the next day how you found my dogs. But there were no reports of a shooting. After a few days I decided you hadn't seen enough to make you dangerous. But then you decided to talk to Jarvis about the video." The gun moved erratically. "What do you want? Money?"

"No, I don't—"

"You must have thought you could milk us." She came closer, still blocking the only escape. "That's a crime, you know. Extortion."

Macayla digested this new information, and anger flushed through her. "But there is no body, so no crime." She could have bitten her tongue off. But the fear was wearing off and a weird kind of exasperation was taking its place.

She nodded. "Jarvis is good for some things. I called him to meet me after the, ah, accident. He took care of things. But one never knows what might turn up here or there."

Macayla shuddered. A man's life reduced to here-or-there remains. Chilling.

"I don't want money, Mrs. Henley. And I don't care what you did. The police have no evidence. The video shows nothing clearly. It's just a blurry infrared video. We all thought it was a man."

"Don't lie."

"It's the truth. But you should know that you can't get rid of me as easily as you did Nico. People know I'm here tonight. You can't explain away my disappearance."

"You'd be surprised what I can do. My dad always said a smart person could get away with anything, as long as there are no eyewitnesses."

The cell phone in her hand suddenly buzzed, a sound so unexpected that Macayla dropped it in surprise.

"Leave it. You don't need it."

"I take my phone everywhere." The snappish answer was a sure sign to Macayla that she was about to lose it big time. "I want my phone." She bent over to pick it up.

"Touch it and I'll drop you here and worry about the rest later."

Macayla froze, assaulted by a memory as clear as the reality before her. The shot. The sound. The burning pain.

She jerked upright. "What do you want?"

"Come downstairs with me." The pistol indicated the doorway.

"Where are we going?"

"Downstairs." She pointed the gun at Macayla's middle.

A tremor began at her knees. Dammit. She could feel the old horror climbing up her spine as they descended the stairway. Did not want to be shot. Again.

Mac's thoughts went into overdrive as they moved through the dark house. Not always delivering things to her advantage.

Never go anywhere isolated with your attacker. Better to stand your ground and fight.

That was the standard principle of every self-defense class. Except that fighting required having an equal chance. Gun versus body was not a fair fight. And she was already in an isolated location.

If I'm shot inside, the mess it would make would make it easier for the police to solve my murder, some insane part of Macayla's brain delivered up.

The rest of her mind, the sane part, was weighing the odds of her getting away without being shot at all. A boat perhaps?

Run for it. The house was huge. She could hide long enough to make a call. If she had her phone. Or could reach the one in the kitchen. Or knew which doors in the house had locks on them.

Go on the offensive. She could try her luck at tackling her opponent. Being so much shorter, she might even be able to catch Sara low on her hips and knock her flat on her back. But then what? Grapple for the gun? She noticed that Sara held the gun with authority, as if she was accustomed to using it. Mac had never shot a handgun.

Shot. Yes.

"Open the back door. Move. Now."

"Yes." She was moving. Opening the back door.

"Outside." Sara Henley had to shout the last word.

The wind enveloped Macayla in a cool mist as she stepped outside. The heat of the day had been sucked out of the night by the storm.

That's when she saw it, the boat tied to the end of the pier. She spun around. "Where are we going?" Macayla planted her feet.

"Get. In. There." With each word, Mrs. Henley prodded her in the middle with the gun muzzle.

Something came over Macayla, something dark and ugly, shrouding her thoughts in the most primitive urge to survive. She swung around and then back, grabbing the gun muzzle in both hands.

The gun went off.

She was falling.

She didn't ever hit water.

She'd toppled over into the bottom of the boat. Her head connected with something hard.

CHAPTER TWENTY-SIX

Oliver jerked awake, uncertain what had startled him until he saw that Jackeroo had come to full alert and was staring at the house. That meant his partner had seen or heard something.

He checked the front first. The security lights were still on so there'd been no loss of power. The gate was still closed. From what he could see, nothing stirred within. All windows were dark.

"What do you hear, old man?" He sat up, stroking his partner. Then he realized it was really quiet. The wind had died to mere breaths of energy. Rain was now a soft drizzle that silently ran down the car windows. The distant flickers of lightning no longer seemed a threat. It felt as if the night was exhausted, or taking a time-out.

He scotched the impulse to text Macayla. She would probably tear him a new one for waking her. He really did wish she had let him stay with her. Too many things were going on that pointed to trouble, though he couldn't tell from which direction yet.

This strange new feeling of wanting to be with her constantly hadn't eased since he'd come back to St. Petersburg. It wasn't just the carnal hunger she aroused in him. That was good, yeah. But Macayla's company was good, too.

A line from an old-school song ran through his thoughts. He couldn't quite pull it together. Something about wanting to make love with one's clothes on. It had never made sense to him before. But being with Macayla made him feel damn close to that emotion. When she touched him, just the easiest gesture, it registered all the way down to his dick. He didn't need to be balls-deep inside her to feel the connection that had always eluded him outside the bedroom, backseat, beach, wherever he'd loved a woman. With Macayla any and everything was entertaining. Happiness was as simple as watching a smile develop on her cute face. Hers was the nicest face he'd ever seen.

But he needed to be careful. The emotions so new to him were bursting out of him. He'd made a mistake earlier today when she'd asked him why he was turning down work. He'd recovered enough to say it was because she was in trouble. He saw that that's not what she wanted to hear. But the real answer was more intimidating, for him.

I think you might be the most important relationship in my life since I fell for Sharon Jumbuck when I was twelve, that time we went to Alice Springs.

That was pathetic, even if it was true. He didn't want to scare her off. They'd spent less than four full days in each other's company. But he wasn't going to skip out on whatever this was until he figured out whatever this was. And that was going to take time, and effort, and tenaciousness.

He looked at Jackeroo. "We need to buy property in St. Petersburg. Yeah?"

Jackeroo tilted his head to one side, his concentration broken for the moment.

"Yeah, that sounds way too stalker-y at this point. Keep Macayla out of jail. First priority. House shopping later. Maybe next week."

Jackeroo's ears suddenly pricked forward and he stood up, facing the house.

That's when Oliver heard it. The sound that Jackeroo, with his better hearing, had probably been tracking for several minutes. The distant sound of a boat on the bay. It was coming their way, humming in the dark like an annoying mosquito.

The engine sounded too light to be the Coast Guard or marine police. More likely a sport boat. Who was out on a night like this? Some young fool. Those who knew coastal weather would know better than to go out in a small boat after a major storm, when the bay would remain rough for hours after. Add in the darkness and the jackass was risking an accident. Or worse, drowning.

Just when he thought about getting out to check on where it was headed, the motor died.

Jackeroo sat down, his paws dancing impatiently on the seat.

"You need a walk?" Oliver reached for the leash then thought better of it. No one would care about a bit of poop on a lawn. In weather like this it would be washed away.

He opened the door and let Jackeroo out. The rain didn't seem quite as light once he was out in it. He whistled to his partner for a walk, hoping to get it over quickly.

But Jackeroo had other ideas. The shepherd ran over to the security gate and stood, staring through the bars.

"What's up? You missing Macayla, too? Come on. I'm getting soaked. We'll find a way to get her to let us stay tomorrow." But as he turned away, a light went on upstairs.

He paused. Macayla making a middle-of-the-night bathroom run? Probably.

But Jackeroo began to whine and paw the gate. Not like him to be needlessly concerned.

Oliver stood and stared at the light from a single window. And he waited. Finally he saw a shadow move past. Tall and thin. Not Macayla.

Jackeroo began to bark, sharp sounds of alarm.

Oliver waited, uncertain of what to do. Then he pulled out his phone and called Macayla's number. The phone rang and rang. But no answer.

Something was wrong. Jackeroo knew it before he did. But he had no idea what it could be. He started to press the security code to the gate she'd given him but realized that it would be heard within the house. If something serious was wrong, he didn't want to tip off anyone that he was here.

Instead, he reached own and lifted Jackeroo up to the top of the stucco wall, then hoisted himself up and vaulted over. He lifted Jackeroo down.

"Quiet." He gave his partner the *no bark* hand sign.

Jackeroo moved quickly but quietly to the pair of glass front doors.

Oliver reached them in time to see Macayla walking past and then a second figure followed. Tall, dressed for the weather. Short hair. A man. But it was the silhouette of a hand holding a gun that sent his heart into overdrive.

Something raw and powerful swept through him. He didn't know how or why. But the details didn't matter at the moment. Someone had gotten to Macayla. The boat! That's what Jackeroo had heard. The intruder must have come from the bay, the only way that wasn't guarded by security.

He pulled out his phone and called 911, asking to be

patched through to the city's marine police. His words were simple. *Abduction. By boat.* He gave the location. *Hurry.*

His hands tightened into fists as he resisted punching in the code to the door. The noise would alert the man on the inside to Oliver's presence. He watched, drawing careful breaths until they reached the back door. They were going out into the night.

He gritted his teeth and waited. A guy with a gun would be nervous. He didn't want Macayla shot because he acted too soon. But sweat popped on his upper lip, and his teeth lost a fair amount of enamel as he watched them exit onto the patio. He didn't have a weapon but he'd find something once he was through the door. Kitchens were always good for a nice sharp blade.

The minute they were outside, he punched in the code, heard the beep, and was through the door.

Lightning reflected on the water gave the great room its only illumination, but beyond the windows he could see Mac and her abductor talking. No, arguing.

And then Macayla was lunging for the gun.

A coarse cry tore from Oliver's throat as lightning flashed.

He thought he heard a shot but it was too late. Macayla had disappeared off the edge of the pier.

He tore thought the house as the man jumped into the boat and cast off.

He yelled a warning as he reached the beginning of the pier, but the boat had roared to life and was moving away.

Something squeezed tight inside him as he looked out over the water. Had Macayla gone in, or was she on the boat? He didn't know.

Then he realized Jackeroo was no longer beside him. Had he leaped into the water after Macayla?

It took him two agonizing seconds to notice that the dark hump at the back of the fast-disappearing boat was Jackeroo.

"Shit."

CHAPTER TWENTY-SEVEN

Macayla dimly heard and felt the boat's inboard motor purring. She hadn't completely lost consciousness. But all she could do was lie sprawled between contour seats and gulp water splashing into her face by fresh rain. Another wave of murky storm clouds rushed by overhead. Her pajama tank and bottoms were soaked through.

It took a few more seconds to realize she wasn't tied up or chained or anything. Nor was she dead. She opened her eyes.

Sara Henley was at the controls, one hand on the steering wheel, the other still clutching the gun. So much for disarming her opponent.

Macayla closed her eyes as the boat gained speed, the front of the hull rising out of the water as storm-tossed waves slapped underneath, jolting the boat in hard thuds that jarred her teeth. Was something broken or had she been wounded? She curled her hands into fists, then tried to move each leg just a little. Nothing seemed injured.

Except her back. It hurt like everything. Something dug into her left shoulder but that wasn't a problem. She was alive.

She lay there, trying to gather her strength and not choke on the rain that began falling harder and harder. The wind was rising again as the lightning gathered in intensity.

She'd have only one chance. One chance to bolt upright and launch herself at the woman behind the wheel. After that it was a matter of controlling the gun. Getting it out of her hand. Tossing it overboard. A lot of coordinated effort for a body she wasn't sure could stay upright at the moment.

She sat up, eyes on the woman ahead of her. But Sara was no longer paying attention as the boat cut across open water. She was running the boat without lights. Not wanting to be seen. Dangerous for a boat running at minimum speed. Suicidal for everyone but an expert who knew the bay's every secret.

A foghorn sounded very close as lights flared ahead of them, brilliant beams that raked the smaller boat they were in.

"Tampa Bay Marine Patrol. Ahoy!" The words blasted across the water. "Cut your engines. Repeat. Cut your engines."

A second foghorn sounded, impossible to ignore. A big boat, a Coast Guard vessel this time, brought up its lights and appeared out of the gloom on their left.

"Help me. Help!" Macayla was certain she said the words. But they were ripped away by the wind. And then the sight of the rescue boat vanished as the boat she was in made a sudden lurch.

Under the glare of patrol boat lights, Macayla looked around to see the woman had spun the wheel to the right and was pushing the throttle to full power.

"No. No. Stop!" The boat continued at horrifying speed,

plunging them again into darkness as the boat plowed black water and drenched them with incoming seas.

"Stop! You'll kill us!"

Macayla grabbed at the handrails on the side of the boat as she slowly made her way toward the starboard side where Sara was at the controls. She could see Sara's outline as she fought to keep the boat under control with both hands.

Both hands.

Macayla launched herself at the woman, using both her arms to form a band to trap Sara's arms at her sides. She had no plan but to wrench her from the controls.

It happened so fast she never even knew what happened first. One second they were motoring through the darkness as the opposite shore drew steadily larger. The next they collided with something underneath the boat. It stopped the vessel so abruptly that Macayla's grip was ripped loose as both she and Sara were tossed upward.

Once at summer camp she'd jumped off a water-ski ramp, soaring suddenly upward, too late to turn back. This felt like that. Except. She wasn't wearing skis, or holding on to the towrope, and she wasn't going to land gracefully.

Macayla was in the water. The waves were slapping at her cheeks like a dozen chilled hands. She must have blacked out for a few seconds after they hit something, a jetty. A buoy. A sandbar. But now she was fully alert in the darkness, with the wind keening in her ears and the salt water of the bay heaving in and around her.

She heard a cry. A woman's voice, howling above the sounds of the storm.

Macayla squashed the impulse to answer back. Even in the darkness with the deadly push–pull of the rough water around her, she feared being found by Sara Henley.

She tossed her head, trying to hear the direction of the sound, but was dunked by a wave she could not see rushing in to break over her. She came up sputtering seawater. Her eyes stung from salt and sand stirred up from the bottom by the storm. In the distance she could see two boats with lights on high moving steadily her way. But she didn't cry out for help. The fear was back, and stronger than ever.

Sara Henley was out here somewhere in the black water with her.

Don't panic. Panic will drown you. She remembered the words from her first swim instructor. Tread water. Even dogs and cats can tread water.

No need to fear anything. The Coast Guard was on the way. She would be rescued as long as she stayed afloat.

That's when she saw the lights of the marine vessels swing away. Oh god! They'd lost sight of their little boat.

She heard Sara cry out again, this time a little closer.

Mac felt her lungs fill to echo that cry but didn't. Who would hear them in the storm? Did she dare answer?

Surely Sara, who must be in the water as she was, had lost her gun when the boat struck something and tossed them overboard. Even if she'd managed to hang on to the weapon, it would have to be waterlogged by now, and ineffective.

Macayla gulped a mouthful of salt water as a wave hit her, only to spit it out. She knew so little about guns. They didn't mix with water. But how long before that was true? Maybe she should strike out on her own.

She swung her head right and left, looking for any sight of land that would give her a clue to her location. The only lights she could see between being dunked by whitecaps were at a distance. The shoreline. The patrol boats were running parallel to the shore, slowly moving farther away.

It's okay. You're okay. She'd been a strong swimmer all

her life. She should be able to make it to shore. But this was different. Every muscle in her body ached. Just staying afloat in the choppy water was costing her precious energy. Distances were deceptive in the dark. She didn't know if she could swim that far. Or if she had the strength to counter the current that seemed to be running beneath her at a crosscurrent with the shore.

Sara Henley cried out again, weaker this time. Maybe she was hurt.

The instinct to help rose up in Macayla, surprising her. It wasn't goodness, or bravery, or any finer feeling. It was the basic gut-level response to someone in trouble. Even if that someone had planned to murder her.

Macayla ignored the impulse. And then felt something splashing in the water near her. Shark? Porpoise? Sara?

She reached out to push it away until her hand met the furry muscularity of a dog. Dog? It licked her face and she gasped in surprise, all but submerging.

As she came to the surface something bumped her shoulder and then banged into the back of her skull so hard she saw stars and bit her tongue.

She fought to stay afloat, hand on the mysterious dog's collar, as something large prodded her again and again. She reached out to push it away and felt a hard heavy smoothness beneath her hands. Fiberglass. The boat. It lay dead in the water, its engines ripped by what it had hit.

She swore as it bounced away, only to rear up and nearly overtop her as it rode the waves pulsing on the storm winds. But she didn't swim away. It dawned on her that she, and the dog paddling beside her, would be safer out of the water than in it.

She remembered seeing in the light of the patrol boats that this boat had a flat surface at the rear called a swim platform. That's how they could board.

She floated alongside the behemoth in the dark, trying to get to the rear of the vessel. As she did so, she called to the dog in the water with her. "Here, boy. Heel. Good dog, heel."

As fantastical as it seemed, saving the dog became her first priority. And that gave her extra determination.

Finally, she reached the rear of the boat. Grappling with the bar across the back, she managed to get one foot up on the rear platform. The moment she did, a wave sent the boat rising high and fast.

This must be what it's like to ride a bull at the rodeo, she thought as she grimly held on. The next smack against the waves all but wrenched her arms from their sockets. But she wasn't going back in the water. Not if she could help it. Inside the boat. That was the only safe place.

She heaved and pulled, cursing like a sailor until she had one leg and half her torso on the platform.

She lay there, aware that at any moment she could be tossed off. But her energy was gone.

She may have passed out, or maybe she just closed her eyes. But the next sensation was that of being licked by a dog.

The lick surprised her and she opened her eyes to find Jackeroo swimming alongside the platform as he scrambled to get on board. She grabbed him by the collar and helped him up.

Only then did she realize that she could see because light was again shining down on her, from another boat.

She heard a splash and then someone was hoisting himself up on the platform beside her. She focused her eyes after what seemed a long time. Oliver was there, sitting beside her in a Coast Guard vest, his Aussie smile at full wattage.

"If you wanted to swim, you could have used the pool."

He touched her face very gently, as if she might shatter. "You okay?"

Mac tried to nod but her neck no longer seemed to work. "Sara Henley. She's out there."

Oliver turned and shouted something she didn't quite understand. But it didn't matter. Jackeroo had climbed up on her, to share his heat and hers. And Oliver was there. It was going to be okay. Really, really okay.

Macayla opened her eyes to a ceiling that looked oddly familiar. For the past twenty-four hours, whenever she'd opened her eyes it was to the ceiling of a hospital room. She hadn't wanted to stay but the emergency room doctor said she was exhausted, suffering from hypothermia, and had some bad scrapes from barnacles on her legs that would fester if not properly treated. And she'd swallowed far more salt water than was good for a person. So she stayed, and fretted about how to pay another enormous bill.

She sighed and turned her face to the window where a perfectly beautiful coastal day was happening on the other side of the glass. The storm had passed.

She knew from having been visited by the police and the Coast Guard that Sara Henley had been found, still in the boat. Though technically under arrest for kidnapping and murder, Sara was in worse shape than Macayla, having suffered several broken bones, and was currently in a room down the hall. She'd confessed to the police, so the charges would stick.

Macayla had corroborated what she could, giving the details of her kidnapping. And Sara's admission of Nico Nadella's death, though his body had not yet been discovered. She was allowed to speculate on a few things, like the Henleys' attempts to frame her for dognapping to discredit her and have her put in jail. She was assured that when things were sorted out, those charges would be dropped, too.

Someone knocked on her door. Oliver poked his head through. "Are you decent? Please tell me the answer's no."

Macayla smiled. "Can I go home now?"

He came through the door holding a huge gift bag, which he set on the floor by the bed. "Yes. I took care of everything."

"You." She felt her peaceful moment evaporate under his snarky smile. She put a hand on his chest to prevent him from kissing her when he leaned in. She knew what he'd done.

"You can't pay my bills."

"Why not?" He leaned in harder, pressing the full weight of his upper body against her hand. She took her hand away. Touching him was dangerous, no matter the reason.

"What do you call a woman who takes money from a man?"

"Lucky?"

She swatted at him but missed because her reflexes were still slow and he was fast. He leaned in and kissed her shoulder. "You're many things, Macayla, but a gold digger isn't one of them. I can afford it. I'm happy to do it."

She eyed him suspiciously. "You're wealthy, aren't you?"

"I don't know. I can't count, remember?"

This time she landed a fist on his ear.

"*Ow.* You're violent. I had no idea." He folded his fingers over hers, completely enveloping her hand in his.

"I only strike when you say really dumb things. You can so count. How rich are you?"

"Bill Gates wouldn't consider me rich."

"But I would. So, what else should I know about you?"

"I don't own a home." He leaned in and kissed her properly. "I do own three cars. And a motorcycle. Maybe two. Not sure anymore. I keep clothing on five continents because I hate packing. I work a lot. And I don't call anyplace home."

"That's pathetic."

"I know. So do you feel sorry for me? And let's not forget Jackeroo. He jumped on that boat with the desire to save you."

Though she'd heard the story of Oliver's attempt to save her, she still couldn't quite work out why his dog would leap aboard a strange boat. "He's crazier than you. Why would he do that?"

"I don't know. Jack's always liked the water. He probably thought you were going for a ride without him."

They both knew that wasn't true. Trying to save Jackeroo had probably given her the strength to save her own life. Still, if she went down that road, she'd start crying, and she'd been soggy enough to last a while.

She dredged up a smile for her gorgeous savior. "You brought the Coast Guard and Tampa Bay Marine Patrol. I suppose I do owe you both a debt."

Oliver grinned. "Does that mean you're offering me and my K-9 a space to call home? I have a brand-new memory foam mattress propped up in the hallway outside."

"I only have one good closet."

"Yeah, about that. Not enough, even for me. We'll have to move."

"I can't—"

He put a finger on her lips. "We can afford what we want. We both work. We share the load. Okay?"

"What about Jackeroo?"

"He's good as ever. Spent the night at the vet's. I needed to be here with you."

Macayla rolled her eyes. "You chose me over your partner?"

"Yes, well, he started it. Showing off his James Bond antics by leaping aboard. Girls love that shit. What's a poor ordinary fella like me to do?" The dimple appeared in his beard. "I brought you a gift."

He reached down into a big colorful bag that said GET WELL SOON on the side. He lifted out an animal.

It was a puppy. A silver Labrador puppy with a big blue bow around his neck.

"*Oooh!*" She reached for him with both hands and settled him on her tummy. "You shouldn't have brought a dog to the hospital. It's against the rules."

"Still a stickler for rules!" He sounded disgusted. "I thought it was time you got back in the business of having your own pet. What's a Pet Detective without one?"

"Silver Lab. They're expensive. I hope he's a rescue."

"Will you always be bringing up money? Because a woman who worries about a man spending too much money on her is—kinda cute. And to answer your question, yes. He was pulled from a raid on a puppy mill and flown in by a rescue group I've worked with in the past. He has some issues but the vet says with proper care, he'll be fine."

"I'm sorry I questioned you. It's a wonderful gift." She held the puppy up. "*He's* a wonderful gift."

Oliver glanced over at the door and then pulled back the covers and gathered her in his arms and set her on his lap, puppy and all. "I thought I'd lost you for a moment the other night. It felt like shit and I wanted to pull down the sky. Can you *not* do that again?"

"What?"

"Be brave and heroic. And wonderful?"

She didn't get to answer because he kissed her and the puppy smushed between them took exception and struggled up to lick her on the chin.

CHAPTER TWENTY-EIGHT

There were so many of them. Everywhere Macayla looked out across the expansive grounds of Harmonie Kennels she saw clusters of men and women in uniform.

There were police officers and sheriffs' deputies, state troopers, SWAT team members, and even firefighters, all in dress uniform. At the far end of the drive, a contingent of military people were emerging from a convoy of three Humvees. Many of them had K-9s in their arms or on leashes. Their alertness and responsiveness to their handlers signaled that these were professional K-9 teams.

Oliver had used words like *small* and *intimate* when describing the wedding he was inviting her to. Even so, she knew she'd feel out of place, especially among a tight group of friends. But he'd said that he wanted her to meet the most important people in his life. And who turned down a chance to meet the most important people in the life of someone you cared about?

He hadn't said anything about a wedding that included military and law enforcement maneuvers.

Now he wasn't even here to greet her.

She'd gotten a text when her flight arrived in Richmond, telling her that a last-minute problem had cropped up and he couldn't meet her flight. But he'd arranged for a rental car for her, and left her instructions for the drive to Harmonie Kennels. He said he'd be back in time for the wedding. Great.

As she stood indecisively next to her rented car, a contingent of three walked by with the letters FBI emblazoned on their backs. They were all headed toward a grassy area at the far end of the pasture where rows of white chairs formed two semicircles around a gazebo decorated with grapevines and deep-red flowers she couldn't recognize from this distance.

"Do you suppose the president is invited?" Macayla murmured under her breath as she cuddled her armful of Lab puppy. Security was tight enough.

The man at the gate had checked her credentials against his clipboard before offering her a smile. "Welcome, ma'am. Drive right through and park on the right wherever you find a place. Your packet contains all you need to know. Make yourself at home." He ended that little speech with a snappy military-type salute. Now she understood why. She was the only civilian she'd seen so far.

The packet included a seat assignment for both the service and the reception.

After another soothing pat and kiss on his velvet-soft head, she tucked Pickle back into his carrier and adjusted the windows to be certain he had enough air. She'd decided on the name Pickle for no reason other than it made her smile, and he responded to it. But she wasn't about to bring Pickle among the throng of shepherds, Malinois, and other large dogs strolling past. Even for Macayla, the sheer number and assortment of law enforcement personnel was intimidating. Poor little Pickle would be terrified of that alpha-dog K-9 gathering.

The day was warmish but not hot. It was safe for a dog in a car parked in the shade, as long as she kept checking on him.

Macayla blew out her breath as she joined the crowd walking in the direction of the gazebo. But her gaze kept straying to the old farmhouse, in pristine shape, and its surroundings tucked into the river valley of the Shenandoah Mountains. So this was the famed kennel. Even she knew a bit about it.

She'd been amazed when Oliver first told her who his best friend was marrying. Harmonie Kennels and Yardley Summers, the bride and part owner of the kennels, were K-9 legends. You didn't have to be a K-9 handler to know the name Yardley Summers. She even appeared on TV from time to time when an expert on K-9 teams was needed.

In the male-dominated field of K-9 law enforcement, Yardley Summers was both an enigma and a rock star. Rumor tagged her as everything from retired Special Ops to a sometimes still-operative spook. Oliver said she never admitted to any of that. But what she did have was access to the highest echelons of both the political and military arenas. One of the top K-9 law enforcement training facilities in the country, the business had been run for the past year by her half brother, Law Battise.

Macayla glanced around, hoping for a glimpse of her missing man friend. All she saw were groups of men who looked like they could be models in K-9 recruitment advertisements. Was it a requirement to be hot to be a K-9 officer? It sure seemed like it, if this was a representative sample. Oliver fit right in. As much as a man of his size and outrageous sexiness could. She'd bet a week's salary he sported the only man bun at the wedding.

3

That thought made her laugh out loud as she passed a group who smiled back at her in a totally appreciative male way that made her aware in every cell of her body that she was female. Wow. Just wow. She smiled but kept moving.

Walking more quickly, she passed buildings marked CLASSROOMS, BUNKHOUSE, and GYM. The sprawling facility included a dining hall, a series of canine training suites, and, farther on, barracks for handlers. Finally she passed the temperature-controlled low-roofed barn that served as the accommodation for the animals Harmonie Kennels bought and/or trained for law enforcement and the military.

No one seemed to be about so Macayla tried a door. It was unlocked; she stepped inside. Almost immediately she realized her mistake.

A woman stood just inside. She turned on Macayla with an expression that was anything but inviting.

"Who are you?"

Macayla stopped short. At five foot nine with long dark-red mahogany tresses and coal-black eyes, Yardley Summers was instantly recognizable though Macayla had only seen pictures of her. At the moment, her long-legged curviness was mostly hidden beneath military fatigues and a windbreaker. Still, there was no mistaking her for anyone else.

"You must be Yardley Summers. I'm Macayla." She held out her hand.

The taller woman didn't bother to shake hands. "What are you doing in my kennels?

"I'm sorry. I didn't know this area was off limits."

The woman folded her arms, giving Macayla a drill sergeant's penetrating stare. "I asked what you're doing here."

"I'm a guest at your wedding. Oliver Kelly invited me.

He's not here and I don't know anyone so I just thought I'd look about. A bit." Macayla's smile faltered. Clearly she'd breached some rule of kennel etiquette. "I'll just be going."

"Not necessary. I know who you are." Yardley smirked. "The Pet Detective."

Ouch. Macayla felt her face burn with the snark the woman had put on her profession. During the past weeks, the media had put every kind of spin imaginable on the story of a "cute" and "wacky" Pet Detective who'd broken the case of a wealthy philanthropist couple who'd committed murder. Some had dredged up her past as a heroine who once took a bullet while protecting a child. The result was that the notoriety made it impossible for her to continue working in the field for Jefferina. A PI who couldn't be anonymous on the job wasn't worth much. She'd been basically unemployed for several weeks.

Yardley was still eyeing her as though she were a perspective canine for purchase who didn't meet her standards. "So you're Oliver's girlfriend."

Macayla pulled herself together. No one got to talk to her as if she were a mongrel. "Oliver and I aren't really in a formal relationship. Early days and all that."

Yardley shrugged. "What can I do for you?"

"Nothing. I didn't mean to bother you. Honestly, I thought I'd chat with the dogs. But I'll just leave."

"No need. I'm checking on that Dutch Shepherd." She pointed to a nearby crate. Though *crate* was a stingy name for the six-by-eight-foot area each of the dogs inhabited alone. "You know dogs. See anything unusual about him?"

Macayla moved closer, watching as the dog with a rough salt-and-pepper coat rose and came to the front of the crate to be petted. She frowned as she watched him move. "It appears that he's got a strained ligament in his right hind leg. It's not bad enough that he's limping but he's not placing as much weight on it as the other three limbs. He should see a vet before he does more injury and goes lame."

Yardley's expression didn't change, so Mac wasn't certain what the trainer thought of her remarks. "Any other dog catch your eye?"

Macayla looked around, taking her time as she walked between cages. She moved quickly over to the one containing Jackeroo. "Hey, big fella. Where's your lesser half?"

He barked in greeting, a bright happy sound of recognition. She reached through the bars and gave the Australian Shepherd a scritch but she didn't linger there. She wasn't certain why she was being tested but she knew she was. So she moved on.

"This guy over here." She paused and pointed to a mid-sized dog with a thick yellowish-gray coat, pointed snout, erect ears, and the white face mask of a wolf. "He seems pretty unhappy about something. Anxious is maybe a better word. He—" She broke off and turned back to her interrogator. "Listen to me. Telling you about dogs. How arrogant is that?"

"He's a Czech wolf dog. Ever see one before?"

"No." Macayla shrugged. "Do you know who he belongs to?"

"Yes. Me."

"Oh. Well. *Hm.* Put both feet in my mouth and chewed, didn't I?"

"I know Oleg is unhappy but I'm not sure why."

"I'd guess that he's frustrated. Lots of changes going on. New people. Travel."

Yardley's expression soured. "Oleg and I do search and rescue for a living. He's always traveling and meeting new people."

"Okay then." Macayla tried to think of something to say

that wouldn't make her sound even more idiotic. "Have there been any unusual upheavals in his life lately?"

Yardley came over and put her fingers through the wire, but Oleg backed up and sat down. "You mean other than the fact that his handler is three months' pregnant, about to get married, and terrified of screwing up her marriage and her child?"

"Ah." Macayla smiled. "That would be enough to upset your pack."

Yardley wheeled away from the cage. "This is my brother's fault. All these people and all this fuss." She waved a hand in the general direction of the land beyond the windows. "This is payback for me trying to run his life a while back when he was in a bad way. I told him that all I wanted was a small wedding with maybe six to ten people. Law, that's my brother, invited the horde you see here tearing up the grass."

"Yes, I can see why you'd hate having lots of friends witness your wedding to the man you love above all others." Macayla couldn't stop herself. "Has your brother always been a bully?"

Yardley's eyes narrowed. "Law's not a bully. He's a good brother. If not for him, Kye and I—" She paused and gave Mac a knowing glance. "You always speak your mind?"

"Probably too often. Not my most attractive feature."

"A trait we share." Yardley nearly smiled. "What do you recommend I do about Oleg?"

"You're going to think I'm wacky."

"I already figured out you're not Oliver's usual type."

Macayla decided not to ask. But, oh, it was tempting. "I'd recommend a doggy massage."

"Dog massage. You do them, of course."

"Yes, but usually on more docile animals, pets. And I've given them a bath and trimmed their nails before we get that intimate."

Yardley laughed at last. "You're an unusual woman. What if I hold him, are you game for a little physical therapy on my dog?"

Macayla glanced at the imposing wolf dog, whose yellow eyes were watching her every move. She could almost swear he understood her every word. Spooky. "Do you have time? With the wedding to get ready for?"

Yardley shrugged. "Oleg's supposed walk down the aisle with Law and me. If he takes a chunk out of a guest that will be bad."

"Okay. But I suppose I should try to get in touch with Oliver again first."

"You can't. I sent him to Richmond for last-minute items. Best man duties and all that. For some reason he's not answering his phone. Probably because the bachelor party ran on until sunrise, and he's pissed I mustered him out after two hours' sleep. Or his phone died because he forgot to plug it in. I usually wouldn't mind his giving me attitude but he almost always forgets at least one thing on the lists I give him. And it's important he gets it all today."

"He's got a pretty good memory. Maybe if you just read him the list."

Yardley slanted a long look at Macayla. "You know, don't you?"

"I don't know what you're talking about."

She wasn't about to admit she knew about Oliver's dyslexia when she was pretty certain he'd told her that none of his colleagues knew. But maybe they did, and respected his privacy by not asking him about it.

Yardley stared at her until she was ready to scratch.

"Loyal, too. I'm liking you better and better, Macayla Burkett. Oliver's never brought a girl home before."

Macayla gave her a vague noncommittal look—annoyed by the term *girl*—and then quickly shifted her gaze away out the window.

Yardley followed her gaze. "Oh, look. Kelly's back."

As Macayla headed for the exit, Yardley spoke again. "I know I'm being a misery. The third month of pregnancy is making me crazier than usual."

Macayla turned back. "I can imagine there are a lot of stresses in your life today. Even if they are happy ones."

She nodded. "You don't have to say yes. But would you consider trying a massage on Oleg?"

There was a funny mix of hope and expectation of rejection on Yardley's face. Macayla couldn't help but wonder about what life had done to this strong woman to prepare her to be disappointed.

"I'm game." She looked down at her dress and heels. "Got a place where I can change?"

An hour and a half later, Macayla found a seat near the back row of semicircular chairs next to a pretty woman with dark hair who cradled a baby as everyone prepared for the ceremony to begin. She'd seen Oliver only briefly and from a distance when she went to feed, water, and walk Pickle. He'd merely waved at her, his height and beard making him a standout among standouts. Disappointed by his lack of welcome, even if he was on call as best man, she had decided to simply pretend she was on her own.

She introduced herself to her seat mate. The mother was a police officer, Cole Jamison Lucca. And the three-month-old in her arms was named Gabriel John Lucca, after his father's father and brother, his mother explained.

Macayla cooed at the happy bundle with deep-blue eyes and thick dark hair. "He's gorgeous. Of course, that seems to be a requirement for men in this crowd."

Cole gave her a puzzled look. "What are you talking about?"

"Haven't you noticed?" She glanced about for a prime example. She didn't have to look far. One was striding toward her. Lean of body and dark-haired, the man gave off the kind of suppressed sexual energy that women craved and other men envied. Though he was dressed nicely, something about him seemed a bit dangerous and wild. Maybe it was the expression on his face, like he'd seen something that he intended to make his. A little astonished by her assessment, Macayla turned back to Cole and pointed discreetly. "For instance, who the heck is that?"

The woman looked up and her face lit up like a switch had been flipped. "Oh, that's just my husband, Scott."

Macayla nodded. Just Scott. Of course he was.

She barely glanced up when the man said, "Excuse me," as he stepped past her to sit next to Cole and her baby. He kissed his wife quickly and then bent to brush his lips over the top of the baby's head before leaning past his family to say, "Hi, I'm Scott Lucca. And you are?"

"Macayla."

He shook her hand, an experience she thought she should not think was so singular. More than ever, she wished Oliver was sitting beside her.

The procession music, provided by a flutist and a drummer, was hauntingly sweet. The groom, a handsome man of Polynesian heritage, and Oliver, both looking heartbreakingly handsome in matching cream linen shirts and trousers with a lei around each of their necks, moved into position at the front of the gazebo.

Macayla turned in her seat to see only one bridesmaid,

a woman with a nimbus of bright red-gold curls leading the procession. She wore a sage-green dress and carried a bouquet of autumn flowers.

Next came Yardley. She wore a gown of simple cream buckskin with fringe falling from the sleeves, the bodice, and the uneven hem. The butter-soft leather draped over her body in a flattering silhouette. Her long hair was parted in the middle and fell over her shoulders like a dark-red waterfall. The ends were tied with matching leather strips. Her only jewelry was a collar of jade turquoise and bone from which hung a pendant made of mother-of-pearl, turquoise, and shiny black feathers.

Beside her on her left Oleg walked easily on his leash. Her brother Law accompanied her on her right. It was easy to believe they were related. Tall and oh so handsome, he shared not so much his sister's features as her easy and confident way of walking. Oliver said he'd lost a leg in Afghanistan. She could not tell by his walk today.

The sweet fall air was soon laced with the odors of cedar and smoky burning sage as the celebration began with a smudging to rid the service of bad spirits and create a place for new beginnings. The couple made their vows in whispers, holding an eagle feather in their left hands. Macayla didn't know the significance of each part of the ceremony but it was clear by the time the couple was wrapped in a ceremonial blanket for the final blessing that these acts held a great deal of meaning for them. It was beautiful. Simple. And her eyes were no longer dry.

She tried to catch Oliver's gaze as the wedding party walked back down the carpet rolled out in the grass, but he didn't return her smile because the redhead on his arm had attracted his attention by leaning in against him with easy familiarity and pressed her hand against his chest as she whispered things only he could hear. The laughter that erupted from him seemed much too intimate for Macayla's peace of mind.

Her temper flared and she looked quickly away. Everyone here seemed to know everyone else. Was the redhead an old girlfriend? A former fling? Competition?

Mulling that over, she went back to the car to check on Pickle while the wedding photos were being taken.

Those questions were still very much on her mind when she had made her way to the open-sided tent where the reception had been laid. It was dark now, twilight where the tent glowed like a lantern from the many twinkle lights.

"Finally." She was snared by the waist and pulled in close by Oliver, who'd been standing just inside the entry waiting for her. He caught her face in his hands and kissed her. It was a thorough kiss, long and deep and very personal. When he pulled back he was grinning that Aussie grin she'd learned to love. "Crikey. I thought I'd never get a chance to do that."

"You've been busy, I see." She glanced deliberately at the redhead standing nearby, who was now talking to a man who looked very unhappy.

Either Oliver didn't catch her glance or he chose to ignore it. "Remind me to elope. I never want this much to-do on my account. Ever."

Oliver held on to her waist as he steered her toward one of the tables at the front of the tent. "You met Yardley, I hear."

"Yes." Macayla hesitated. "I went into the kennels without asking. She wasn't happy about that. Did she tell you?"

He glanced at her. "I heard nothing about that. She likes you."

"How do you know?"

"She told Kye that you were a show-off know-it-all and that BARKS should talk you into coming to Hawaii to see

our search-and-rescue setup. We're in need of a stress relief program for our SAR K-9s, and you're good with
dogs."

Macayla brightened. "Yardley Summers said I'm good
with dogs?"

"I know. There's no higher compliment. So you'll think
about it?"

"I'll think about." But she pulled back as he was about
to pull out a chair for her. "Dance?"

He shrugged. "Okay."

She went easily into his arms, and he seemed at ease
on the floor, moving them together to a slow country tune
she couldn't remember the words to but could hum along
with anyway. Yet she couldn't concentrate on being happy.
Being a woman, there was a question she needed to ask.
"I saw you flirting with the maid of honor."

He looked down at her, his blue eyes bright with the reflected light of the hundreds of tiny lights strung in the
ceiling of the tent. "Who?"

Macayla nodded toward the curly redhead, who'd moved
onto the dance floor with a hunk who had FBI stenciled
across the shoulders of the jacket he wore.

"Oh, that's just Georgiana. And to be correct, she was
flirting with me. She and Brad, the guy she's dancing with,
are an on-and-off thing. Mostly because they keep winding
up on the opposite sides of the law. She's a photojournalist
who takes on some hairy assignments. Just happened again.
She took a case he asked her not to. So he walked out.
She's determined to get him back, on her terms."

"Just as long as *you're* not one of those terms."

He grinned. "Jealous?"

"I don't know. Never had the feeling before. Does wanting to snatch her glorious red hair out by the roots sound
like jealousy?"

"It'll do." He leaned in close and kissed her behind an ear. "Just so you know, I've made it known I'm in a relationship."

Macayla leaned away from him and gave him a look. "With whom?" But she couldn't keep a big fat smile from appearing on her face. "You're pretty sure of yourself."

"The way you look at me, I'd have to be made of asbestos not to feel the heat."

Macayla blushed. "Definitely arrogant."

He slid a hand tighter around her waist and drew her in against him. "So, are you coming to Hawaii?"

"When I can afford a ticket."

"Still hung up on earning your own way."

"Always have. Always will."

"What if I gave you some opportunities to earn that tick—"

Macayla cut him off by reaching up and tugging his head down until her inviting mouth found his. It was all the encouragement he needed to stop dancing as he deepened the kiss and lifted her up against him.

"Get a room!"

Startled, they looked around to find Kye, the groom, shaking his head at them in mock disgust. "Trust an Aussie to try to steal the thunder from his best friend's wedding."

Oliver glanced down at Macayla, a playful smile on his lips. "Did I ever confess that I actually did strip for a living? Just one summer."

Macayla shook her head. "Oh no. I fell for that once."

"Because I've been practicing some of my old moves just to impress you."

She smiled but it didn't quite reach her eyes. He noticed immediately. He took her hand. "Come with me. We need to talk."

They left the light and music and laughter under the

tent, and walked until they were secluded in shadow under a tree near the edge of the woods. Only then did he turn to her and pull her into his arms. One hand firmly on her waist, he brushed his free hand slowly over her head until he cupped her chin. "I know I tease a lot. I'm not good at being serious. But what you did today, coming here for me, it means a lot."

Macayla smiled. "Glad to be of service."

He frowned. "Don't. Don't make light of it. Always before, when I liked a woman, it was always about the sex. This is different. I don't know how to be what I want to be around you. But I'm trying."

"What are you trying to be?"

He leaned his forehead against hers. "Someone you'd like to keep seeing. Outside the bedroom."

"You don't have to try, Oliver. You had me at g'day."

He leaned back to try to catch her expression in the dark. "I never say g'day."

Macayla just smiled. Then she rose up on tiptoe in her very high heels and kissed him like her world and his depended on it being the very best kiss in the whole wide world.

And judging by the feelings spiraling up through her, it was that good.

ACKNOWLEDGMENTS

Dear Reader,

I hope you've enjoyed the K-9 Rescue Series as much as I have writing it. I've learned so much about working K-9 teams and respect with fresh appreciation all that they can and do in service of our citizens and country.

If you are enjoying the series, please let me know: DDayresftw@gmail.com.

I know you're wondering, where are the links to those hot Australian Alpha males? So, just for you: https://youtu.be/sJgPYtHbM58

> All best!
> Woof!
> D.D. Ayres